Creepy Campfire Quarterly
#4

I0457351

Edited by
Jennifer Word

Creepy Campfire Quarterly #4

Compilation Copyright © 2016 EMP Publishing
Atchison, KS
www.emppublishing.com

ISBN-13: 978-0-9980860-1-9
ISBN-10: 0-9980860-1-0

"Where The Dead Men Lose Their Bones" first appeared in *Welcome to Nod #22*, Spring 2000, copyright © 2000 Ken Goldman
"The Warmbloods" copyright © 2016 Jenean McBrearty
"The Ultimate Prison" copyright © 2016 Larry Lefkowitz
"Sebastian's Girls" copyright © 2016 Ellen Denton
"All the Time in the World" copyright © 2016 Luke Walker
"Sapphire Moon" copyright © 2016 Richard W. Black
"Tooong!" copyright © 2016 Randy D. Rubin
"The Undiscovered" copyright © 2016 Jeffrey B. Burton
"Pan-Dimensional Monsters Hate Anger Management" copyright © 2016 Michael Shimek
"Cookies" copyright © 2016 Matthew Weber
"Axe Murders on the Harpeth Turnpike" copyright © 2016 B. C. Nance
"Romero & Juliet" was first read and recorded by *Liars' League*, hosted by *Slings & Arrows* in April 2014, copyright © 2014 Liam Hogan
"PERIODS" was previously published by *Pseudopod* in the fall of 2008, copyright © 2008 Florence Ann Marlowe
"Cuppa Joe" copyright © 2016 Craig Faustus Buck
"The Punchline is Cthulhu" copyright © 2016 Jamie Wahls
"Xmas" first appeared in *Morpheus Tales #27* by Morpheus Tales Publishing, October 14, 2015, copyright © 2015 Calvin Demmer
"Sinker" copyright © 2016 Robert Hart

Cover design by MaxMart © 2016 Jennifer Word

Printed in the United States of America

CONTENTS

Introduction

So here you are, sitting by the campfire all warm and toasty. Some hot dogs cook over the flames, and marshmallows turn brown on sticks. Your friends or fellow campers are laughing and having one hell of a good time, and maybe a few of the luckier guys have the prettiest girls snuggling close. Favorite songs are sung in off-key unison, and the laughter seems contagious. This moment will stay with you for a long time because it's perfect.

Well, not quite perfect. One thing is missing that WILL make this moment memorable. No campfire would be truly unforgettable without that creepy tale, the one you knew all along was coming. Because here, while you sit close to the crackling flames and the firefly sparks are dancing before you, everything seems so right and safe — right here and now, you want to feel scared enough to wet your pants. It's a ritual; a necessary rite of passage every Boy Scout or overnight camper understands — a trial by fire, if you will.

Scare me, damn you. Scare me half-to-death!

Back when I was a high school teacher, I tried to bring a little of that campfire experience into my classroom during selected lessons on Poe, or when I felt daring enough to read aloud one of my own horror tales. (I taught a course on Horror and Science Fiction in Film & Literature, so I could easily pull that off without worrying about losing my job.) I'd turn the lights down and go into Vincent Price mode. Channeling my inner thespian, I even managed a sardonic snicker.

"Listen closely, kids, for I have a story to tell..."

Okay, for some, my stories didn't always work, but fortunately I had many tales and I knew that eventually — *well, hoo-hah! I got you this time, didn't I?* Maybe a crackling fire in the classroom would've helped, but sooner or later, I knew *something* would get through to chill the marrow of those young bones. I took it as a challenge.

That's where we (authors) come in, thank you very much. We're here to provide a little of the ol' Booga-Booga that a night by the campfire requires. These woods are the right place, and the darkness that lurks just beyond the reassuring firelight will provide the atmosphere.

Sit close, will you? It will make the storytelling so much better.

1

Let's begin, shall we?

Here's a tale that may cause you to reconsider those late-hour subway rides, where the tunnels are always dark and cold. You don't really know what's with you under the ground, do you? Those twisting tunnels, they're like one immense tomb — with tracks that may not lead to where you want to go. The question is — where do those rusty tracks lead?

Sit close to the fire, campers, and I'll tell you...

Ken Goldman
August, 2016
Narberth, PA

Where The Dead Men Lose Their Bones

Ken Goldman

"I think we are in rats' alley. Where the dead men lost their bones…"

– T.S. Eliot
The Wasteland (1922)

Getting a little piece of ass on the subway during the middle of the night... Hell, what kid wouldn't nurse a woodie just thinking about doing it right there on the MTA?
    ["Oh my God, Billy! ... Hold me... Oh my God...!"]
    It seemed like a good idea at the time...

Midway through the Labor Day weekend, Billy again felt like a horn dog, and he knew that tonight, Miss September and a Kleenex would not suffice. Hungry for someone who did not have a staple in her navel, he found himself cruising the East Village night spots.

Frankie Blue's was awash with human bodies, but this holiday weekend the shark frenzy on the dance floor seemed especially fierce. Spotting a likely candidate, Billy mashed out his cigarette at the bar and ran his fingers through a buzz cut which, like so many in the crowd, contained streaks of hair gone prematurely green. He moved in for the kill among the throng packed ass-to-ass.

Although the girl in the denim skirt would not have been his first choice a few weeks earlier, she outclassed the Goth types and tongue-pierced Vampirella wannabes who frequented Frankie's. Her face might have been plain and maybe her tits belonged more properly on a pygmy, but in Billy's eyes, the girl with the mousy hair and the prominent overbite would do nicely. He tapped the bean pole who was her dance partner and waited for him to perform a disappearing act.

"I'm Billy."

"Cecilia. Call me Cee. You into scavenging other guys' girls, are you, Billy?" she shouted to him over the din of a throbbing bass without losing the tempo of her gyrations.

"Carpe diem, Cee," he answered with a Billy Idol sneer, although he hoped to seize a lot more than the day. That thought kept his hard-on twitching through several spasmodic numbers by The Roots and Beenie Man while the couple joined the group-gasm that passed for dancing at Frankie's. After fifteen frenetic minutes of dance floor convulsions and a couple of cold draughts from Suzette who tended bar, Billy managed a semblance of focus, enough to catch the fragments of Cee's conversation he could hear from his stool.

"...sales rep at Mandee's, near Hutchinson Parkway... saving for my own apartment..."

Working girl in the city, direct from central casting.

Yada, yada, and yada...

When time arrived to determine just how congenial this sales girl really was, Billy slugged down the last of his Coors. His kiss came from out of nowhere like some kind of sucker punch, but Cecilia-call-me-Cee didn't push him away. His teeth scraped her overbite and the girl didn't really respond much to him, although her tongue tentatively brushed against his. The brief taste of her proved encouragement enough to advance to Phase Two.

"It's warm as a bitch in here. Let's get some air."

The girl could not mistake the irony of Billy's suggestion of getting fresh air in the midst of a sanitation workers strike. With an ephemeral blush, she smiled and mumbled, "Why not?" Her consent was as good as a checkered flag waving Billy in. Within two minutes, both were through the door.

Because the garbage strike was into its third week, Avenue A was hardly conducive to a midnight stroll. Crud overflowed the dozens of receptacles that lined the alleyways, creating a stink that made it all the way to the curb, and Billy wondered if New York flies ever slept. On 2nd Avenue, a bloated brown rat scampered across their path, the remnants of some thick scrap of mystery meat hanging from pointed teeth. It stopped for a moment to stare belligerently at them, then continued towards the teeming bins.

"Filthy little fuckers get pretty ballsy with all this shit lying around, don't they?" Billy muttered. He slipped his arm around Cee and she clung closer to him. In the Village this passed as a romantic moment. Somewhere between a walk-down Caribbean candle shop and another that specialized in gimmicky bar mitzvah items, the girl stopped cold.

"So, where are we going, William? You planning to have your way with me here in some alley? Just you, me, and the rats? I can't tell you how wet the thought is making me."

Billy had no idea where they were going. He wanted to take her anywhere reasonably private that provided opportunity to slide his hands south of her bikini line. But discounting the demands of his hot-wired hormones, he was beginning to like Cee and the paradox of her being so wise-assed while looking like the girl who always raised her hand in Algebra class.

"I was thinking maybe the park. Stop at Starbuck's, find a bench and just sit for a while, discuss your Beanie Baby collection, strangle a rat or two."

"Tempting," Cee acknowledged, turning towards the derelict sleeping on the subway grate she had practically tripped over moments earlier. A tone of genuine foreboding kicked in. "Look, Billy, for real. I'm not sure we should..."

Passing the darkened crevice of an art gallery, a semblance of clear thinking returned, and Billy weighed the logistics of Cee's point. Could he get something going surrounded by winos, scavenging fur balls, and three weeks of garbage? On these streets it was difficult to feel much of anything except the urge to puke. Worse, his appearing like some drooling school kid out to cop a feel might bogus the entire situation. A passing subway rumbled beneath them, its thunder reverberating from the grate near his feet. In that moment, Cee spoke his very thoughts.

"You said you lived in Queens...?"

He wasn't sure where this was going, uncertain if the girl's mind operated on the same frequency as his.

"Uh huh..."

"I live on the way. We take the same subway home, the 'A' train from Washington Square. Late nights the Spring Street Station is open. It isn't far."

The girl's smile oozed peaches and cream, suggesting possibilities entirely incongruous. If the effect were intentional, Billy had struck the mother lode.

Maybe she wanted a little taste of him right there on the subway? Possibly wanted to do it balls-out the second time, on her couch alongside her high school graduation photo, with Mom and Dad asleep upstairs and the dog resting on the carpet. Hell, past midnight, an empty subway car seemed a creative alternative to a quick dry-hump in the back of a taxi. It took all of his effort not to *drag* her along the sidewalk like some life-sized love doll so they would not miss the next train. If luck and the MTA were with him, they might catch an express, and there was a long interval between the JFK and Broad Channel stations during the hour's ride to Queens. Maybe, if the last car were empty and the girl wasn't just yanking his chain...

"Come on!" she said. "We have a train to catch!"

Cee raced ahead of him.

It seemed like a good idea at the time.

***

They stood at the tracks beneath Spring Street, Billy surveying the entire length of the station. He saw no one on the dim platform, and satisfied that luck remained with him, he kissed Cee again. Her response proved considerably more enthusiastic now. Wrapping her fingers around his neck, she drew him closer while her tongue explored his mouth. He continued kissing her as the subway rumbled into the station, illuminating it with strobing lights and making the impassioned couple appear part of some flickering, old-time movie.

This train was one of those dinosaurs belonging to the older fleet from maybe the early '50s that the Transit Authority sometimes used late at night when riders were sparse. The cars were noisier and rumbled a lot more than the modern models, but there was something genuinely picturesque and 'I Love New York' about them. As Billy had hoped, the last car was completely empty, but both waited for the doors to slide shut before taking a seat. The two were yanked backwards as the subway howled into the vacant darkness.

Billy craned his neck to view the forward car which seemed empty also, and turning to Cee, he noticed she was checking, too. They shared smiles during a moment that seemed so free of bullshit that kissing her again convinced him this weekend belonged in the win column.

Billy slid his hand to Cee's breast. "Maybe I should make a few local stops along the way." That earned him a giggle.

"No need to stop," she said smiling, and leaned into him. They kissed for several minutes, and Billy kept right on going even when the train took a sharp and unexpected turn. With his tongue still deep inside her mouth, a realization slowly sank in. He managed to pull himself from the girl.

[No need to stop ... No need to ... stop ...]

"We haven't stopped," he said.

"What?"

"There are supposed to be stations along here. Canal Street. Chambers. This train hasn't–"

"I wasn't paying attention," Cee giggled. "I was a little distracted, you know. Anyway, maybe this is an express. Like your hands on my ass."

He looked through the dusty window into the darkness and his jaw dropped. Something clearly had gone gonzo. A couple of beers and a stiff one might have dulled his perspective. Maybe they had stepped inside a train that was supposed to be out of service?

"There's no Southbound track going the other way," Cee pointed out. "I think we're in some kind of utility tunnel. Has this ever happened to you before?"

"Shit, no."

A rancid stench filled the rail car. Billy turned to Cee.

"You smell something funny?"

She sniffed.

"There's nothing funny about *that* smell..."

Garbage. There was no doubt about it. Billy tried to smile but he felt his lip twitch. "We may be under one of those refuse sites the city is using during the strike. Christ, if New York has a butt crack, I think we found it."

The lights flickered once. A moment passed and they flickered again. The train slowed.

"Billy? What's–?"

He stared through the window as the wheels came to a squealing stop. The doors remained closed while yowling subway echoes resonated through the tunnel, fading like distant ghosts. A lengthy silence followed, a stillness as empty as the tunnel was huge. They had arrived at some kind of platform that could not properly be called a station. There were no street indicators and few lights – dim bulbs, really – not enough to provide any decent illumination of the murky shadows that were impossible to determine as either posts or people.

Billy could not see anything in motion outside, but he had the uneasy feeling there was something in the darkness moving with a determined slowness, something watching and perhaps waiting. He sat frozen, unwilling to run the risk of revealing himself and sweating even in the cold damp of the tunnel. Cee must have been feeling the same. She did not move.

The lamps inside the train again strobed wildly as if they were shorting out, replacing the couple's confused expressions with colorless, stop-action masks. In the next instant, the lights blinked out altogether and the subterranean world went black.

"Billy!"

"It's okay. They'll probably be back on in a minute."

But light did not come, and inside the darkened rail car, Billy instinctively reached for Cee's hand. Hers felt clammy with cold sweat, and she squeezed his hand hard.

"Jesus Christ, Billy! What's happening?"

"Maybe I should go to the first car, see what's going on," he offered, not certain he favored his own suggestion. "There's got to be someone running the train, right? Maybe if I can just find–"

"No, Billy! Don't leave me here! Please don't!"

A *whoosh!* interrupted her. The subway tube's dank coldness filled the car with the chill of a meat locker. Billy could not clearly see it happen, but he knew doors had slid open.

"Power failure, maybe?" Cee offered.

"I don't think so. Something opened the doors. And that means there's someone running this train. There's lights on inside the tunnel, too, not that they're lighting much. See for yourself."

She looked through windows caked with black dust.

"See what? I don't see anything! Aren't there other passengers bitching anywhere on this whole goddamned train? Who's driving this thing? What's going on?"

"I don't know."

"Shit, Billy. Shitshitshit..."

He heard thumping on the floor pads like something scurrying through the open door. Coming through and coming through and coming through, there was a scampering at their feet so close that if he probed the floor with his Nike, Billy knew he would touch...

...touch what?

Cee heard it too, a scampering accompanied by shrill squeaking sounds like violin strings plucked by a madman.

"Something's in here with us! Oh Christ, Billy, they're all around!"

Instinctively, they pulled their legs from the floor, crouching together on the seat like huddled children.

"Shhh!"

Billy pulled his Bic from his pocket. Snapping it on, he already knew what he would see. Still, he gawked when he spotted them.

At first, there were only the eyes and teeth in the undulating darkness, but then lumpy shapes formed and Billy recognized for certain what had been keeping them company inside the stalled subway train.

Huge, bloated brown rats squirmed along the floor in squeaking, furry heaps, their tails thick tangled strands of flesh. There were dozens of them, and they crawled over one another skulking in stop/starts towards the couple cringing on the seat. More of them were wiggling from the platform and into the train, their movements on the floor pads a cacophony of light thumps, their legion swelling in dark waves.

"Garbage must've brought them out of their holes," Billy whispered. "For weeks they've had themselves one hell of a banquet, got themselves good and fat. Goddamned disease carriers eat anything, even each other. Now they want more than garbage."

The lighter, low on fuel, flickered. A heavy rat that felt like a small dog catapulted itself into Billy's lap. The boy remained perfectly still while his heart did the funky chicken. The chunky rodent paused upright on his thigh. Billy could hear it sniffing the air. Then it sprinted off.

Cee's screams suddenly filled the old railway car. Billy fumbled trying to reactivate his lighter. Getting it going, he saw the husky rat had flung itself onto her. The fat little fur ball was agile and had attached itself to her face, the scaly tail extending past the girl's eye while its mouth snapped wildly at her lips. Cee tried tearing into it, her nails digging deep into rat flesh. The creature squealed in pain and fury, but it did not release its grip. Thick veins of blood dripped down Cee's cheek, purple rivulets that smeared her complexion, gone pale in the fire light.

"Billy! Oh my God, Billy! Get it off! Please, get it off!"

The rat continued gnawing as Billy squashed the flame into sticky, matted fur, the rodent's barbecued pelt giving off a rotted stink. Shrieking, the rat still would not budge. Tearing blindly at it with both hands, Billy felt a damp trickle along his wrist that he realized was Cee's blood. Tugging harder, he feared he might shred the flesh right from the girl's face. He pinched the rat's jaws, and it struggled trying to shake itself free. Finally, the rat loosened its grip. Billy tossed it like a ticking grenade clear across the aisle, then heard it thud against a window, its protesting squeak cut short.

Cee could not stop flailing at the air as if she expected the next one to drop from the ceiling.

"Get them away! Oh God, get them away!"

Another rat climbed up Billy's chest, tearing through his shirt and embedding taloned claws into his skin like thick needles. He felt the cold snout poke his throat. This one wanted *his* face, wanted to sink its teeth deep into the soft flesh of *his* neck.

"Get off me, motherfucker! Get–!"

He managed to twist the claws from him, ripping shreds from his own skin as he did. The rat hit the floor like a kid's deflated toy.

But now other rats snapped near his ankles. One, more ambitious than the others, climbed into his lap. It tore and chewed its way towards his face even as he shook another from his foot. There were many more on the way. Billy could hear a platoon of them thumping along the floor.

[...thub thub thub...]
[...thubthubthubthub...]

The rats would not stop coming until they had wrenched the skin from their bones like sticky cheese, tearing at them as if he and the girl were serving up a buffet. Struggling to keep the lighter's flame alive to fend the new intruders off, he felt a sudden stabbing pain as a corpulent rat sank a string of sharpened pencil points into his wrist.

The Bic fell to the floor. Darkness and Cee's screams filled the rail car.

Panic overtook him. Billy slammed the rat against the window and kept slamming. It clung stubbornly with the persistence of an adhesive, shaking its head and clenching more firmly. Smashing the tenacious bastard into the plexiglass, Billy felt something inside the rat crunch. Seizing his chance, he squeezed the head hard, twisting the rodent's thick neck like a bottle cap until the bone inside snapped. When the animal's vicious squirming stopped cold, Billy tossed the bloodied creature into the writhing pile swarming the floor. He turned to Cee in a blackness so pitch he could see only a charcoal sketch of her.

"You okay?"

"I'm bleeding so bad, Billy."

"We'll get out of here," he told her, aware of the idiocy of his remark, aware, too, that he hadn't the slightest idea how to do it.

"There's someone out there ..." Cee said.

"What?"

"Someone's outside the train, there in the tunnel ... people ... a lot of them are walking on the tracks straight ahead! Look!"

Cee was right. Billy couldn't tell how many were approaching further up the tracks. He saw only the long trails of light beams bobbing in the darkness. There might have been a dozen flashlights, maybe more. They were some kind of rescue party come to find them, maybe tunnel workers or passengers from one of the other cars. Billy didn't care. The two of them pounded on the windows.

"In here! The last car! We're in here!"

A wash of light at the sliding door caused the rodents to scatter towards the other exits. A tall, stick-figured man silhouetted in shadows entered first, and stomping his heavy boot, he nailed one of the rats on the run. The creature made a dull farting sound like a crushed water balloon, writhing on the floor and kicking ridiculously at nothing. The man kept stomping until its writhing slowed, then stopped.

"Thank God... *Oh, thank God!*" Cee muttered. Billy held her close, uncertain if her shudders were hers or his. Other shadowy figures entered the car behind the leader, stomping at anything that moved near their feet as if the entire group were doing some grotesque square dance. The activity must have scared the rat shit out of the mangy swarm. In thick rows, they scurried from the train.

The tall man removed his cap and wiped his forehead. "Grubby little subway cooties. Must be a million nestin' inside these tunnels, but I ain't never seen 'em do this before. Refuse site upstairs prob'ly made 'em bolder and more 'thusiastic for some midnight treats. These track rats can't never seem to get enough, and runnin' in packs, they'll do some serious damage. You the only ones in here?"

His lantern's high intensity light revealed only tattered seats and a few dead rodents on the floor. The man's companions silently entered the train, their faces hidden in the wash of illumination as their lamps pierced the darkness like searching beacons. Satisfied the rail car had emptied, the cluster of rescuers ventured forward into the aisle.

"You two okay?" the stick-figured man asked.

"This girl was bitten pretty badly. I think she needs a doctor," Billy said.

The man's filthy clothes suggested he had seen a lot more of the underground transit system than most would care to. When he leaned forward to examine the girl, Billy noticed he wore the tattered hat of an MTA train conductor.

"Are we in some kind of utility tunnel?"

"That's just where you are," the man answered. He aimed a high-powered wash of light into her face to inspect the girl's cheek closely.

"Naw, ... she ain't hurt."

"Of course she is!" Billy shouted. "Christ, look at her! She's bleeding!"

"Ain't hurt, I'm tellin' you," the stick-man insisted. He aimed the light again at Cee, smearing his thumb on the girl's bloodied cheek. "You see? It's just a scratch. You're not hurt, are you, little girl?"

Cee stared uneasily at Billy as if she expected him to speak for her, but the boy had no ready response. He managed a semblance of composure that seemed all the more uncertain for his attempt.

"Mister, she's hurt pretty bad," he tried again. "A few minutes ago, a rat the size of a bread loaf was chewing on her face. I wrestled one of those bastards off me, too. These rats are rabid and I'm pretty sure we both need some medical attention."

The tall man scratched the oily hair beneath his cap as if this information took a powerful effort to assimilate. Finally, he turned to those who stood behind him, addressing a tub of lard with a wispy beard, whose belly spilled from his soot-streaked t-shirt like a fleshy beach ball.

"We'll ask my boy, here. These kids look hurt to you, Jeremiah?"

The husky kid stepped forward, bringing his face level with Cee's. He spread another wash of light on her. Leaning in, he licked a thick stream of blood from her chin.

"This one seems fine to me, Pa. Least she's a whole lot better than this rat, here."

He scooped the rodent from the floor. It was still alive, although barely, but it shimmied wildly in his pudgy hand as he held it close to his face. "Then again, I guess most anything looks fine compared to what you find livin' down here in these tunnels." He bit off the rat's head.

Billy said nothing, just sat by Cee, nodding in agreement like an idiot.

"You get to understand them garbage-eatin' fur sacks, though," Stick-man continued. "Sometimes, you learn from 'em how to play real dirty just to get some food to feed your family. This city don't act too kindly towards its vagrants, you know? You sometimes got to set your own rat traps, so-to-speak. Like I been teachin' my Jeremiah, when these old trains go clunkin' through these tunnels so late at night..."

He handed the conductor's cap to the fat kid.

"All aboard!" the boy said, smiling through teeth that resembled smashed crockery. The bearded kid urged those behind him forward, and in the shadows, Billy couldn't determine how many were inside the rail car. He could barely make out faces belonging to those who stood muttering in the brightness of the hand-held lamps. They hardly seemed like faces at all. It was impossible to tell their features as male or female. Their shapes were all *wrong*.

The man knelt to pick up the rodent he had stomped into pulp, sinking his teeth deep into what meat remained of its stomach. Sticky ropes of entrails dripped down his chin.

"'Course, these little gray-backs sometimes will do as appetizers. Ain't that much substance to 'em, though, nothin' no sane man would ever call tasty. On the other hand..."

The tall man snapped off his lantern. Taking his cue, his family did the same, each high-beam, in turn, yielding gradually to the shadows. In moments, the rail car went as black and silent as a tomb.

Billy trembled, cold and shivering in the darkness. He could hear Cee whimpering to herself.

"Billy... oh God, Billy..."

[It seemed like such a good idea... such a good idea...]

The couple crouched together, holding each other. For one wildly irrational moment, Billy wondered if he should kiss Cee one last time, try to salvage something, anything.

You set your own rat traps, so-to-speak...

Together, the tall man and the tub-of-guts named Jeremiah, moved toward the pair.

"You go first, son. We'll leave the girl for the others. Ain't good to be greedy."

"Thanks, Pa."

"Oh God, Billy! ... Please hold me... Oh my God...!"

Cee's shrieks turned to hysteria. Billy could not stop himself from screaming, too.

Then they were on him.

The Warmbloods

Jenean McBrearty

I call them Warmbloods. The ones who feed us regularly, but not anything we like to eat. I call that misplaced philanthropy. My friend, Georgette, calls it torture.

We don't have to eat, technically. The undead can't die of starvation or Avian Flu or atherosclerosis. But we can suffer. Oh, yes. Never doubt it. Our psyches can deteriorate incrementally. Our self-esteem can wilt like any dead flower, the bloom of life evaporating with every insult.

We live here, in what they call a safe-space, but it's a prison. An ancient term for a sealed-off place where like-and-like learn to hate each other because they are suffocating from sameness. Everyone turning ghostly pale. Hollow-eyed. Decayed. Leprous. What are we supposed to do all day? Contemplate our sins?

Okay. Here's one of mine. I call it, "My Trip to the Zoo Sin."

***

It occurred on a typically beautiful San Diego morning at the World Famous San Diego Zoo—that's what all the brochures called it. The name was always preceded by the description that drew attention to its stature which, I'm sure they hoped, would keep people from littering the pathways with napkins and melting ice cream cone mishaps.

I was doing my primate study, an anthropology course assignment that required students to observe a monkey, chimpanzee, orangutan, or gorilla for a few hours and note its behavior. Stare at a human relative long enough, and one will see their own self reflected back, get over one's human-centric world-view, and accept evolution. One will return to the classroom humbled, more appreciative of the small niche humans occupy on earth, which will turn human hubris into brotherhood. The primates are just like us, only hairier, and, not having the capacity for idle chatter, probably easier to get along with.

I chose to stare at Gorilla Gorilla Gorilla, a huge, silver-backed male who audaciously stared back at me for the entire three hours that I sat near the edge of his enclosure. I wanted him to do something; jump around, throw shit at me, peel a banana, swing in the tire attached to a tree limb, beat his chest—*vocalize*. So, I said as much. Not in a teasing, "you're boring," kind of way, but in a friendly, conversational tone that, hopefully, would get him to move closer to me—so I could see the whites of his eyes.

I wrote: *he looks dead*, in my notebook. *He just stares in my direction, and I don't know if he's looking at me or through me or past me. I don't know if he likes my madras shirt and my tan Bermuda shorts, and my brown leather sandals. I don't know if he's hungry.* Not that it mattered because I read the sign, **Please Do Not Feed**, and I sure as hell didn't want to risk killing the old guy off with half of a well-meant, well-thrown, peanut butter and jelly sandwich.

I looked at my watch. An hour had passed and no one had come to feed him. Maybe he'd been fed at sunup, or maybe the waiter hadn't come yet and he was waiting. *Ask what gorillas eat and when*, I wrote, determined not to leave until I made contact with whoever was in charge of feeding. I know I was starved. I raided my backpack and gobbled down the peanut butter and jelly, and the egg salad, and finished off a bottle of Sunny Delight.

Finally, around eleven, a girl in a khaki uniform drove up in a golf cart and threw the old guy a few bananas. "Morning snack," she said.

"Don't worry, I haven't given him a bite of anything," I assured her.

She waited with me a few minutes, the gorilla still sitting like a sphinx, and then sighed. "I told them this wasn't going to work," she murmured to herself.

"What?" I said. "What wasn't going to work?"

"See that brown stuffed bag over there behind him? It's supposed to be a toy. Something he can rough and tumble with. He doesn't want to play. He's waiting for his mate to come back. Gorillas aren't known for monogamy. They're more the love her, and her, and her, and leave 'em type. But Shiloh was different. He was really sweet on her. She got an infection, and we didn't know it left her blind in the eye. She did okay in the hospital. But the day we brought her back, she fell into the safety pit and died. He thought we were going to bring her back. Probably still thinks we will. We brought him another female. He ignored her."

When the girl left, I waited a few minutes and then I left, too. Before my three hours were up. I cheated. On the assignment. An unforgivable sin for a student dedicated to keeping a 4.0 GPA. But that wasn't the BIG sin. The big sin was leaving the old guy to grieve alone when I could have stayed and talked to him about Shiloh.

Maybe said a prayer with him. Explained that God loved him and that life was worth living even when you lose someone you love. I could have listened to his silence. Like one primate to another. And I could have gone back. The same way I could have gone back to the Pine Tree Retirement Community to see my grandmother before she passed.

***

The Warmbloods wear khaki uniforms too. I watch them from the parapets as they unload our rations onto pallets that will be lowered inside the wall by the drones. They work quickly and without conversation. They never smile. The meat they are loading looks and smells as bad as any other rotting flesh, including ours. I once wrote a note and stuffed it between the pallet slats: *Can't you at least try to make the food look appetizing?* Nothing changed, but then, I don't know if the note survived a journey back over the wall. Maybe it fell through the cracks.

***

"What do you expect?" Georgette asked me.

"I don't expect anything," I told her. "I hope that one of these days, I'll see a crate of strawberries and a couple of cans of Reddi-Wip."

"Hope? Isn't that what Warmbloods do when they know they're going to die?" She laughed because none of us Zombies wanted to die. We had all hoped that being Zombies would be a happy medium between real life and extinction. We hoped we'd still be able to smell and taste and have sex. But we were foolish. At least, I was.

And stupid. One afternoon, my friend Roger and I decided to hitch a ride on one of the mail-drop drones, and got to see inside the ghetto wall. We were sophomores in high school and got caught smoking weed instead of going to P.E. class. We got community service and probation, and were sentenced to work for Zombie Services three Saturdays in a row. After we delivered the slaughterhouse leftovers, the boss wanted to know if we'd deliver the mail. "Do extra duty, and I'll let you off the hook for next Saturday," he promised. We agreed.

We fastened the mail pallet to the drone and climbed aboard, taking aerial pictures with our cell phones. "People will pay good money to see what life is like inside the ghetto," Roger had assured me, and we took hundreds of pictures. Silly us. We thought we'd see a bunch of naked, dead people frolicking in the grass. Maybe smoking weed or swilling beer. At the very least, we expected to see a little Zombie tits and ass. But, it seems, boobs and butts are the first parts of the body to decay. All we saw was the saggy, baggy elephant skin hanging off ashy-white stick people. Nobody was kissing, much less screwing. The zombies didn't even hold hands. Not even the young ones.

"Maybe we caught them on a bad day," Roger suggested.

"Or maybe they always sit and lay around doing nothing. Too weak to jog or dance," I said, and I remember I got very afraid.

"It's better than being stuck in a box underground for all eternity," Roger said, and I agreed with him. Then. Roger un-died first. I remember him telling me he'd opted for Zombie Conversion on his hospital bed, and said he'd be waiting for me inside. "We'll liven up their existence," he vowed.

***

It hasn't worked out that way. He and Georgette and I spend hours making plans to organize some activity or another—a 5K Fun Run, say—and then find an excuse not to move. Too dreary. Too hot. Too cold. Even though we can no longer feel hot or cold, and the Zombie ghetto enclosure gets as much sun as any other place in San Diego. Some of the Old Timers tell us not to worry or plan. Eventually, our minds will deteriorate like our butts and we won't care what we do or don't do from one day to the next. I used to think the Old Timers had just eaten one too many sour grapes. Now I listen to the dead poets talk about feasting on regret.

"Who doesn't regret something?" Georgette reminds me.

The question sends me into silence. Sometimes I walk along the parapets and look out over the countryside of the living. I could jump, I tell myself. Even if I break a bone or two, it wouldn't hurt. Still, I'd be crippled because I couldn't mend, and I'd never be able to run a 5K.

"What do you regret, Georgette?" I asked her once.

"I regret being foolish. I regret not learning to drive safely. I regret not living long enough to get old. Perhaps death wouldn't have seemed so awful if I'd been wobbly and ugly."

I haven't told her I regret getting into that car with her. I'm afraid to finish the conversation. It might sound too much like I blame her for where I am and it's not her fault. I could have chosen not to convert.

***

Zombies are dangerous to Warmbloods. We remind them they may have to make a difficult choice someday. They may not die outright. Like in an explosion, or drowning, or a gunshot to the head. They may linger. They may fear the end so much that they opt to be undead. They may opt to become gorillas. To sit and stare at, through, or past those doing their primate observations. A monkey, a chimpanzee, an orangutan. Or a Zombie, separated from the Warmbloods who live just beyond the wall and the twelve-foot pit that is easily fallen into when one is blind in one eye. Warmbloods, who can behave as cold-blooded and be as dead to kindness as I am.

The Ultimate Prison
Larry Lefkowitz

Twenty thousand years after it left, the gutted ship beached itself on the Earth like a dead whale. Twenty thousand earth years – two ship years. The inhabitants of the ship who survived were two years older. In the space of their journey, seven hundred generations had been born and died on Earth.

Of the original colony of one hundred thousand sent into space faster than the speed of light, less than three thousand remained. In a year's travel in each direction – as the judicial sentence had specified, as the ship's system had been programmed in conformity therewith – most of the original penal colony had died.

The first to succumb had been the colony's commander, chosen upon his record as head of the New York area's most powerful criminal family. Murdered two weeks out. A succession of self-appointed and clique-appointed chiefs succeeded the first, sometimes in sole authority, sometimes as joint chiefs. The ship, large as a city, quickly developed its own areas. Except that each one was a private turf.

That the ship was not destroyed in the process could be attributed less to curiosity than ambition. Curiosity on the part of the prisoners to see what Earth would be like when they returned. Ambition – to rule the place. Oh, they knew well, each of the battlers for the spoils, that Earth would be advanced – far beyond the time of their departure – when they returned. Twenty thousand years advanced. The sentence had made this quite explicit; it was *the* penal aspect. An unknown penalty that appealed to its framers.

But the criminals thought they would outwit the creative punishment – or "beat the rap" as they phrased it. They figured the same strife they carried in their hearts would occur on Earth, such calculations had fueled their thoughts while they were streaking out and back in their prison ship. If Earth would be a jungle, so much the better. They were used to jungles, had warred all their lives in them, mostly of their own making. Had warred in the ship as well, again in jungles of their own or their rivals' making. The ship's engines were intact, its guidance system online, a result of the only law 'obeyed' in their jungle-ship: a product of their survival instincts plus the possible spoils awaiting them upon their return. The less vital parts of the ship were a mass of rubble; confinement areas knocked out of the ship's innards, whole blocks suzerained to one party or another. A ship of fiefs more than thieves – and murderers, and the other assorted riff-raff that 21st Century Earth had consigned to the 221st Century.

Those alive to return home were among the toughest, or luckiest, or more likely, the canniest. The winners of the wars. Alliances, betrayals, and occasional live-and-let-live, that allowed three thousand hardened types, divided into a number of groups under their bosses, to disembark from their ship on its return.

***

Their shock could not have been greater. Jointly, severally, alone, they had imagined a desert, or a jungle or, at the other end of speculation, a magnificent future Earth so fantastic that they vied to conjure it up. And if they did imagine it not twenty thousand years in the future in terms of progression – then at least ten thousand, or five hundred, factoring in intervening wars, conventional or atomic – surely to have passed the point where they had left it.

And yet, Earth was much as they *had* left it; the same cities, the unaltered streets. Maybe seedier than they remembered, but otherwise unchanged.

They were flabbergasted. They did not have time to be so for long, however. They were quickly and brutally rounded up by men and women tougher than they, and better armed.

"What gives?"

"What's going on?" they queried their captors.

They got their answer when they were led into the familiar-looking building. They were forced into cell blocks. They were back in prison.

***

A loudspeaker answered their questions as soon as they were inside. They each clung to their cell's bars, plunged into a future Earth none of them had ever speculated could exist. They listened to the harbinger as he delivered their new sentence with glee.

"Yeah, we know," the voice thundered. "You want to know what happened. The blasted Earth you pictured. Or the paradise. Well, it ain't the Earth destroyed and it ain't the Earth in Eden and splendor. And you want to know why? Because *your* prison ship wasn't the *only* one sent for a two-year, lightning, yo-yo trip twenty thousand years ago. Every so often, other ships were sent. And other ships returned. And the suckers who landed on Earth were no match for us *first guys* sent off.

"Yeah, the Earth had been almost destroyed a few times in those twenty thousand years. But the good guys came out on top in the end. They built a fantastic world, all right. A fancy kind of place where everyone sat around contemplating art and refined thought. Well, they were no match for us guys and gals of twenty thousand years ago. They never knew what hit 'em. Most of them went nuts at the *idea* of us. Committed suicide in masses. The others, we hunted down. They were too weak to be our slaves. Lucky for your shipment, or we would have finished you off the moment you landed. Now, you're needed. As slaves. The privilege of the bosses. That's the only 'improvement' over the old days. Ain't no human rights groups anymore.

"You'll be good workers, we know. You are the best of your ship. *We* won out on Earth. Your bad luck was that we were sent out a few years *before* you. You should have been caught faster. Hah, hah.

"There were four ships in all sent twenty thousand years ago, before the punishment was eliminated as too cruel or too vague – I forget the basis of the decision, I ain't too good on law. Hah, hah.

"One ship never made it back. They must have been stupid cons and somehow destroyed their ship – not an easy thing to do. Or maybe the auto-return was faulty and they're still traveling. The third ship returned a couple of years back and we were waiting for 'em like we were for you. They were pretty good workers, but a lot of 'em died on us. Took us a while to get the knack. You should last longer. You seem tougher...

"Oh, sure, you can try your luck. Try to take over. Good luck, we give fancy funerals. Plenty of flowers. Limousines. The works. Fortunately, a few things haven't changed in twenty thousand years."

Sebastian's Girls

Ellen Denton

"More wine, Lisa?"

"Sure. Thanks, Sebastian. I meant to tell you, I love that little orange orchard you have out back."

"Actually, those are tangerines. I'll have to also show you the new vegetable garden in the side yard later. The carrots and beans you're eating came from there, grown by yours truly."

"Wish I had a yard to grow stuff like that. All I've got is that little concrete terrace with some flower pots on it. You've done some really nice things with the place since the last time I was here."

He grinned at her. "Well, you can always marry me. If you do, I'll even throw in letting you cook and clean for me, just to sweeten the deal."

She shook her head and took another bite of her braised salmon. It was just like old times, when they would humorously banter back and forth at their dinners about him wanting to marry her.

The cotton summer top she was wearing tonight – white, the neckline down low on her shoulders with red and blue flowers around it – made her look like a charming little gypsy. She caught him staring admiringly at her breasts, and with mock sternness, said, "Eyes up!"

He feigned a look of hurt and surprised innocence as he raised his hazel eyes to her teasing blue ones.

***

"Okay, here we go. Home movies, as promised."

After much fiddling, he had the projector set up and took a seat next to Lisa on the couch. In a few minutes, they were both laughing – Lisa so hard that she had tears running down her face.

"I didn't realize you were such a cute kid when you were three."

They were looking at a movie clip of him standing up in a kiddie-pool, with his swimming trunks being yanked down by the family dog.

"I'm even cuter *now* with my shorts off."

"Yeah, I'll bet."

***

"This has been really nice, Sebastian. And yes, I would like to do it again soon."

"At your service, Madam. How about if I pick you up next week, same time? I promise you a feast fit for a queen. I can also rent some real videos we can watch afterwards."

"Okay, it's a date. I'll see you Tuesday."

All the curtains in both the dining and living room, where he now stood saying goodnight to her, were firmly closed, with not even a slit on the side providing an outsiders' view into either room. He always made very sure of that whenever they ate or watched movies together – because if someone did happen to venture into his yard, peek in and see a skeleton propped up at the dinner table dressed in a gypsy blouse and long-haired red wig, or sitting beside him on the living room couch – they just wouldn't understand.

***

After getting her body settled back into its storage crate in the basement, he returned to the dining room to clear off the table and do the dishes.

He imagined he heard the phone ring, so picked it up. It was Claire. The sexy, throaty sound of her voice on the other end of the line made his pulse quicken. He confirmed the arrangements for her to come over tomorrow for their Wednesday night chess game. By the time he hung up the phone, he had a full-blown erection.

He was relieved that she hadn't called when Lisa was there. That could have been awkward. With six dead, potential brides now in storage in his basement, it was sometimes hard to keep track of who he was dating and when.

***

He stood behind a magazine rack pretending to be reading something while watching the girl move toward a checkout line with her shopping cart. He'd been surreptitiously stalking her all over the store, aisle-to-aisle, for the last fifteen minutes. Now was the time to make his move.

He stepped out from behind the rack and closed the distance between them. When he got close to her, he turned, started walking backwards and raised his hand as though in a goodbye gesture to someone.

"I'll catch you later, Maryanne! Send my love to your parents."

As he waved, he kept stepping backwards fast so that he rammed hard into the girl, who had started to turn at the sound of his shouted farewell.

He spun around to her with a look of concerned surprise. "Oh my God! I am SO sorry." He placed his hand on the girl's shoulder. "Are you okay?"

Her initially annoyed expression softened. "I'm fine." She turned away, was about to start toward the checkout lane again, when he lightly put his hand on her arm.

"I feel like a complete jerk. Truly, I'm sorry. I'm Sebastian, by the way." He held out his hand to her. He had a sheepish expression on his face that he'd earlier practiced over and over in front of a mirror until it looked real.

She hesitated, shrugged slightly and shook his hand. "Janet."

"Janet. Let me make it up to you. Can I give you a ride home or something? Seriously, this isn't a pick-up line and I'm not a serial killer or anything, but it's not every day I bang into a girl as pretty as you."

She laughed. "If that's not a pick-up line, I'll eat my hat, but no, I don't need a ride. Honestly, it's okay."

"In that case, wait here for *just* a moment." In response to her puzzled expression, he held up a finger, then sprinted across the supermarket to a display of potted plants and flowers near the entrance. He returned with a bouquet of yellow roses and got down on one knee.

The girl smiled, a little embarrassed, and looked around at the people who were watching the romantic scenario of Sebastian on his knee holding out the bouquet to her. The onlookers smiled too.

"Janet, I insist you at least let me grace your day with this truly lovely bouquet. See, I can even spout poetry in your presence. You are an inspiration."

"Okay, okay." The girl, laughing now, took the bouquet. His boyish good looks and light-hearted civility tended to have a certain appeal to the women he culled out as possible prospects.

He stood up again. "Now I've got an excuse to walk with you, at least to the checkout counter, so I can pay for the flowers."

It was Saturday afternoon and crowded, so every checkout line stretched out and back into the aisles. They chatted while they waited to get to the front of theirs. By the time they'd left the store, Janet with the bouquet, and Sebastian wheeling her cart of groceries to her car, they'd made a dinner date for Sunday evening.

***

Back at home, he pulled out a new spiral notebook from the supply he kept in the storage space beneath the basement stairs. In painfully neat, uniform, straight up-and-down print letters, he wrote JANET on the front cover, then began his notes with the information on their encounter at the supermarket. He included every minute detail, from the clanking sound of her shopping cart when she swung it impatiently around the corner of the crowded produce aisle, to the small, loose thread, which he estimated to be about half an inch long, peeking out from the bottom of her right pant leg.

After he set the pencil and notebook aside, he sat back with a sense of satisfaction. He had five women, their skeletons nicely clothed and packed away in crates, a sixth, Robin, in an air and temperature controlled tank with Dermestid Beetles cleaning the flesh off the bones, and a seventh, empty tank for the new arrival, soon to join them, come Sunday.

He got up and took a peek into the tank containing Robin's almost-skeleton. The beetles swarmed like river rapids over the skull and into and out of the now empty eye sockets. At this rate, Robin would likely be done by the weekend.

He only kept the lid of the tank open for a couple of seconds, but one of the tiny Dermestids had escaped and was crawling in uncertain circles on the side of it.

"Get over here, you little fugitive!" He captured the bug with a pair of tweezers and dropped it back into the tank. He knew their breeding potential and didn't want to risk even the possibility of any of them getting upstairs and ruining the carpets or furniture.

***

The Italian restaurant where he and Janet were now seated in a booth near the back was small and cozy. Wine, candlelight, and a basket of warm, sliced bread gave a comfortable, easy feel to their conversation.

She had shining, blonde hair that fell in soft curls to just above her shoulders, but he had already decided on a straight, jet black wig for her. He had one stored in a hat box he'd been saving for someone

25

with just her pale complexion. The contrast would be stunning. He was contemplating this while looking at her attentively as she talked on and on about her job as an assistant manager at some trendy downtown boutique.

He needed to maneuver the conversation onto the subject of her apartment.

"So, Janet, what made you decide to move here to Chicago from the idyllic little town in Vermont you grew up in?"

"I just wanted to expand my horizons and have more of a career than working as a cashier and stock girl in the town's one automotive shop. The owner of the boutique I'm at now said that I'm on track to becoming a full manager. He plans to open a new branch next year."

"I can totally see that with you because of your looks and outgoing personality. I think people probably just take to you naturally."

"It's nice of you to say that, Sebastian." She smiled and looked away modestly.

"By the way, I didn't see all the rooms when I picked you up this evening, but you have a really nice apartment. Did the living room come already furnished like that?"

"Oh, no, I actually pulled that together piece by piece after I moved here; most of it is thrift store and flea market finds. You can find some great stuff at those places."

Sebastian raised his eyebrows and did his best to look impressed. "I would never have guessed that. It looks like it's all from one coordinated set. Each piece and color harmonizes with every other piece."

The girl nodded, pleased.

Sebastian continued. "By the way, I also noticed some wood shelves stacked on the floor below the window. Are you planning on putting them up on the wall or something?"

"Yes. I want to have something for knick-knacks and potted plants. I just have to get some brackets to set the shelves on. For a girl, I'm pretty good with a hammer and nails."

"Janet, damn! If brackets are all you need, I have some you're welcome to use. I have almost identical shelves at my place and a whole box of brackets that look great with that color wood. When I drive you home later, I can stop quickly at my place and bring you out a whole handful of them. What do you have – four shelves?"

"Yes, but are you sure, Sebastian? What if you need them later?"

"Not a problem. The ones I have left over now in my garage have been sitting there unused for the last two years. They may as well be put to work on those shelves of yours."

"Well, thanks! I really appreciate it. That's–"

She stopped talking and they both looked up and smiled at the waiter who had just arrived at their table with their food; linguini with white clam sauce for him and veal scaloppini baked in Marsala sauce for her.

They smiled at each other and started to eat.

***

"It's just a few blocks further down this street."

He was driving slowly down Rosemond toward the cul-de-sac that contained his house. Five years ago, when he purchased the property, he had chosen this location with care. Only two houses occupied the cul-de-sac, which were separated by wide, bowery landscaping. The other house contained an elderly couple who, he discovered in casual conversation with them when inspecting the property, spent much of the year away at a condo they owned in Los Angeles, where their children and grandchildren now lived.

"Nice neighborhood, Sebastian! I can see why you bought a house here. It's beautiful and quiet. I bet this area has great schools, too."

"Well, Janet, you can always marry me, and this can all be yours." He had just pulled into the U-shaped driveway at the front of his house. "I'll even throw in letting you cook for me every night, just to sweeten the deal." He winked at her and turned off the ignition.

***

"My garage is a mess, so I'm not going to invite you down there, but I'd love to show you the house. Also, my kitchen is kind of dated and I've been thinking of getting a renovation done. I'd love to hear your ideas on it. I mean, you can wait here in the car if you want, while I chase up the brackets from the garage, but since I'm not a murderer or rapist or anything, I thought you might like to come in and maybe give me some decorating ideas." He smiled at her, first with good-natured humor, and then with frank sincerity.

She paused only for a moment. "I'd love to."

***

"I'll only be a few minutes in the garage; I'm pretty sure I know where I stored those brackets. Can I get you something? Soda, tea, coffee...?"

"No, I'm fine." She was standing in his dining room looking at some Delftware pottery on the fireplace mantel. "These are really nice, Sebastian. They must have cost a fortune!"

"Oh, hell no, those are imitations I mainly got on eBay and at thrift stores. I'm like you, when it comes to searching for great decorating bargains. They look like the real thing though, don't they?"

"They do!"

He beamed at her with feigned pride and could tell she was feeling pleased and in control because she made *him* feel proud and smart.

"Okay, well, the kitchen is right through that swinging door that-a-way, and the garage is right through this one." He held his arms out windmill style and pointed at the two doors at opposite sides of the room. "I'm going to leave you for a few minutes. Feel free to roam around the house. But I really would like to have your thoughts on what I should do with the kitchen."

She smiled, nodded, and headed for the kitchen, while he disappeared down into the basement.

***

He opened a drawer in his tool chest and selected one of his three stiletto knives. He looked admiringly at its slender profile and needle-like point, considered how it was the ideal weapon for inflicting mortal injury at close range – easy to conceal and causing less bleeding than other killing blades or clunky kitchen knives. With his easy-to-clean, vinyl kitchen flooring, sopping up what bleeding did occur was always a piece of cake. He stopped musing dreamily about the knife and brought his attention back to the task at hand. He picked up several brackets of different sizes from a bucket under his work bench, stuck the stiletto into a specially-made slit inside his jacket, and started back upstairs. He hoped she was still in the kitchen. It would make this really easy.

***

He walked through the swinging door leading from the dining room into the kitchen, holding a bracket in each hand. "I forgot – I have two types of brackets and plenty of each. Which one?"

She took both and turned them this way and that. "This thinner one. Let me show you something that I think will work wonders in your kitchen. This room has a great period feel to it which I think you can keep, while still modernizing the space."

He opened his eyes wide as though with surprise and avid interest and followed her to the part of the room containing the sink and counter space. Her back was turned to him, and he now paid no attention at all to whatever she was saying as she gestured at the sink and the kitchen window. Her voice was a meaningless drone, drowned out by the blood pounding in his ears. He was directly behind her, pulling the stiletto from his pocket, felt an erection starting—and then a phone rang.

He jerked his hand from his jacket and turned away from her, acting like he thought it was his house phone ringing, but he knew it wasn't. He just needed a moment to compose himself again before turning back to her.

"Sorry about this," she muttered, and pulled a cell phone from her own jacket pocket.

"Oh, hi Jean! She mouthed the words "my sister" at him. "No, I'm not at home. I'm with....," She looked over at him and smiled, "my new friend, Sebastian."

He smiled back at her warmly, but inwardly, he was in a freaked-out fury. She may have just ruined the whole thing by telling this 'Jean' his name.

As he watched her on the phone, he calmed down some. She hadn't yet said his last name, and a first name alone wouldn't create much of a trail when she was reported missing. As long as she didn't mention that or where he lived, it would be okay.

"YES, Jean. He's really nice. YEEEES, he's a gentleman." She smiled at Sebastian, shook her head, and rolled her eyes. "No, it's not a "hippy-pad"; it's a beautiful, old house in an upscale part of the city called Rosemond." She used her finger to make circles around her head, to indicate her sister was crazy.

Sebastian smiled conspiratorially with her, while digging his nails into the flesh of his own legs through his pants pockets. "Sebastian from Rosemond." The dumb bitch had just fucked everything up. He wouldn't be able to go through with it now and wanted to smash her over the head with a cast iron frying pan, just to vent his fury.

"I gotta run, Jean. I'll call you tomorrow, okay?" She snapped the cell phone shut. "Sorry, Sebastian. Jean is six years older than me; our mother died four years ago, and Jean's acted like a mother hen to me ever since. She's good people, though. She's coming from Vermont to visit in around three weeks, so maybe you'll get to meet her."

"That would be cool, especially if she's as nice as you." He smiled at her warmly again, but inwardly felt like punching her in the face for blabbing to her sister about where he lived. "Anyway, let me grab those brackets for you, and I'll get you home so you can get your beauty rest."

***

He dropped her off at her apartment complex, told her he'd call soon, and gave her a cheery smile and wave when she turned back to him before entering the building. On the way home, he drove way over the speed limit on the parkway, weaving in and out of traffic and chewing on the inside of his cheek.

He almost side-swiped another car, got his bearings, and realized he'd driven two exits past his own. He got off on the next one and headed back towards his house along the surface streets.

***

He carried Lindsey upstairs from the basement and placed her gently on his bed.

"I really need you now, babe. I'll pay double." He opened his wallet and began thumbing out bills onto the bedside table.

"That's okay, Sebastian. This will be a freebie. You look like you had a hard night."

She was propped up against several pillows, her black negligee open, enough below the waist to seductively expose part of her pelvic area. He stared at her a moment, still quivering inside with frustration and disappointment at the unexpected turn of events with Janet, and then started to whimper.

"Come here, Sebastian." Lindsey's voice was low and evocative, as it always was, the way a pro's *should* be.

He got onto the bed and slid over to her, pulled one of her arms over his shoulder, and buried his face in the long, perfumed wig falling over the skeleton's neck and face bones.

***

"You need to get off the streets, Lindsey. 'High-priced hooker' is not exactly my idea of a safe occupation. You know that I would marry you. All you've got to do is say yes."

It was morning and he was carrying her back down the basement stairs.

"Thanks, Sebastian, but I like our current arrangement just as it is, at least, for now."

He sighed and placed her back into her crate, gazing at her wistfully a moment longer before shutting the lid.

He was halfway back up the basement stairs when he heard Lindsey's voice, muffled and echoing from inside her box.

"Sebastian, that little snag you told me about with your new girlfriend – Janet and her sister – we need to have a party. That's the solution to everything, you know."

Claire's voice now rose up with a hollow sound from the crate next to Lindsey's. "Yes! Something nice, though – elegant – a dinner party. You can kill two birds with one stone, so to speak."

Six muffled female voices now started chattering back and forth excitedly, throwing out menu suggestions and asking to borrow jewelry and shoes from each other.

He turned around on the basement stairs and looked down at the crates with a light in his eyes and a grin across his face that really did look like it went from ear-to-ear.

***

The following Sunday, he was on his second date with Janet. They'd had several long, intimate phone conversations during the week, and she'd invited him to her house for dinner. He brought a bottle of good wine for the occasion, and now, the meal finished, they sipped and talked, easily moving from one subject to the next – her comfortable and contented – him skillfully pretending to be.

"Janet, I'm going out of town for around ten days – a work-related thing, but when I get back on the third – well, didn't you mention that your sister was coming to visit around then?"

"Yep. She's coming on the fifth."

"Perfect. I'm hosting a dinner party on the sixth. I'd like to invite both you and your sister. This way I can get to meet her, plus it will be one less day you'll have to cook for her."

"I'll drink to that!" She raised her wine glass to him in a mock toast. "I'd love to, Sebastian. That would be great."

"Okay, then! It's settled."

***

The rest of the evening progressed as planned. Soft music played in the background while they talked and finished off the wine. No matter what she was saying, he looked at her with interest and affection, while inwardly feeling like an itching, ticking time bomb.

At the end of the evening, she walked him to the door.

"So, Janet, I'll call you during the week, and then as soon as I'm back in town, I'll get that dinner party set up. I think it would be nice if you and your sister came early, before the other six guests, so that I can get a chance to know her a little on a one-to-one basis. I want to make a good impression on her. I hope she likes me!"

As he'd hoped, Janet appeared pleased with where things seemed to be going. "Of course she will, Sebastian."

They stood for a moment at the still-closed door. There was an awkward beat of silence as she looked at him expectantly. He clenched back a wave of nausea, and leaned down, brushing his lips gently against hers.

"I like you, Janet. I want to do this right."

She beamed and nodded. "Me, too."

She pulled the door open for him. He stepped out into the hallway, did a little soft-shoe just to amuse her, and gave her a wave and smile as he backed away.

***

Janet and her sister, Jean, sat on a sofa in the living room with Sebastian in a chair turned caddy-corner towards them, so that the seating arrangement formed an intimate conversation area. There were glasses of wine and a tray of appetizers on the table between them.

Jean had warmed up to Sebastian quickly and they all now laughed, talked, drank, and snacked. Sebastian, skilled at gracious hosting, was a good listener, and as he leaned forward with interest at a story Jean was rambling on about, wished he could stuff a sock in her mouth to shut her up. He knew he just had to be patient. The tasteless and odorless Rohypnol he'd placed in their drinks would soon enough take care of them both. He could have put a toxic, fatal drug into the wine to kill them, instead of just something to put them to sleep, but he didn't want to risk his corpse-cleaning bugs getting sick or even killed from an ingested poison. It also still gave him the stabbing to look forward to later in the evening.

***

After Janet had slumped over unconscious on the couch, spilling what was left in her wine glass in the process, Jean – groggy but still awake – seemed to finally get what was going on, opened her eyes wide in terror, sputtered some unintelligible words at him, and groped a cell phone out of her purse. Sebastian realized that since she was somewhat on the heavy side, he probably should have put more of the drug into her drink. He yanked the phone out of her hand, and straddling her on the couch, pressed a throw cushion over her face. Even in her drugged state, she was surprisingly strong, almost bucking him off twice, but she finally stopped struggling and sagged back, unconscious.

He went out the front door and into the garage, then up the stairs from there to the dining room. He would normally have just walked from the living room to the kitchen and from there into the dining room, but before Janet and Jean arrived, he'd barricaded that room from inside by pushing a heavy storage box up against the door. He couldn't risk either of the sisters looking in there. Not until it was actually time for dinner.

He now moved the box so that the dining room door could open again, and one-by-one, dragged the two new, soon-to-be corpses into the room and got them propped up in chairs.

He finally addressed the six women already seated around the table. "You did great, girls. I really appreciate all of you being quiet while we were in the living room."

"Well, Sebastian, you said it was going to be a special surprise party for them. It wouldn't have been much of a surprise if they could hear us women gabbing in here." It was Marie, his number four, who had just stated the obvious.

Sebastian thought she looked stunning tonight in a green silk blouse and black leather mini-skirt. "Very true."

He now turned to Claire, sitting to Marie's right. "I could use some help bringing in the serving dishes. You up for it?"

"Of course, Sebastian, but it's going to cost you an extra chess game this week."

"No problem. I've got a few new strategies I plan to try out on you the next time we play. Say goodbye to ever check-mating me again."

"Oh, we'll see about that!"

She looked at him provocatively, and he returned the look with a playful expression of his own. Her dark, empty eye sockets were magnified to almost twice their size by the thick-lensed eyeglasses she wore.

Sebastian always felt that glasses made a woman look less attractive, but Claire was definitely the exception.

***

After killing the two sisters, he got Janet settled into her tank with the beetles, then started carrying Jean down the basement stairs to hers. He didn't anticipate how her extra weight would affect his balance, got his feet tangled up in each other, and tumbled down the stairs with her, breaking his neck in the process. It took him three days to die – alone and in agony – on the basement floor.

***

The nice old couple who lived in the other house returned from a stay in Los Angeles and, noticing the odor seeping from Sebastian's garage, called the police.

Two officers entered the house, and as they started walking down the basement stairs, the cop in front stopped in his tracks. He was trying to figure out why the basement floor was *moving*. It wasn't until he got almost to the bottom step that he realized the two long, black mounds on the floor were human bodies under a carpet of swarming beetles – the proliferate offspring of those few escapees Sebastian failed to notice before he shut Janet into her tank.

All the Time in the World

Luke Walker

♩ ♪ ♫ ♬

Freddie King made it to the kitchen table a few seconds before his legs gave way. Naked, he fell into the chair, rested his head on his hands and wept. Although the nearest mirror was back in the bedroom, the dawn light shining through the crack in the curtains and making the corner of the glass gleam as always, he saw himself as if in reflection. Fat. Bald. Old. Naked. Shaking and crying like a kid who hadn't got his way before throwing a major wobbler.

Forcing any humour into that self-image failed miserably. Freddie let his hot tears soak his palms and was glad to see nothing but the faint red behind his eyes.

Helen.

Helen clawing her way out of her grave.

Helen. Her hands as pure and white as they'd been in life, but now caked with crumbling earth; dirt embedded below her smooth nails because she'd been punching and tearing at the ground they'd buried her in to get to the surface. To get to him as he stood over her grave, crying as much as he wept now.

"Jesus Christ." Freddie's mutter caught on the second word. He forced himself to take a few trembling breaths which helped a little. Then, with an extreme level of effort, he lowered his hands, splayed them in his lap and stared at the blind over the window. Warm morning light peeked around its edges. Another nice June day. Another nice day of being a widower, and another day of making it through to the evening, the night, the sleep.

Before he had the chance to stop it, a terrible question rose.

Would it have been better if she'd been rotting?

Freddie groaned. What an idea; his Helen, bones exposed, flesh mouldering, worms and insects burrowing into the holes they'd made in her body. Or, his Helen as she'd been in the dream: untouched by death, whole and healthy – the woman he'd known for the best part of fifty years – looking like they'd buried her alive as she shoved and pushed at the ground to stab her fingers through it like white flowers; then her face, speckled with mud, looming up at his feet.

35

And her eyes. He couldn't forget her eyes. Wide and hurt and confused. She'd had no idea she was dead. That was the worst. No idea days and months had gone on without her, the uncaring world happy to keep turning despite her absence and despite Freddie's terrible ache right in the centre of his gut.

Fredddddddieeee.

She'd cried his name, the word dragged out for long, awful seconds full of her betrayal of being buried before she knew she was dead.

Freddie managed to stand. He poured a glass of water at the sink and drank it with one hand still on the cool metal of the tap. His head, always quick and clever when it came to the numbers, gave him the answer to the question he hadn't known he was asking.

"A hundred and eighty days. That's what... five thousand hours?"

Yes, his mind agreed dourly. *Yes, it is.*

"Wonderful. Minutes?"

That, he couldn't work out. Not too quickly, in any case. Five thousand hours since Helen had hit the floor at The George—her aneurysm a death sentence—was more than enough to know. Freddie saw it again while he stared at the clean white of the kitchen blind.

***

Sunday dinner in the pub, the place busy enough, although not like it'd been back in their early days of running The George. Men, for the most part at their tables, talking, laughing, a few papers being read; the fire burning and warming against a particularly sharp January while the strong white of the daylight shone on the floor—and Freddie walking the length of the bar to a couple of regulars—all calling with good and boisterous humour and waving their empty glasses as if they'd been standing there for hours, not seconds. One, Sam Henderson, beginning to frown, his hand and glass lowering and his gaze behind Freddie, who followed the line of sight, turning to see Helen leaning against the pumps, two hands digging deeply into the thin flesh of her back.

Then Helen falling to the floor. Helen dying in the time it took Freddie to run to his soon-to-be-corpse of a wife.

***

One hundred and eighty days later, here he was in his little flat—the life of running The King George with his wife for over thirty years—nothing but a memory covered in dust and cobwebs. Much like Helen would be now.

Freddie closed his eyes, wishing the nasty, snide whispers inside would crumble into dirt and blow away. Even if it meant nothing in the day but weeding he didn't want to do, TV he wasn't interested in and absolutely no human contact with any of the other old farts in the building, all of that was just fine. It was everything outside the pub, his marriage; everything a million miles away from the long ago days of 1969 and being introduced to his boss's sister.

Long ago days of their first date; of that Bond film and him thinking as George Lazenby held the body of his new bride:

She's the one.

Freddie kept his eyes closed and his hand on the cold tap. It was only after several moments passed that he realised he'd been humming ♩♪ *We Have All the Time in the World* ♩♪ since collapsing to the chair.

Humming their wedding song while he wept for his wife.

♩ ♪ ♫ ♬

Standing against the wall with a beer in hand, Freddie saw Tony trying to make his way across the garden, and it was a little relief to see his son stopped by the running children and the adults who wanted to tell him the food was something special.

Keep him talking, Freddie thought at the people, most of whom he didn't know or care to. A few of Tony and Sheila's neighbours, some friends. While Freddie was happy to see his grandkids clearly enjoying the barbecue, he couldn't pretend he had the strength or focus for this. Half past three, last time he'd seen the clock in the kitchen. Another fifteen minutes should do it. Then home to wonder if he was going mental or what.

Unable to stop the image, Freddie saw himself a few hours after waking from his nightmare exactly a week ago—hand on the remote control, frowning and unsure if he honestly could hear background music on the news or if he was simply imagining it. He'd changed the channel and there it was, again—the soft mutter of Louis Armstrong behind the newsreader at her desk. The bizarre memory played over and over to reassure Freddie that, yes, he was going mental; losing his shit, a nutcase, a loony, a...—

"Dad?"

Tony had managed to make it through the gauntlet of milling children and slightly pissed adults, all carrying their plates of burgers and sausages, all drinking those little, shitty bottles of lager Freddie couldn't stand but had drunk at least eight of since arriving at noon, and still he could not escape the sight of himself, mouth open a bit while he stared at the telly like some old fart who couldn't work out how to turn it on.

"Dad?" Tony said again, and Freddie looked at his son. He had to blink a few times before the boy came into focus.

Boy? He's... what? Thirty-eight, now? Thirty-nine?

Freddie wasn't sure, and knowing Helen would tell him with a mixture of amusement and exasperation was a sting he welcomed. If nothing else, it took a few seconds of focus from the question growing louder: when would he dare to turn the TV on, again? Dare to check if the song had gone away?

"All right, son?"

"Dad. *You* okay? You look tired."

"Yeah. Fine." Freddie nodded repeatedly to show just how fine he was.

At the door to the rear of the house, a couple of the kids emerged, both carrying plastic cups full to the brim of Coke. Freddie wondered if he should say they shouldn't be drinking too much of the stuff and then realised he was thinking that only because Helen would have said so. He did his best to focus on Tony's face and clear concern. Hard to do when he wanted to dig a finger deep into his ear and stab the echo of the song away.

"Me and Sheila been talking, Dad." Tony studied the smooth grass. He kept the garden tidy, did Tony, and Freddie always admired that. The boy took care of his own as he'd been raised to do so in the pub.

"It's not great for you in that flat, is it?" Tony asked, eyes still on the garden.

"It's fine. It's a nice place. Good people. Good area."

"No, that's not what I mean."

Obviously aware he couldn't stare at the green for their entire conversation, Tony glanced up to his father for barely two seconds, then appraised the back of his house while all around, voices and laughter, conversation and human contact joined in the good heat of the summer.

"I mean... you don't have much going on there. Do you see any of the other people who live there?"

"Sometimes, son. Sometimes. It's fine. Really. I'll sort it. Just need a bit of time."

♪ *Time* ♪, Louis agreed, and Freddie saw himself standing at the kitchen sink a week before, humming their wedding song without hearing the little sound. Humming it because it'd been in his head since the second of waking from the nightmare and it apparently wanted to escape through his mouth. Problem was, it hadn't gone anywhere. If anything, it had grown to live in the TV, which meant maybe he really was a nutcase, now.

Unconvinced, Tony faced his dad directly and met the older man's steady gaze.

Here it comes, Freddie thought and couldn't be surprised. He and Helen had raised their only son well. He'd been a good kid for the most part and had become a decent man who knew what was right. And *right* was sorting out his old man's life, now that his old man's life had fallen deep into a dark hole.

"Look, Dad. I'm not going to say anything daft like come and live with us. You've got your own place and that's good. Better than staying in the pub. We all know that would have been a shit idea after Mum... after. That was your place. Both of you. And now things have changed, *you* need to change. Talk to people. Talk to your neighbours. See your mates. I ran into Sam Henderson and Billy Upton the other day. They said you haven't been in touch with anyone from The George in months, Dad. You're welcome there; that couple who bought it weren't giving you any bullshit about that, and all the regulars would love to see you. Why don't you sort a pint out somewhere with them?"

At least he didn't say go for a pint with them **in** *The George.*

Tony's cheeks were bright red, and a line of sweat that Freddie suspected had sod-all to do with the heat, dotted the boy's brow. Had they ever spoken so honestly to each other? If so, it hadn't been in more than twenty years. Probably since the ups and downs of Tony's teenage years. While Freddie had unconsciously considered himself to be the sort of dad his boy could talk to without any awkward rubbish getting in the way, maybe that had never been clear, and maybe thirty-odd years of being happy to present himself as the jovial but always in control landlord of a locals' pub meant now, he and Tony couldn't open up to each other without red cheeks and sweaty foreheads.

"I just think things don't have to be so shit for you, Dad."

And that was that. The boy finished his little speech and stood motionless, waiting for the standard, '*It's fine, really. Don't worry about me*'. Seconds trickled by—Freddie lived outside himself. He saw the two of them close together—the beads of moisture running down their little bottles of pissy French lager—the unbroken sunlight coating the green of the garden, and the reds and yellows of the flowerbed running its perimeter. And all over the place, his grandchildren playing with the neighbours' kids while adults scoffed their burgers and hot dogs and some awful pop song blared out of Tony's iPod.

Okay, son. Here it is. I think I might be going mental. I turn on the telly and I hear the song me and your mum had for our wedding dance. And this morning, I heard it on the radio. Faint and in the background, but there, behind every song and every second of the DJ talking. I haven't dared put the TV on since Wednesday. I can't listen to anything or try to watch anything because everything has that soundtrack. Everything. So what do you think about that?

"I—" Freddie began.

The song on the iPod abruptly finished. No, that wasn't right. It cut off mid-warble from some teenage boy. Not a fade-out or a smooth ending, but a sudden, jagged silence right in the middle of a word.

"Dad?"

The pleasant opening bars, the gentle flow of the tune, and then the gruff but somehow still-smooth growl of Louis Armstrong answered Tony—and Freddie could do nothing but stand with his mouth open—gaping at his son.

♩♪♫♬

Freddie folded his arms over his chest and stood utterly still. All through the cemetery, the heat of the day faded into evening warmth. Birds sung a little in the trees, the soft trill fitting perfectly for the area. The occasional car drove by out on Loder Road. The summer night closed in, the sun going down at his back in a huge sheet of red while he stood beside Helen's grave with no idea what to do or say. He swallowed. It caught in his throat, a dry click, like a snapping twig.

Another week had passed. Oddly, the moments after his nightmare a fortnight ago existed in two states: right beside him—as if time hadn't moved—and also years before. They could have belonged in the early days of his and Helen's relationship, before the pub and marriage and parenthood. And becoming a widower. Couldn't forget that.

I miss you, Helen. I really do, but I tell you what. I don't miss that bloody song. Not one bit. If I never hear it again, then that's fine with me. Just fine. And the funny thing is, I used to love it. Every time I heard it, I thought of nothing but you. You and our dance. I know you might assume I'd think of our first date, of the pictures and that Bond film, but I always go to our dance when I hear the song. And now, I never want to hear it again. Not one more time.

He took a mental breath. The ghost of the song played in memory. He'd sat on the sofa for an hour that morning, struggling to click the simple button which would turn the TV on, *knowing* Louis Armstrong would be there on every channel, desperate to believe that wouldn't happen.

Click.

And the image coming to life, the woman behind the desk as she'd been days before. No time at all could have passed. Then, a second— surely no more than that, of the only sound—the woman's calm voice.

Closing in as if speeding down the motorway, Louis Armstrong singing his lovely song now turned loathsome, no longer as background but as an overpowering storm of noise.

"Me and Tony spoke the other day. His party." For a moment, Freddie's one-sided conversation failed. Had it been the other day? Or longer? Time felt to be stretching like it was made of old glue. Freddie still managed to go through the motions of day-to-day life, or at least, he thought he did. No hunger gnawed at his belly; no thirst made his throat sting or ache, and he smelled fine, so presumably he was taking care of normal business, but even so, he didn't really know anything but the idea – he'd lost the plot. Lost it in the biggest way possible. Time was a thin line, frayed, pulling apart while he sat in the middle of it.

"The other day," Freddie told his dead wife. "He thinks I've got a problem. Thinks I've had it since you passed, Helen. And you know what? Maybe the boy's right. Maybe I need to see people. Talk to them. Maybe this going for a week or more without talking to anyone isn't right and maybe I just sort of fell into this when you died. That's the odd thing. I didn't plan on shutting everyone out. I didn't imagine myself living in the flat. I don't even know how it happened; I can't *see* how it happened, but... well, here I am. You're in the ground and here I am."

Yep. As simple as that.

Freddie let out a sob that wracked his chest. At once, self-loathing claimed him. What the hell was he doing? Standing in a boneyard while the sun went down, like some mad bastard, talking to his dead wife and assaulted by a song he used to love. Was that him, now?

"No, it's not!" Freddie shouted and whirled around. Nobody in sight to see his grief and confusion. The only movement was the gentle wave of the leaves and the bend of the thinner tree branches. Running beside the path that wound its way through the centre of the cemetery, short, tidy blades of grass trembled.

Bending double, Freddie coughed out another sob, not wanting to let it go. Better to keep it inside and relish the nasty pain of it, because he *deserved* that old ache.

"I'm going mad, Helen," he whispered. "Actually mad."

He stared at the patch of grass under and around his feet, not seeing the green. Instead, he saw his nightmare from a fortnight before, and himself standing at Helen's grave, immobile, while she pushed at the earth, creating little mounds that sent mud pattering to the sides. Her fingers broke free first, didn't they? Then her face, and her eyes – so very wide and confused at what had been done to her.

You could join Helen.

The idea came without any drama or even much emotion. It was a suggestion with as much strength as choosing his dinner every night, and containing its own power. No need to shout it, or make a song-and-dance about ending his life, the misery and loneliness. And even if there was nothing else after all his days and nights, at least he'd get away from that *bloody song* living on the radio and TV.

"Do you want that, Helen?" Freddie asked the air.

Birds sang again in the rows of old trees. Helen's headstone took the late sun, the grey stone bleeding a little red at the edges.

The chance to join his wife, six months apart; to be with her again and not have to let go of their fifty years together.

With his one mistake.

Freddie closed his eyes against the sunset on his wife's grave. It had been months, maybe years, since he thought of that mistake. It belonged in another life, when he'd been someone else. A young, stupid man, scared of the future and what he was getting into with a wife-to-be and a pub to run.

Is that what you're telling yourself? You did it because you were scared and wanted to cock everything up so you could walk away from it? Is that really what you're saying?

Freddie started crying, disgusted with himself and unable to stop. And in those tears, he realised he'd lied seconds before. It had most definitely not been years since his mind picked over those long-dead events. They'd been with him—always in the background—for the last six months. Non-stop. A scab he'd picked at since the doctor came through to the little waiting room and said, *"I'm sorry, Mr. King. I am so very sorry."* The memory and guilt broke through the little box he'd buried them in and they'd been stuck to the dark for the long, terrible days while his life fell apart.

And he could not be sorrier.

That's what I'm saying. Oh, God. That's what I'm saying. I'm sorry, Helen. You deserved better than me doing that to you and I know you would have forgiven me if I'd told you, but you still deserved more.

Thought fell apart, the pieces swallowed by guilt. All Freddie had as the evening wound down was the deep hurt of the wish that he and his sister-in-law had not betrayed Helen. It was only the once, but more than enough – forever more than enough. And the length of time did not change a thing or even come into it as an issue. He'd done what he did—Georgina did the same—and then, the wedding, and the first dance, and Satchmo's happy growl, beckoning him and Helen to the floor of the Dalry's Working Men's Club, and welcoming them to the start of their life.

And now you've got nothing but your little flat, a son who thinks you're a wreck, and a dead wife. Oh, and a dead sister-in-law you could never get on with. That's everything you have.

Freddie straightened, tears easing while the shame remained healthy and strong. He cocked his head.

Coming in like a black wave, horror roared down.

Satchmo had broken free from the TV and radio.

The song played on the breeze, drifting through the trees and over the tidy grass, living on the air like the warm currents.

♩ ♪ ♫ ♬

Freddie elbowed the bedroom door open, staggered forward and walked straight into the wall. A lightning bolt crashed through his skull and didn't do a thing to dislodge Louis Armstrong. He pressed his forehead against the wallpaper, twisting, scratching his skin, mumbling as he did so. If there were actual words slipping from his mouth, he didn't know what they were. He knew nothing, least of all, why he'd smashed the door open and walked into the bedroom.

Freddie pulled away from the wall and looked around with hot, bleary eyes. The bed, its covers a sweat-soaked pile at the foot; the chest of drawers, each one yanked fully open because he'd been looking for... he didn't know what or when. And the window on the other side of the room sealed, despite the day's heat. Keep the air out. Yep. Keep the breeze outside, so Louis couldn't get in. Not that it really mattered, because old Satchmo was still in his head, singing that ♩*fucking song*♩.

Roaring, Freddie swung his fist at the chest. The two photos of Helen, the aftershave and little clock flew to the wall, a bottle cracking. At once, the aroma of the aftershave rose, cloying and terrible. Freddie bounced between wall and wardrobe, and passed through the hallway, each door open, each window shut. He made it to the living room and stood in the centre of the carpet, head cocked as he tried to make sense of why the white below his feet was much brighter than usual. *Sunshine*, he realised, after several long moments. Lunchtime. Noon. The sun strong, its light falling through the patio doors to make the carpet shine and the wall beside the telly glow.

The telly.

Freddie stabbed at the buttons on its sides, swearing and raging when nothing happened. By luck more than intent, his throbbing fingers found the right button and the screen blossomed. He lunged for the remote on the little table—the mess of his incoherent thoughts mumbling—telling him that he should turn the volume way up and drown out everything else.

As he punched the remote, unable to focus on how to increase the volume, the image came into focus. BBC News, the young guy behind his desk talking but not speaking.

He sang.

Freddie howled and hammered on the remote. Again, through luck, he found the right button. The channel changed. Sky News.

And a *singing* newsreader, the woman relaxed on her chair, legs crossed and smiling as she *crooned.*

Every channel was the same. No speech, no discussion, only everyone singing, ♩ *We Have All the Time in the World* ♩.

The remote fell from Freddie's hands. He lunged back to the door, veering over the carpet, forced to use the wall as support. Between kitchen and living room, he managed to think for a few seconds.

Five days. No sleep. Five days of hearing nothing but the same song, and now it lived in the air and in his head, as well as on the TV. His and Helen's first dance lived everywhere, and while that could not possibly be true, it *was*. For today, for tomorrow, for the rest of his life.

"No!" Freddie roared the word and kicked the kitchen door open. It bashed into the wall; he barely heard the impact. At the sink, he yanked open the drawer, spilling cutlery to the floor. Freddie slid the longest knife free and watched light turn the blade a shining silver.

"No," he whispered. This would not be his life. Mental or not, he'd control what happened, now. He'd get away from the song.

Laughing and crying in equal measure, Freddie placed the knife against his wrist, took a few sharp breaths – and then froze.

In the back of his exhausted, hurting mind, an idea yelled for his attention and managed to slip through Louis Armstrong's voice only for a second, but it was long enough.

Staring at the white door of the fridge and no more seeing it than he'd seen the grass below his feet a week before, Freddie lifted the knife and placed the blade against the join of his left ear and skull.

With slow, methodical strokes, he *cut*.

There was no simple pain. There was agony, sharp and clear, all at once.

He continued cutting.

Blood rained to Freddie's shoulder, splattering on his arm before dribbling down his side, leg, and onto the floor.

He sawed back and forth, screaming, not hearing himself. After thirty seconds, his hand was too wet to pull on his ear. He let go, still screaming, head burning, and sliced at the dangling flesh. Gore painted his cheek and mouth red; blood slipped between his lips and he spat against the fridge. Flecks struck it, became running beads and smears. Bellowing his sobs, Freddie continued slicing. His ear hung by a thick stretch of flesh and cartilage. Catching himself on the side of his head with the knife, Freddie opened several deep gashes. The torture couldn't be narrowed down to a single wound; each wide groove in the skin and bone made doing so impossible to pinpoint, because each added its own, separate voice to a shrieking, discordant song. He dropped to his knees, landing in a red puddle. With a saturated hand, he gripped the remains of his ear and yanked.

Flesh shredded, but stubbornly held firm.

"Off. Come off." Crying it over and over, Freddie brought the knife down on the hanging meat a final time, and his ear hit the floor with a wet plop.

Roaring laughter and tears, Freddie grabbed his other ear.

The knife came down again.

Again.

Again.

Hacking, Freddie got through half of the job before the dim sounds of yelling voices and rapid hammering registered. Frantic to finish what he'd started, he stretched his remaining ear as far as he could and sawed with frenetic speed. He'd caught the flesh at the right angle; it went faster than the first attack. He broke cartilage and tugged. *Hard.* Everything had gone beyond agony now. He knew nothing but the flames stretching through his skull and the deluge of blood pouring down his sides and turning the floor into a killing pit.

Movement on the hall carpet: shadows, running.

They sprinted to the kitchen doorway, Freddie's neighbours, the people he'd barely spoken to over the last six months. They'd smashed his door down while others yelled for help on their phones, calling the police because someone was dying in flat number three; someone was being murdered in there.

They saw Freddie – his terrible wounds, and their screams bounced off the walls.

Freddie heard those screams but they were muffled. He could have been underwater. With vision blurring and shaking, he stared at the people he didn't know and heard their horror from faraway.

The song, though – that remained as close as always.

If there was an edge to go over, Freddie went with his last thoughts; as close to rational as he could manage.

Helen, I am so sorry, so sorry, so sorry.

He wept. Sight collapsed into nonsense for a moment before he managed to blink. Louis Armstrong sang in his burning skull and each face looming from the doorway rolled and shook. Each face shivered.

Freddie's vision levelled, and he shrieked at the sight of five people—for all had become Helen—staring down at him with her eyes hurt and betrayed.

Freddie screeched no words. His sound was the animal noise of his horror, and the wails bounced and rebounded off the white walls and the streaming blood.

A lone word broke free from Freddie's mouth.

"Helen."

Moving a second faster than the first of his neighbours could run for the knife, Freddie raised the blade and plunged it towards his eyes.

♩ ♪ ♫ ♬

Sapphire Moon

Richard W. Black

Constance Ratcliff loved her husband. Friends who knew the couple best thought she was foolish. Well, so be it. Patrick Ratcliff loved his life and every aspect of it, which included his wife, but he was not restricted to her. While Constance gave everything to her marriage, it was to Patrick merely a piece of a larger life, that of a Master of the Universe. There were only a few like him, men with unlimited wealth and power to whom nothing was seemingly forbidden and everything was for the taking. Such men never worried about consequences; for them, there were none they could not overcome.

Constance discovered the home while racing her car along the country roads when she had to escape the city to clear her head. She mistook the winding private drive leading to it as a lonely country road. The Latino lawn crew caring for the property stretched her high school Spanish when she spoke with them. They could only shake their heads when she drove away and ignored their warnings.

The realtor was all too happy to rearrange her schedule to show it. Though it was called a home, it was really a mansion with several bedrooms, a large dining room, a study and a huge kitchen that needed remodeling. But the most stunning was the large ballroom at the entry which opened to the second level with an interior balcony that wrapped around it and a large staircase. The real estate agent avoided her pointed questions with smiles and lies, and Constance knew she had found the home that would save her marriage. Initially, Patrick was not interested in leaving his penthouse condo and the city in which he thrived. However, Constance knew her husband and enticed him with images of the mansion as a trophy of his success, and even more so, when he realized that his wife would be *out* of the city during the day while he would be *in* it; he saw the world of possibilities for a Master of the Universe.

After they signed the papers and took possession, they went to the local restaurant, a casual business with great food and the center of the community life. Friendly locals learned that they were the owners and were more than happy to tell their new neighbors the story of the mansion and the tale of Sapphire Moon.

***

It began with Tyler Moon, a self-made man with a fortune from the arms business. With his wealth, he built a large mansion on a sprawling piece of land his new young bride named Sapphire Estate. The hopes of Tyler and Elizabeth Moon for a big family that would fill the many rooms and bring them joy were dashed when she died giving birth to their first child, a daughter. However, to his delight, Tyler Moon found the qualities of Elizabeth in the girl he named Sapphire, after the Estate, and he showered her with gifts and affection.

On Sapphire's sixteenth birthday, he gave her a necklace of silver with a matching locket that contained his portrait on one side and that of Elizabeth on the other. The young woman kept it under her clothing at all times as her most prized possession.

Then, Sapphire fell in love with handsome and charismatic Franklin Lee. She completely gave him her heart and asked nothing but that he reciprocate. They were truly in love.

At an early age, Sapphire took on the role of the Harvest Ball hostess, the annual event founded by Elizabeth and continued by Tyler in her memory. The servants of Sapphire Estate loved Miss Sapphire and put their hearts into helping her with the preparations. But the event would take on a special meaning for years to come as the couple decided to use it to announce their engagement and wedding.

Motor cars lined the road to the mansion that night and deposited the cream of the city's social elite, dressed in their best formal wear, at the front door. In the large ballroom, they found the finest foods, best wines and champagnes. A small orchestra perched on the second floor landing played favorite dance music.

For her entrance, Sapphire was stunning in her light blue gown, deep dark eyes and flowing black hair. Descending the main staircase unescorted, there could not have been a more beautiful woman in attendance. People ceased chatting, moved to the side and watched as Franklin led her out onto the dance floor while the orchestra played a waltz. It was a magical moment of love which Tyler took in with pride from among his guests. Sapphire was in love with a good man, she would marry him, fill the mansion with grandchildren and live happily ever after. What more could a father want for his daughter?

The couple was the center of attention at the Harvest Ball. Every man wanted to dance with Sapphire and all of the women wished they were in Franklin's arms on the dance floor. The dance ended and they kissed. Then their social obligations separated them but Sapphire caught glimpses of her love through the crowd from time-to-time. The party eased into the night and eventually, the contented guests began taking their leave.

To Tyler's surprise, Sapphire was nowhere to be found as he bid the guests farewell. Franklin approached him, concerned that his fiancée was missing. The rest of the guests forgotten, the men went in search of Sapphire with the help of the servants. They found her in the garden; her dress was torn and bloody, and her body savagely mauled. Her last moments of life had been violent and painful. At her side was the silver locket and chain. A despondent father held the shattered body of his child and wept. Franklin took charge, called the police and helped them with their investigation, while the usually strong Tyler Moon fell apart with grief. Eventually, the police had to admit that they were short of evidence and leads in finding the killer. It was an age before advanced forensic crime technology, when unsolved murders were not uncommon.

There would be no cold grave for Sapphire Moon; a loving father could not imagine her lying in the ground, nor being parted from her. So Tyler built a crypt for her in the garden where she had died, made of soft-colored, pearl-white stone, lined inside with lightly colored hardwood and windows to allow in the light of the sun to warm her during the day and the moon to comfort her at night. In the center was a marble pedestal upon which was laid a cushion where Tyler placed his daughter.

Meanwhile, the head police detective had the unfortunate duty to meet with Tyler Moon and Franklin Lee. He informed them that they had exhausted all their leads, and interviewed every guest several times, yet nevertheless, the search for Sapphire's murderer had gone cold. The detectives would not give up, he assured the two men, but, for the present, the case was transferred to the cold case files. As the detective left, Franklin sadly expressed his view that the killer would never be found.

Franklin Lee was the city's most eligible bachelor, there were women who clamored for his attention, and the dead were... well, dead. And as far as he was concerned, it was time to move on with his life.

Tyler Moon could not. He sold his companies and devoted his life to finding the killer. As the anniversary of Sapphire's murder approached, he became obsessed with tracking down the guilty party. After one visit to the police station for an update on the case, he became convinced that the detectives would never solve the murder of his precious Sapphire Moon. With a copy of the police file, he hired a private detective. Nevertheless, it also brought no results. Each day, the grieving father sat in his study with the view of the garden. The crypt among the well-cared for flowers and plants was a constant reminder of the hole in his heart. It was his old housekeeper who provided him with an option he had never considered.

Margaret was French Creole and a Catholic woman of faith who treated the spirit world with respect. She constantly wore a medallion held by a leather strap around her neck that fell out one morning while setting Tyler's breakfast tray on his desk. She knew that her employer sat behind his desk and constantly gazed for hours at the crypt through the large windows. But that morning, Mr. Moon's eyes were on the medallion swinging by the leather strap. She saw this and the object of his attention and quickly returned it under her clothing.

"Where did you get that?" he asked Margaret.

Had the innocent woman known what horrors her answer would bring, she might have been tempted to lie. She did not know, however, and so she told her employer about the old woman known too well by the locals, who both feared and revered her.

The old shack was in the woods near a bend in the river. Tyler parked out of sight of the road that followed the flow of the river, in fear that his car would be recognized. He checked to see that no one was about and then lightly knocked on the door. It eased open and an old woman appeared in the crack.

"What you want?" she demanded.

"I want to find the killer of my daughter."

Again she demanded, "What you want?"

He was about to repeat his statement when he thought better of it. Instead, he contemplated a moment. His tone was angry and vengeful, "I want to find out who killed my daughter, rip out their heart and smear their blood on her tomb, so that I can see it to my dying day."

"For all magic, you must pay a great price."

Tyler shook his head, "I am a wealthy man. I will give it all to have what I want."

The old woman laughed and opened the door for him.

She was exactly as Tyler imagined she would be. Dressed in old clothing, brown and rough and held in place by a rope belt, she was covered with jewelry but nothing that would be considered valuable. They were made of shells, bones, old bits of wood, animal claws and feathers. Her straggling hair hung loose. One term to describe her immediately came to mind: old hag.

The single room shack was filled with all kinds of tools of the dark arts. There were dried herbs hanging everywhere and in jars. Clay pots of every type and size were scattered on work tables, filled the shelves and covered the floor. In one corner was a cabinet with a sink, a hand pump and an old cot with homespun woven blankets. She motioned to an aged wooden chair.

"Sit," she growled. "Touch nothing."

He obeyed.

The old woman searched among her clay pots and glass jars until she located everything she required. Taking out a large mixing bowl, she combined many of the items. Finally, she looked at Tyler.

"Do you have a thing of her?" she demanded. "Something of her soul."

His hand involuntarily touched the silver chain and locket under his shirt. He had kept it when he laid his daughter in her eternal tomb. It was a piece of her, of him and her mother, that united all three. How could he part with it?

She seemed to read his thoughts. "Only the most powerful spell can bring what you seek."

Reluctantly, Tyler Moon gave the old hag the necklace and locket. To his horror, she dropped it into the bowl and it started to smoke as though on fire. His reflex was to grab it.

"Don't you move," she commanded.

Staring intently into the dark smoke, she frowned as she concentrated. "Her killer, no one knows but the girl, and she ain't telling no one."

"Can you ask her?" Tyler inquired hopefully. "Tell her that her father will avenge her, if she will only tell me who murdered her."

"She won't tell. Ain't no one to take vengeance but her."

The smoke dissipated and the old hag staggered back, drained of all her energy.

Within the bowl, there was nothing left but ashes.

Tyler could only shake his head in sorrow. "If she will not tell us, then how will I ever find who took her from me?"

The old woman emptied the ashes into a clay jar and sealed it with a lid.

"Bring together all who might have guilt." She raised the jar. "Sprinkle these on her body. She will or won't show the way to the blameworthy. It is for her spirit to decide."

The meeting was over. There would be no more questions, nor answers. Tyler Moon took the jar carefully in both hands and walked to the door, but then stopped and turned back.

"What is your fee?"

The old woman sat on a stool, her head down and face concealed by her gray, matted hair. She did not look up as she spoke.

"Vengeance does not a spirit give peace. Many who sought it, they are roaming the earth still. You think long in time before you wake that beautiful young girl. For the price will be paid for generations to come."

Tyler considered the words and briefly thought about giving back the ashes. Nevertheless, he did not. He dug a large wad of cash from his pocket, thought about how much he should give, then placed *all* of it on a table beside the door and quietly left.

Those who had attended the previous year were surprised to receive invitations to the Harvest Ball at Sapphire Estate. Whispered curiosity about why that strange, grieving old man would hold the event made it too great a mystery for any of them to refuse, so everyone responded with plans to attend.

The night had a macabre magic to it. The mansion never looked as splendid or more haunting. The guests included Franklin Lee and the Lee family. Most of those invited celebrated Tyler's courage to continue the event his wife had begun and daughter had carried on as hostess with such grace. The orchestra played. Guests ate, drank and danced; it began as a wonderful night for all. No one noticed Tyler slip away.

Out in the garden, Tyler unlocked the door to the crypt. Rusty hinges creaked as he pushed it open. Inside was what remained of the body of his daughter, slowly decaying under a silk sheet. Pulling the sheet back, tears filled his eyes as he opened the clay jar and spread the ashes over the corpse in the light blue gown, a replica of the one in which she had died. He then realized that the old woman had not given him further instructions. Sighing, he returned the silk sheet over the body, walked from the tomb, secured and relocked the door. Making the trek back to the ballroom, he wondered how his beloved

Sapphire would identify her murderer or even *if* she would identify that wicked person.

In the ballroom, Franklin led his new fiancée, Susanne Morgan, out onto the dance floor, just as Tyler Moon entered. In a tribute to Franklin and the memory of Sapphire, the couple was left to dance alone by the guests. Tyler felt a pain in his heart as the scene reminded him of a year ago.

Suddenly, the wind kicked up outside the mansion, blew open windows and doors and extinguished the lights. People froze in fear. In the moonlight, a silhouette of a woman in a light blue dress appeared in the doorway to the garden. As the mesmerized attendees watched, Sapphire Moon seemed to glide across the dance floor to face Franklin, who was unable to move. Terrorized, Susanne staggered several steps backward, then tripped over her dress and fell. Wisely, she stayed on the floor.

In the terrible quiet, as not a soul moved, Sapphire regarded Franklin as though he were a strange curiosity. Circling around the frightened man, she examined him closely, almost but not quite touching him, her face inches from his.

"Sapphire Moon," Franklin finally cried, his body shaking. "You're dead!"

They were his last words.

"You should know," replied Sapphire, her lips near to his ear and her voice a haunting whisper.

Yet, in the stillness of the room, her words echoed off the walls.

She continued in her soft voice, "I gave you my heart and you betrayed it with another. Then you killed me to hide your guilt."

Sapphire's hand shot out and penetrated Franklin's chest below the ribcage. When it emerged, she held his heart, dripping blood onto the floor.

"So, I shall take *your* heart."

She showed it to the dead man, his eyes wide with horror, the only part of his body able to move. Blood drained out from both the heart and the few arteries from the severed organ that still hung from the hole in his chest.

Franklin tried to speak again, tried to say something. Perhaps it was to beg forgiveness, but most who were present thought he was merely begging for his life. A useless gesture, he was already dead. Sapphire floated on a cushion of air, back to the doorway, the pumping organ still in her hand, and glanced over her shoulder. There was a twinkle in her eyes, and then she was gone. At that very moment, the body of Franklin Lee dropped to the floor with a thud and was soon surrounded by a pool of blood.

Susanne, lying a few feet away, screamed.

The Harvest Ball was over. The guests fled but they immediately spread the word to the community and city, though few who had not attended believed the story. The police were never called.

The Lee family quietly took away the body of Franklin. Days later, an obituary in the city newspapers announced the untimely death of Franklin Lee from heart failure. He was buried at what was billed a private ceremony. In fact, only his mother bothered to attend. Whispered gossip told the real story of the scandalous behavior of Franklin one year earlier – an unfaithful man who jumped from one woman to another – and people filled in the blanks. The night of the ball, Sapphire discovered him in the garden with another woman in an amorous embrace. They fought and he angrily beat her to death. Rumors had it that the Lee family paid the police to quietly close the cold case homicide file of Sapphire Moon, determining that she was killed by a homeless man who had died soon after.

The morning following the Harvest Ball, while the servants cleaned up from the event and talked softly among themselves, Tyler sat in his study where he had been since the previous night. He watched the sunlight through the large windows work its way into the sky and over the white crypt he had built for his daughter. The light revealed that the white stone was now stained red with the blood of Franklin Lee, and the remains of his heart lay in front of the door to the vault. Until his death, rarely did a day go by that Tyler did not savor the sight.

Local legend did not stop there.

Tyler Moon passed on and was buried with his beloved Elizabeth. Sapphire Estate was sold and resold, but always, its haunted history remained with it, because the red stains on white stones of the tomb *never* faded. In fact, some claimed that they were as bright and visible as they had been on the morning when Tyler first saw them in the sunlight and even *moist* to the touch. What fueled the tale were the occasional police reports of men in the community gone mysteriously missing. They all had one thing in common; they were said to have cheated on their wives. Their fates were stored away in cold case files and their wives' names as persons of interest, kept quiet by the police, as were the shriveling hearts found at the locked door to the crypt of Sapphire Moon. No bodies were located to go with them.

On windy nights, the women in the town were fond of warning their men that it just might be Sapphire Moon roaming the countryside in search of vengeance. Unfaithful men were admonished to change their ways if they wished to keep their hearts firmly in their chests, for Sapphire Moon might just pluck them out and smear their blood on the white stone walls of her tomb.

***

Stunned, Patrick glanced at the faces of the locals after they had finished the story. Then, they smiled impishly and he laughed, assuming they were just playing with the new folks in the community. To show that he was a good sport, he paid everyone's check and left a healthy tip.

The large moving van delivered the possessions of the Ratcliffs to their new home and the couple began settling in.

One dark night not too long after, Patrick slipped back into the mansion of Sapphire Estate after investigating the old crypt. He grabbed a handful of tissues from the box on his desk and rapidly worked to remove the substance from his hands, then threw them into the trashcan. He sat at his desk in the study, converted into his new office and brooded.

Constance was in another part of the mansion unpacking endless boxes. She had made a point of prioritizing his office as the third room she set up and established as livable, after their bedroom and the kitchen. She even took responsibility for arranging to have the computer support people from his firm install everything he needed to work from home. On the desk were multiple monitors displaying the financial markets in every country so the Master of the Universe could watch over his kingdom. But tonight, his thoughts were on the tomb he could see so clearly out his windows. His eyes seemed constantly drawn to it. It was unreasonable, he knew, but he could not stop. He had returned from what was not his first excursion into the garden.

Suddenly, someone moved in the bushes. There was a person out there. A woman – she wore a light blue dress that shimmered in the moonlight. She moved gracefully through the foliage seemingly without disturbing a single leaf or branch. Where did she come from?

"Is something wrong?"

Patrick nearly leaped out of his skin. Then he realized that Constance was in the doorway and took a deep breath to regain his composure before turning to her with all the calm he could muster.

"What?" he asked innocently. Did his voice shake? He did not know.

"I thought something was wrong, the way you were staring out the window," she replied casually.

She had a box in her hands. "I found your shot glass collection. It was mismarked," she continued. "I thought it would look good on the shelves."

He forced a smile. "Sounds good. I'll do it."

When he took the box from her, she kissed him. Her face sparkled with delight.

"I think we'll be so happy here," she said.

Glancing down, she saw the trashcan and snatched it up before he could react. "It's remarkable how much trash we generate just moving in."

She was on her way from the room when she added, "I feel like we're starting a new life."

Then she was gone.

Patrick sat the box of glasses on a shelf, but before he opened it, he snatched up his cell phone. His heart was beating so fast that he thought it would explode out of his chest, and he involuntarily placed a hand over it.

Monique was a sensual, buxom blonde, deprived brains as compensation for a great body and a wild sexual appetite. Patrick had met her when Constance was on a trip to the West Coast. He had been bored, so he went out with his buddies to add to his shot glass collection. Hopping from bar to bar, the men peeled off as they picked up women. The blonde bombshell gold-digger saw money and chiseled good looks in one package, and zeroed in on the unsuspecting straggler from the herd. They had a one-night stand that led to an eventual affair. Patrick had no desire to divorce his wife, he was in love with Constance, but he felt the sexual power of Monique and she was like a drug he could not resist. Gradually, he began believing that he could keep both of them; he actually deserved to have both women. Was he not one of the financial Masters of the Universe?

Everything was suddenly quite different from the perspective of Sapphire Estate. He could very well lose more than Constance; he could lose his life. He might just be a dead man walking. His hand went once more to his chest and beating heart.

Out of the corner of his eye, he thought he saw someone move in the garden again. Or was it the wind in the trees? And was that a voice whispering his name?

Fearfully, as the phone rang, he eased over to the windows of the office and watched a blue light drift through the garden, near the crypt.

Patrick knew that there were no excuses which could help him easily escape this house and go back to his life in the city. He had bragged to *all* his friends, clients and colleagues about the great deal he had negotiated for the property and how *wonderful* life was in the country. His reputation was on the line. Constance was happy and content. She was planning a big party... a ball. The Master of the Universe was the mansion's prisoner.

Monique answered, and without much in the way of small talk, he ended their relationship. He also terminated the call before she could protest or talk him into meeting her. He blocked her number, put the phone down and returned to the windows; the figure he thought was there was no longer visible. For a moment, he thought the stone tomb had a glow inside but then it disappeared.

Forcing his body away from the windows, Patrick unpacked the glasses from the box and arranged them on the shelves. He fought to keep his hands from shaking. Gradually, his breathing returned to normal and his pulse slowed. He felt his chest; his heart was still there and beating normally. He closed his eyes tightly and resolved to be a good husband. It was the right thing to do. Yes, that was it, the right thing.

In the hallway outside the office, Constance leaned against the wall, clutching the trashcan after listening to Patrick's phone call, with an expression of satisfaction, or perhaps, relief.

She remembered the day she stumbled on the small community. She sat in the corner of the restaurant, and with the terrified belief that Patrick would be lost to her, she could not bear it. She overheard the locals tell the ghostly story to some poor couple interested in Sapphire Estate, who fled after hearing it.

If nothing else, she knew her husband and those with whom he worked; superstitious creatures, afraid of anything that might jinx their lives, jobs or the financial markets. These brave Masters of the Universe feared anything that could tear their power and wealth from them.

She noticed the contents of the trashcan in her hands. Gently, she picked up one tissue; it was stained red – blood red. She dropped it back into the container.

As magic came with a great price, she would put her trust in the hope that her marriage would be saved by the fact that the spirit of Sapphire Moon could never be at peace so long as an unfaithful man walked near her garden. She prayed her man *would* be faithful, but the only thing she was absolutely certain about, was that she would love him, regardless, until the day he died…

Tooong!
Randy D. Rubin

1

So this is where it all ends. A lifetime, one-decade shy of a century, gonna end right here in this cold, lonely 'hoss-pistol' bed.

John Jack Pryor thought-whispered to himself. The respirator hissed in tandem with his own wheeze as he labored for each breath of air. The plastic mask that delivered his oxygen made John Jack feel slightly claustrophobic but the cool dry air was somewhat comforting when he pulled it into what was left of his lungs. Every inhalation was laborious, like trying to drink peanut butter through a cocktail straw – likewise, every exhalation was a conscientious sigh of relief.

John Jack used to say, "it was like... being on the verge... of the worst... coughing fit... of my life, just... taking a deep breath. It has to... be done slowly... so's not to... choke me ... into a hissy fit. And the mucusey shit... always comin' up... out of my throat. It's nasty tastin'... stuff... feelin' like a... wad of smashed taters... and tastin' like... dirty copper pennies."

That's how old John Jack would have said it back then—back when he could talk and sing and cuss and tell the dirtiest jokes and the funniest stories—before they had to remove John Jack's cancerous voice box, a large piece of his esophagus and trachea, and for the kicker, half of his lady-licker. The Big 'C' took hold and pretty much ate them away back in '94, and ol' John Jack Pryor had to hand 'em in, up to the front of the class, along with his three-pack-a-day smoking habit, (*Thank you very much Mister Macho-assed, Mustang ridin', Marlboro Man*).

TOONG... TOONG... TOOONG...

That sound—loud and incessant—was always there in the back of his head, like tribal war drums pounding urgent battle messages...

TOONG... TOONG... Beep-Beep... Beep-Beep...

The monitors around him beeped a steady rhythm, and put on quite a light show of green squiggly lines and amber waves of numbers; the IV dripped its own silent cadence into a tube that fed a smaller hose that fed his sun-dried, withered arm. John Jack tried to doze again but couldn't find that comfortable spot, that place where everything let go and sleep took over, lying on his back so totally supine. Normally, he slept in a slightly leaned-back position in his old recliner. It kept him from choking to death; kept the wheeze demon from oozing out of the dark caverns of hell that were his blackened lungs.

John Jack's long white hair tickled his ear. He didn't have the energy to reach up and give the gristle of it a good scratching. It made him irritable. Everything lately made John Jack irritable. Hell, life in general went marching up his ass with a stiff-bristled chimney brush.

Nurses and other staff members had taken to avoiding his room; their conviviality whittled away by the razor blades of his remarks, the thrusts and parries of his constant fussing and acts of passive-aggressive non-compliance. They only entered Pryor's world at prescribed times to dispense medication, or on the rare occasion, to bathe him or change his IV bags and/or bed linens. Nothing more, and to put it frankly, ol' John Jack was just fine with that.

"Fine as fuckin' frog follicles," ol' John Jack would have said.

He wanted to be left alone to die, quickly and quietly. He absolutely hated what was left of his life, his piddly, impotent existence. He hated the choices he'd been forced to make and the secrets he'd been forced to keep. He hated a world that hated him back in so many different ways, at so many different times. Ol' John Jack Pryor hated everything these days… including himself.

He knew all these things, and John Jack also knew exactly *why* he felt that way.

It was because at one inestimable time in his life, ol' John Jack had stumbled on or over or into… Love. And it really was as all the old sayings went; love can mess your whole life up—love's a bitch—love is a many splendored thang.

But that love 'thang' was a lifetime ago… and he hated that fact, too.

He hated this state-owned hospice, a veritable stable of the dying, and all of its state-employed staff.

Angels of mercy, my wrinkly white ass! Bunch o' so-called care-givers who really don't care about anyone or anything except their paychecks and their paid vacations and their... He jumped the tracks on his train of thought. *Hippocratic oath swearin' hypocrites, the lot of 'em!* John Jack silently raved. They were a despicable lot and he loathed them, each and every one.

At this stage of his miserable existence, he only wanted one visitor to grace his threshold and knock on his door.

TOONG! TOOONG! TOOOONG!

...enter his room and take him away...

TOOOONG! TOOOONG!

Death, himself.

Ironically, even Death avoided ol' John Jack Pryor's room, preferring to taunt and torture, to tease and torment him just a wee bit longer with the agony of life.

2

Now, to say that John Jack Pryor once loved and that this very love eventually led to him hating everything life had to offer, including the living of it—then leave that statement dangling vicariously off a limbo branch—would be down-right cruel as well as confusing...

~

Seventy-five years ago... Sixteen-year-old John-Nathan Jackson Pryor met Sarah Lee-Ann Adams, same age, at The Suffolk Peanut Festival in front of a booth where Sarah had just purchased a bag of freshly roasted goobers for a penny. There were concession stands as far as the eye could see at the festival that stretched along both sides of the peanut hull-paved promenade on that warm, sunny, somewhat humid day. Lemonade was sold by the ladle under starched tarps, or slices of freshly-baked pies and cakes, bought off the tailgates of trucks parked ubiquitously in rows, with homemade signs on handmade easels. There were booths of peanut brittle and peanut butter, hay bale display stands in each makeshift business filled with anything and everything peanut. There were kiosks and stands filled with the aromas of apple butters and jams, cinnamon-laced baked goods, hot buttered popcorn, caramel corn, roasted corn-on-the-cob baptized in a warm kettle of melted butter. There were soft pretzels with mustard, hot dogs with mustard, sardines with mustard.

There were quilts, tatted lace doilies and tablecloths. There was even a bootlegger booth and a hoochie coochie tent in the very back, by the wood's edge, that didn't get to rarin' and roarin' until way past sundown.

Tooong!

In the distance, the muffled oom-pa-pa of a tuba tried its damnedest to keep tempo for a waltz as the Suffolk High School Band more or less screeched through it, much to the embarrassment and dismay of its music director.

People drifted about the promenade slowly and deliberately, basking in the distraction from their everyday rural lives. There were judgings and contests for everything from best new recipe utilizing the almighty peanut, to the traditional 'Best Pie' (double chocolate peanut pudding parfait), 'Best Jam or Jelly' (Peanut Butter and, you guessed it, Jelly-flavored Jelly) 'Best Brittle' (Gracie's Goober Gravel), et al, ad infinitum.

John Jack was horsing around with some of his chums from school—playing keep-away—flicking his friend's earlobes and slap-boxing with the other fellas his age. They had pooled their pennies together to gain admission to the festival. It was during one of these caterwaulin' sprees that John Jack Pryor accidently knocked the afore-mentioned bag of freshly roasted goobers right out of pretty little Sarah's hand when he unintentionally backed up into her while trying to catch the cap snatched off the head of his best friend, Royce Carmichael. When he turned to apologize, she slapped him a grand one across his right cheek. Royce and the other fellas pointed shame fingers and laughed hysterically. It was a fit of folly that had them slapping their knees and holding tight to their bellies.

John Jack didn't care, though—and that was the strange part—for normally he would've cared immensely if someone else had slapped his face in public. And that someone would've inexorably taken a most deleterious ass-whoopin' from young Master John Jack Pryor. But Sarah was that someone who slapped him—who stunned him—shaming him and shaking hold of his soul… and in that very moment, she stole his heart. It was love at first slap.

As she stormed off, John Jack borrowed two pennies from Royce after handing back his cap. There was a strong sense of imperative in his voice; his heart was racing and he couldn't quite figure out why his palms were sweating. His feet wouldn't keep still as his heart pounded even harder in his chest and (*What the hell is taking Royce so long to get two coppers out of his trousers?*) and (*She's getting away!*) and his mouth was going dry as cotton biscuits and (*Hurry up, Royce, 'fore I slug you, slow-poke*) and finally, Royce slapped two penny coins into his palm.

John Jack told his friends that he would catch up to them later. He shot Royce a sly wink and ran his pomade-soaked comb through his slicked-back hair. They had come to the festival to meet girls and, by golly, John Jack felt confident that he had just taken home the grand prize… then lost it last second on a technicality.

He bought Sarah two bags of peanuts to make up for the one he had spilled and caught up to her halfway down the festival's peanut-hulled promenade. On bended knee, he proffered up the peace offering, and apologized as sincerely as he could make it sound. He knew that he probably looked like a love-struck fool but he didn't care. Sarah just stood there looking down at him in silent consternation, one hand cocked on her hip, for what seemed to John Jack like somewhere around half-past eternity. At long last, she rolled her eyes in mock exasperation and snatched up the two bags from his hands.

A tuft of John Jack's wavy blond hair had fallen over one eye as he looked up at Sarah and she thought that he just looked so damned cute in a pathetic, greasy-haired, hick sort of way. She accepted his apology forthwith and allowed him to accompany her for a piece, as she enjoyed the festival. She handed him back one of the bags as they strolled. He cracked and opened every peanut she ate that day and later, Sarah would tell her best friends from school that she thought *that* was "The Most Romantic Thing" that anyone had ever done for her.

Sarah and John Jack talked and laughed and delighted in the enchantment of the Suffolk Peanut Festival that afternoon, as if they had been friends their entire lives. John Jack would later confide to Royce (and subsequently threaten to blacken both his eyes and crack both his lips 'til they bled if he ever so much as breathed a word) that Sarah, even though she didn't know it yet, was gonna be his girl and maybe even, one day… his beloved bride. ("There, it's said. I mean it, Royce-dog! Don't laugh man, I'm serious and I will put a hurtin' on ya!").

From that day until Sarah's untimely passing (mercifully, in her sleep, John Jack always said), they never spent a day of their lives apart. After a proper year of courting, at the ripe old age of seventeen-and-a-half, and a few weeks after graduating high school, they eloped and were married in a little Baptist Chapel outside Moyock, North Carolina (pronounced Norf Kalina). John Jack was so ecstatic and beaming with jubilant pride that he climbed out onto the roof of the church to the steeple bell. He reached into the trouser pocket of his "Sunday-go-to-meetings" and pulled out a horse shoe and proceeded to ring that bell like he was whoopin' its brassy backsides. TOONG! TOONG! TOONG! TOOONG…

~

… Buzz… Buzz… Buzz… Buzz…

John Jack pushed the call button with his thumb as if detonating an explosives charge, hoping to get the attention of a nurse. Something was wrong. The pain in his throat and chest was excruciating. His crimson blood was backing up into his intravenous line and his oxygen tube seemed to be clogged with liquid.

Buzz… Buzz… Buzzz… Buzzzz…

Panic crept into his eyes and his lungs; his feet pointed downward and he gripped a large handful of sheet with his free hand—the hand not detonating nurse bombs.

Buzzz… Buzzzz… Buzzzz… Buzzzz*motherfucker*buzzzz!

His eyes widened and a tear raced for his chin. He scissor-kicked the bed like an Olympic swimmer. He groped even more bed sheet in his sweating fist. He opened his mouth in an almost-silent scream that sounded more like a hoarse whisper, thrashing his head from side-to-side in agony. He pissed himself. He cried out silently. Death was coming for him, catching him off-guard and he wasn't ready.

The call button slipped from his grasp and panic washed over him, smothering John Jack with such totality that he felt as if several wet, wool blankets had been thrown over his helpless frame. He couldn't breathe. His eyes closed. He could feel it in his temples first and it was spreading…

TOONG… TOONG… TOOONG…

BOOM!

The door was pushed open at last. The nurse rammed the medication cart into the door hard, knowing it would both startle and annoy Mister Cantankerous Old Bastard who obviously wanted to practice his antiquated Morse code over the call button and drive everyone at the nurse's station ape-shit.

"Okay, what seems to be the problem Mister… Pryor?"

The nurse had to look down at the foot of John Jack's bed on his chart cover to remember his name. When she looked up and saw him convulsing, she sprang from behind the med cart and went into action. Pushing buttons on monitors and quickly changing the intravenous bag that held John Jack's pain medication, the nurse increased the flow of the drip that cleared the blood from the tube. She then reattached the Pulse-Ox clamp device on his index finger, cleaned the mucous from his oxygen tube in his nose and readjusted it. She picked up the call button and taped it to his bed rail.

"Mister Pryor? I know you can hear me, okay? Open yo' eyes fo' me, Mister Pryor, okay? You've had another panic attack, okay, that's all. You gonna be just fine, okay? I'll send in a 'tendant to change yo' gown and bed linens and bathe yo' bony white ass, okay? You just wants to lay off that call button fo' a spell now, Mister Pryor, okay? Give us a minute's peace out there, please. I'll take yo' chart and make the necessary annotations, okay?"

John Jack's eyes slowly opened as the fire in his temples, throat, and chest subsided. He began to relax, letting go of the fistful of bed sheet. He looked at 'Nurse Okay' with abject loathing, still unable to move. He was hoping that, at long last, Death was coming for him this time. It took him unawares and it scared him.

"Do ya want yo' head up or down, Mister Pryor?" Nurse Okay asked, not really looking at him. He made a 'thumbs-up' gesture with his left hand. He slapped the bedrail to get her full attention and again put his thumb in the air indicating that he wanted his head raised. She looked directly at him, smiled sardonically and said, "Okay," one last time, and then she left the room without raising the head support of the bed.

Tears of rage slipped from the sides of his eyes as he lay there. Yet another annoyance, John Jack thought, as gravity forced his teardrops slowly across his temples and down into the cups of his ears. It was at that moment that John Jack Pryor had a stark revelation—an epiphany of sorts—coming clearly to the realization that the staff at the hospice wanted him gone. In fact, it seemed that they wanted old John Jack to expire as quickly and quietly as was humanly possible, "Thank you very much and if it's not too much to ask."

This last little visit from the Angel of Mercy from the 'okay corral' was the spark that ignited the flames of this reality bonfire. They knew that if he laid flat he could drown in his own juices, especially in his sleep. It was slow torture, that's what it was, John Jack thought. And as if that weren't enough to piss a person off, the piss bathing his lower extremities was starting to sting the decubitus ulcers that had just begun to clear up on the cheeks of his ass and the backs of his legs.

Sting... Sting... Stang... Stung... STOONG... TOONG... TOOONG...

John Jack drifted off into a fitful dream where he was sitting alone in the porch rocker at the container yard and the sky was rapidly darkening. It was as if someone were playing a movie in fast-forward for the movement of the clouds, but slow motion for John Jack and the rest of his perception. Grayer and more voluminous, the clouds rolled across his restricted skyscape, and with such speed. Lower and blacker the sky became, until he felt like he could reach up and into the thunderheads and pull lightning down with his bare hands. In extremely slow motion, he rocked forward and tried to reach up into the sky with one painfully outstretched arm, to grab the reins of the storm, to touch the roiling, billowing clouds as they galloped by. With a raspy whisper, he called out for Sarah to come and witness this obsidian stampede and his mighty attempt at harnessing its power, but thunder stole his 'thunder', and lavender lightning whips cracked the sky. The clouds groaned their displeasure as they ran across the horizon.

Cra-ack... TOONG... TOONG... TOOONG...

Ever so slowly, John Jack settled back into his rocker and rode the chair's backward momentum, allowing his arm to rest at his side. He felt deflated and weak, embarrassed and ashamed. He knew Sarah was gone. He knew, too, that he was no match for the sky. He knew that he was alone and defeated, not knowing what hurt the most—the defeat... or being so alone with it. He rocked forward again as the chair propelled him, forward and ever so slowly forward until...

~

John Jack came awake with a start as if he were about to fall forward onto his face. He gasped. Two big, burly male orderlies were attending to the task of bathing him; one of which had John Jack's bony, see-through ribcage cradled in his arm, bent forward so he could wash his back. A warm terrycloth rag rubbed pink the translucent skin covering his spine. The head of the bed was raised, the bed linen replaced, and a fresh hospice gown was applied. A fresh lamb's wool pad was stretched out under his buttocks and lower extremities. John Jack Pryor was back in the land of the living.

This explains the feeling of falling forward, he deduced. The orderly carefully laid John Jack back onto the mattress. The other began lowering the head of the bed. John Jack vehemently protested, shaking his head. The other gentleman stopped cranking. They packed up their portable washing station and quietly rolled it out of the room. John Jack forced a whistling "Wait!" to them just as the door eased shut.

He smacked the mattress with his hand in anger and frustration, sure that he had missed a chance at getting a small favor. One of the orderlies came back into the room and asked John Jack if he had said something. He motioned the man closer to the bed and asked for a pad of paper and a pen, which came out like "paa pa puh and peh." He also mimed a writing gesture.

"I'll see what I can do, Mister Pryor. No promises, mind you, but I'll see what I can do," Young Master Bather said. Just then, the other orderly popped his head into the room and hurried his partner away with an exasperated, "Come on, we still have four other patients to bathe before knock-off."

John Jack could hear their voices trailing off down the corridor. "What'd the old guy ask for?"

"Something to write wi–" … and they were gone.

He stared up at the holes and the water stains in the acoustic ceiling tiles. *This is surely what hell is supposed to look like*, John Jack thought. He resisted the temptation to count the number of tiles in the ceiling for the umpteenth time, the number of holes in each tile, the number of braces holding up said tiles, and the number of cinder blocks in each wall of his room, et cetera, rooty-toot-poop. Bored he was again, and bored he was destined to remain, it would seem.

He closed his eyes and tried to think of something pleasant, something other than how many units it took to construct his private section of hell. Nothing would take him away from his mundane existence. Nothing came to his mind. He opened his eyes.

Oh, yeah, this is definitely what hell is supposed to look like. Time takes a proverbial shit, the demons monitor you from a station on the opposite side of hell, and the devil makes all your decisions for you.

3

Tears are the grapes grown from the vines of our memories – and their bittersweet wine flowed down John Jack Pryor's face. He craved the silvery-sweet, dry taste of tobacco coursing into his now decrepit, parchment-like lungs. He lusted for the bitter-bitch burn that a swallow of sour mash bourbon from Kentucky's finest bordello bottle would bring his crusty palate. His heart ached for just one last, tender kiss from Sarah's rose petal lips. There was a stifling pain in his heart. He cried as these memories flashed like a slideshow across the otherwise blank white screen of his mind. His chest heaved and clutched, spasming, and at last, relaxed with the exhalation of air. His vision blurred and then cleared as the tears jumped from the rims of his eyes. He clenched his gums together to stifle the emotions, channeling them into something else, something more physically painful and less emotionally excruciating.

Toong... Tooong... Toooong... He could feel his pulse in his temples, pounding against the walls of his head. That sound, that haunting, incessant din. The pain was intensifying. The noise was almost overwhelming, and thunderous... Toong... Tooong... torturous... TOOONG... *murderous*... TOOONG...

~

He was back in the container yard—*his* container yard. The land was a gift from his father. Eighty acres of oil-soaked junkyard bequeathed to John Jack Pryor and aptly named, 'Pryor's Auto Salvage and Welding'. John Jack worked that land up to the very day they picked him up and put him in this hospice-of-the-damned, the day of his last myocardial infarction, they called it. Said ol' John Jack was plum eat-up with the cancer, too—lungs, liver and lymph nodes all ablaze with it.

The sky was black and bilious with thunderclouds, rolling past his field of view at a gallop and splintering the windshield of the sky with whip-cracks of peach-colored lightning. John Jack was at the back of the yard, moving a stack of NYC containers to a new row with his Hyster 2060 heavy-duty forklift. He had just finished welding new hinges on the doors of these "Semi-Trailer" containers and was preparing them for pick-up and delivery to the Transway Trucking Terminal in Chessy, (that was what Sarah called the city of Chesapeake—Chessy.)

Rats as big as purse dogs scurried across the yard as he lifted each container from one spot to the next, settling into place with a mighty TOOONG sound. They were eventually stacked four high and made a formidable wall around the perimeter of John Jack's yard. He stopped to light a fresh "coffin nail" with one hand, shaking the stick up and out of the pack and catching it in his teeth, all the while waiting for the tines of the fork to elevate to the height of the highest container.

Sarah was in the kitchen cooking supper—a pot of 'Cranberry' or 'October' beans—swimming alongside a smoked picnic bone with a cornbread chaser. It was one of John Jack's favorite meals. He would say, "Cut me a Vidalia onion into quarters and serve 'em up with fried taters and a tall glass of sweet tea, then back your ass way up!"

He had moved over to a row of Genstar containers over in the back corner of the yard, blowing black diesel smoke behind him from the Hyster's exhaust pipe as he bounced down and up again over the potholes in the gravel. Hawks circled overhead, riding the wind in search of some hapless rodent they might swoop down and dine on. John Jack loved the hawks, with their fierce beauty and swift unwavering savagery. He once said that if reincarnation was actually a thing, he'd want to come back to Earth as a hawk so he could ride the winds and soar across the sky.

He flicked his cigarette butt into a gleaming puddle of water lightly frosted with diesel fuel that looked like a liquid rainbow across the surface. Lowering his tines again, he spied a slight movement out of the corner of his eye – ever so slight, accompanied by a small noise, like a skittering creature. It wasn't your typical rat or opossum-in-the-weeds kind of noise, either. It wasn't a bird or cat-stalking-prey sort of sound. John Jack was used to those skitterings and would dismiss them as nothing after so many years of tending his yard. This was different. This was the alarming kind of noise, like when a daddy who could normally sleep soundly through a thunderstorm with the television blaring and his wife snoring her nightly bassoon concerto right next to him, wakens in the middle of the night the instant his child's sock-covered foot touches the Berber carpeted floor to get up and go pee. There's an unexplainable intuition that something just isn't quite right in the world.

John Jack noticed that one of the container doors on the bottom of a stack of "K-Lines" next to where he was about to do some container rearranging, was swinging slightly on its hinge. He depressed his clutch and put the Hyster in reverse. He always made sure that the bottom container doors were shut-up tight and sealed with aluminum tape. John Jack didn't like this; it didn't sit well with him. He backed the lift all the way to his house, as if nothing was wrong.

Sarah met him at the door. He put his finger to his mouth as if to indicate silence and then mimed like he was carrying a long arm— rifle or shotgun—it mattered not, then pointed to the back of the yard.

Sarah understood and disappeared from the front door for several seconds. John Jack shook another "cancer stick" from the kindling box and lit it with his trusty Zippo – an invention John Jack swore was the best thing ever made. It never failed, no matter how windy it got. "This bitch'd light inside the innerds of a tornado, by gum," ol' John Jack would declare. He exhaled the smoke but the wind wrapped it around his neck and into his hair, stealing the pleasure of it.

Sarah returned with John Jack's pump shotgun, the one he liked to hunt deer and rabbit with on cold winter mornings. She handed it up to him barrel-first and lifted two shells to him with her other hand. He motioned her back into the house. She closed the door and locked it.

From the corner of his eye, he spied where the edge of the living room curtain was pulled back slightly so she could see. He loaded the shotgun and put the Hyster 2060 in gear.

As he approached the container door, two doves took flight from a scrub of weeds on his left. He never flinched or took his gaze from the open container door at the back of the yard. He drove with the gun across his lap, slowly and deliberately, drawing large amounts of smoke into his lungs and exhaling through his nostrils like some kind of human locomotive. Adrenaline poured into his blood and his muscles tensed up, tightening as he got closer to his target. With the dexterity and prowess of a needlepoint seamstress, he threaded the tines of the forklift into the carrying slots under the top two containers. He lifted them off effortlessly and set them aside in an open area of the yard. The Hyster swung around in a tight circle and the forks were already in the exact position to impale the slots of the bottom container. He pulled back on the fork elevation knob and lifted the container in the air to a height of about thirty feet, setting it aslant on a stack of its brothers so the entrance door would swing open into a thirty-foot drop down to a gravel stop. John Jack put the lift in neutral and cut it off. He raised his shotgun, placing the butt of it on his thigh, his nostrils exhaling more smoke.

"Whoever you are – now would be as good a time as any to open that door and show y'self." John Jack yelled, absently flicking the cigarette away. "Don't make me say it twice, boy, to come out of there."

There was silence, then Tooong... TOOONG... TOOOONG... as the door began swinging open and the end of a shovel handle was visible. "Don't shoot, Mista. Okay?" A voice from inside the container wavered.

"What are you doin' on my propity, boy? This here's private... and it's posted so. So now... what makes you think you can just mosey in here, bust open one of these semi-trailer containers on posted private propity and set up house? You can read, can't you, boy?"

"Mista, I's just sleepin' off a couple bottles of dinner and a tallboy breakfast. No harm meant. I'll just leave the way I come, if'n you'd see fit to settin' this down closer to the ground," the trespasser said. He looked filthy and gaunt, smaller than his clothes and yet, strong in a wiry sort of way. He had a three-day growth of stubble hiding the nuances of his affect and his eyes were "pink with the drink" and only open enough for navigational purposes.

"I'll set her down if'n you give me your word to leave peaceful-like and post haste," ol' John Jack said.

"All right, Mista... my hand to the heavens. I'll skedaddle without so much as a peep. Just don't shoot me with that double thumper you got there."

John Jack fired up the Hyster and set the container down with a thundering TOOONG, maybe just a wee bit too hard. "What's your name, young fella?"

"Albert... Albert Donavan, sir." The younger man staggered from the container and leaned on the shovel as a walking stick. He slammed the door to the container and locked the bar down into the slot. "It's gonna need another seal, Mista. I cut through the other with the shovel blade. And I'll pay fer it... I just needed a..." he lost his train of thought, as he waved his arm at the container, then looked back at ol' John Jack. He hobbled on shaky legs toward the front entrance to the yard. He moved slowly and drunkenly across the gravel. John Jack lit another cigarette from atop the forklift.

From somewhere off behind them, Sarah called out to her husband that his supper was ready. He jumped down from the lift and headed toward the vagabond, on his way toward the house. He still clutched the shotgun, barrel resting over his shoulder, while he smoked. He watched the young drunk from behind and soon caught up to him. He walked with him and offered up a smoke, shaking one out of the pack. Albert thanked him and lit up using a Zippo similar to John's.

"So, where you from, boy?" Ol' John Jack asked.

"Souf Nahfick."

"I got people lives in South Norfolk, too. So's my wife, Sarah. So, why'd you pick my place to sleep off a good drunk, Albert Donavan?"

"Just got laid off at the shipyard. Been there three years, bustin' my tail in the dry dock, buildin' them Navy ships and then outta the blue, they say they don't need a bunch of us no more 'cause the contract hadn't quite run out, but it was runnin' thin, if'n you catch my meanin'. So I hit the titty bars and a few juke joints and got me a bottle or three an' ended up here. Seemed as good a place as any to nurse my wounds."

They continued toward the front of the yard in silence, Albert with his shovel walking stick and John Jack with the double thumper resting on his shoulder.

"You et anything in the last few days, boy?" Ol' John Jack offered from somewhere out of nowhere in particular.

"No sir, can't say as I have. Just drinkin' and chasin' away these out-a-work blues, I reckon."

John Jack stopped and stood about still as a stone, watching Albert Donavan stagger toward his front gates. He sucked in the last burning drawl of his cigarette, held it in his lungs for three seconds or so, and flicked the butt away with his middle finger and thumb. He exhaled an audible sigh.

"First, Mister Donavan, you need to wash up 'round the side of the house, then I'll have the Missus rustle you up a bowl o' beans and a chunk of corn pone for soppins and a onion chunk. If'n you can stomach some solid food, that is. Then maybe we can talk about puttin' you back on the wagon and back to work," Ol' John Jack said, before even *he* knew he was actually formulating the words and making the offer.

Albert Donavan stopped. He didn't turn around. He leaned on his shovel and rubbed the scrub on his cheeks with his free hand and hid the tears that were forming in the corners of his rheumy pink eyes. "That's right kind of you, Sir. I reckon I'm finished drinkin' for a piece. I'll get washed up and meet you on the front porch directly."

Ol' John Jack left him to it, calling out at Sarah to set another place for supper. She came out of the house at a trot, wiping her hands nervously on the towel tucked into the front of her apron. She took her husband's shotgun and stowed it in the house, all the while whispering to John Jack, asking him what had transpired in the yard. He gave her the abbreviated version and said he was doing his Christian duty. Albert Donavan was his name and he would be joining them for supper tonight and working with him around the yard tomorrow, and from there, it was anyone's guess. Sarah smiled at her husband and looked over his shoulder nervously at the front door and the man who was crossing the yard to the side of the house.

4

So it began that Albert Donavan, simply called Albie, worked for and with John Jack for nigh on six years. He proved to be a hell of a welder and yard man, keeping the containers stacked and inventoried, primed, painted and ready for shipment – in short, a very organized man with a keen business savvy. He was the one who suggested to John Jack and Sarah, over supper one night, that they section off the yard and sublet other businesses, like Forney's Firewood Company and the Dreadmere Parts Yard. Both businesses, paying rent on parcels of land fenced in on three sides by containers stacked three high, proved to be very lucrative. Then the used containers that were either forgotten or left behind for non-payment of services were leased as storage units, bringing in even more monthly income. John Jack and Albie became business partners.

Together, they bought the twenty-five-acre piece adjoining John Jack's land and fenced in the whole parcel with containers three high for privacy and security. They sublet it to an automobile repossession company and the money flowed. The sound of cars being prepped for auction or crushed, or broke down for parts and then crushed, along with the constant stacking of containers, made the sounds of thunder incessant—Tooong, Tooong, Toooong, and John Jack would nudge Albie in the ribs or on his arm and say, "That's the sound of money being made by the ton, Son," or "There's gold bein' dropped from the sky in thunderloads, Albie." And life went on all peaceful and profitable and tranquil—and calm—like the eye of a hurricane is serene and taciturn. Six years of unity and contented prosperity, and then...

~

It came to the ass end of that hurricane one unassuming, cloudy day in the autumn of Nineteen-Hundred-and-Twenty-Aught-Some-Such that Albie and ol' John Jack had a massive drop in the barometric pressure of their friendship. John Jack had come into the house to get another pack of smokes, and there in the kitchen, standing way too close to the love of his life, was good ol' Albie, lookin' like the cat who swallowed the canary. Now, in reality, (according to the two of them), Albie was just looking to get to the sink to wash out his eyes. He had ground down a weld and had several slivers and minuscule shavings of metal flecks and dust stuck to the moist rims of his peepers. They were annoying the hell out of him and stinging so bad that he ran into the house.

Sarah was at the sink and thought it was John Jack come for a glass of water or smokes. She was startled to see Albie run in, but immediately saw that something was wrong, so she tried to sidestep out of his way. He went to the same side and she moved to correct as he moved to compensate, and they ended up in each other's way a second time, and just as Albie went to gently move her from in front of the sink, grabbing her upper arms and sliding her to one side, in walked ol' John Jack, and it *looked* as if they were in some sort of embrace. Albie jumped back reflexively, then pulled himself to the sink to wash out his eyes—but the fuse had been lit in the mind of his friend and business partner—and it wasn't long before the jealousy bomb inside John Jack would blow sky high. All the explanations in the world couldn't diffuse that ticking device of paranoia and assumption, once it was lit. And the tempest on the other side of that hurricane's eye grew daily and exponentially, as John Jack's manifest jealousy had him seeing nothing but red, confirming his suspicions with constant, filtered, tunnel-vision scenarios, time and time again.

Sarah tried to calm her husband. She explained away that initial incident after much bellowing from John Jack, even while spraying several hundred gallons of rinsing water directly into Albie's eyes with the sink's dish hose. He was in visible distress and his eyes were blood-red with metallic irritation. John Jack eventually and seemingly succumbed to the truth of the matter, but he never quite fully believed their story, nor let the embers of his rage go completely to cold ash. And everything his wife or Albie did or said from that day forward only reaffirmed John Jack's tainted and infected thoughts.

He kept a watchful eye on Albie now – one that he had figured was never really necessary before. Sarah was and always would be his bright and shiny star whose light shone only for him. She was John Jack's piece of heaven—his private angel—his gift from his Maker. Albie had been his trusted friend, but now John Jack thought of him as a devil sent to steal some of that light—John Jack's private radiance—and maybe even snuff that light out completely. What had seemed   either   divine   providence—or   simply   fortuitous happenstance—six years earlier, John Jack now saw the truth of it all: Albie hadn't drunkenly and accidentally stumbled into his container yard those several years back. No. In fact, John Jack knew now that Albie was the Devil himself, come to take all good things away, including his most treasured possession, his beloved Sarah. The wealth, good fortune and prosperity were Veils of Evil, further devised to blind John Jack to the truth of what Albie was. Why, if John Jack hadn't walked in on those two in the kitchen that first day, he might have gone on forever, never knowing that a den of iniquity was brewing right beneath his nose and inside of his own home, with his very own wife and his best friend and business partner. It reeked of the Devil's most poisonous plans, but John Jack now knew better. He'd never be fooled by the wolf in sheep's clothing that was Albie Donavan ever again. He knew the whole truth now, and could see with unfettered eyes. Albie would not mar his wife, nor take beautiful Sarah away. John Jack would never let Albie succeed. He loved his Sarah too deeply to let that happen. Albie was the Devil on Earth, sent to torment him and steal his precious Sarah away, and John Jack knew that Albie must go.

~

As the days wore on, John Jack came to realize this epiphany more and more, cementing it in his brain and thoroughly coating all his thoughts in its bitterness, its pungent blackness. Within weeks, the tension was so thick between the two men that it made the very air of the salvage yard unbreathable. Cigarettes wouldn't even stay lit. While they worked, there seemed to be more coughing and spitting than talking and enjoying a smoke.

They took to avoiding each other, and Albie felt John Jack's sour, acidic gaze and smoldering, quiet anger burning into the back of his neck and mixing some of Hell's itch with the sweat on the small of his back. It felt warm and sticky and itchy all at the same time. John Jack would just take to watching him from afar, something Albie rarely had to put up with until the incident at the sink, and it gave ol' Albie the Heebie-Jeebie-Jump-Backs. He wanted to say something about it but he really needed another paycheck or two before he beat feet out of there, telling John Jack to take his greasy-assed job and shove it up his Hyster! So, Albie avoided any confrontations and kept his back to his business and his nose to the proverbial grindstone. He would weld up those containers, primer 'em up, paint 'em up pretty, and stack 'em up four high.

Several times a day, Albie or John Jack would take up a chipping hammer or a sledge or a maul and a loud TOOONG, TOOONG, TOOOONG could be heard for miles around, like some muffled basso bell being rung for church services or just for freedom's sake. TOOONG, TOOONG, TOOOONG—chipping that slag off or knocking the hell out of that rust so the primer and paint would stick to the metal. TOOONG, TOOONG, TOOONG...

***

Ting, Ting, Ting-ing, Ting. John Jack could hear the pen hitting the hospital bedrail every time he took it up to write more of his death bed confession. His hand cramped. His eyes stung from the dull fluorescent lighting and the tears burning down the parchment of his cheeks and out of his blackened, ashen soul. His lower lip quivered uncontrollably. He wasn't sure if he could go on. He had to, though. It was inevitable and imperative that he finish this deathbed repentance of his, if he was ever going to find some solace at the end. He had told himself this. He had also reassured himself that he would probably never die if he didn't get this on paper and out of his soul, mind, and ailing heart. He would live forever, he told himself, in pure agony and eternal frustration and pain. That would be his punishment for the evil he had done. He would never be rid of it unless he confessed and had someone take it from him. Without his beloved Sarah, he so wanted death to come for him. He was dying for death to come and take him away. He was oh so finished with this miserable existence he was forced to endure, where all of his functions and fluids went on without him, all his thoughts were polluted, and his dreams were tainted and painted with the evil from his past.

He set the pen down on the bed and rested for a while. There was a plastic water cup with a bent straw sticking out, like the world's smallest periscope, on the tray beside his bed. They had mercifully set him up with ice chips in a small plastic pitcher and drinking water in the matching cup. The ice and the water renewed him, calming his nerves. He leaned back in bed and drew several ragged breaths, envisioning deliciously sweet tobacco smoke in each rusty exhalation. He had visions of his beloved Sarah fetching his cigarettes and whisky as he rocked in his porch chair into the evening. She would finally settle in next to him in her own rocker, sipping sweet tea and knitting something for someone or embroidering a doily or pillowcase. She would sing softly into the twilight breeze as she busied her hands and John Jack figured that to be as close to heaven as any man could hope to ride in a rocker. He sipped his whisky and smoked.

John Jack woke from his recollections of front porch paradise with that dull-pounding boom in the back of his head. It was coming on him again and he whined softly, knowing that it would arrive any minute now with its own sledge hammer.

TOOONG! TOOONG! TOOONG!

It took hold of his teeth and pushed down on them, driving them into his gums.

TOOONG! TOOONG! TOOONG!

It squeezed his temples together, forcing his eyes to want to bulge out of their sockets. His nose had that runny, coppery-nosebleed taste in his sinus cavity and the back of his throat. He winced against the onslaught of the pain. From the window in the door, it looked as though ol' John Jack was grinning. His eyes were closed tightly to keep them in his skull.

TOOONG! TOOONG! TOOONG!

This would have to be his last spell, he thought, between the ringing iron bars of his pain cell. He could not endure another. He just couldn't do it.

TOOONG!

He couldn't stand it.

TOOOONG!

His jaw clenched so tightly against the throbbing agony in his head.

TOOONG!

His neck went rigid and his shoulders ached as if he were saddled with a heavy oaken ox yoke.

TOOONG!

Take me. Take it away from me, Lord. Take this pain, this pounding agony and suffering from me, please, Dear Lord in Heaven.

TOOONG!

Please... and ol' John Jack mercifully lost consciousness.

***

When at last he woke, the pounding had ceased. He opened his eyes slowly and tried to focus on the room and thanked his Maker for the peace and the silence. His mouth and throat were prairie dog dry and he remedied that situation with melted ice chip water. He pissed freely through his catheter into the output bag zip-tied to the side rail of his hospice bed. He tried to shift his ass on the sheepskin pad and couldn't—he was stuck to it from his oozing bed sores. He found the pen under his ass along with the steno pad of paper that the orderly had brought. His IV line fed him his nourishment, but damned if he couldn't swallow down a half-dozen fried eggs and a pound of chewy cooked bacon and some biscuits with apple butter. Maybe a black coffee wash-down at the end, sort of a last meal before sentence was carried out. Ol' John Jack actually smiled that time and it made his face feel good. He took another few sips of water, scratched at several places on his person, rubbed his bristly face, and took up the pen to finish his confession.

5

I reckon I killed Albie Donavan in a fit of jealous rage. I think my true love, Sarah, my beloved angel, my shiny light from heaven and gift from God Almighty Himself, and that rat bastard, son-of-a-bitch, back-stabbin', scurvy drunk, bug-riddled mongrel cur had intimated relations when my back was turned. I can't prove it for one hundred percent surety, but I can damn near almost, 'cause I feel it prickly-like in my bones, the way they look at each other and the way they avoid talkin' plain to each other and several other 'each others' that don't feel or figure right. A man knows! They say a woman knows these things when their mate steps out on them and fools around, but a man knows it too, by God!

I took that worthless son-of-a-bitch into MY world, into MY home, into MY business, into MY friendship, and fed his sorry ass at MY supper table damn near every night and this is how I'm repaid for my kindness. That's just how I feel about the whole situation, that's all. I done what I done justified. JUSTIFIED! Do y'all understand me! What I done, I done for justified reasoning. This is what started it all.

Albie was a worthless drunk. THE END.

(Good Lord, I wish it was that damned easy.)

Albie worked with me through the holiday season a right good piece back. Almost forty-three years back. (Good Gracious has it been that long?) Sarah passed in, well, I don't rightly remember the specific chronological year number any more. What I do recollect is that that low-down son-of-a-bitch took an unhealthy shine to my missus. I could see it in both of them after a spell. The way they eyed each other like they couldn't jump in the sack fast enough or rip each other's coveralls and cover-ups slam off quick enough to suit either of them. I saw it! We'd sit down to supper and every time I'd look at him he was shooting glances over at her and vicey-versey. It was magnetic or something. It had its own tug and pull. It was like an acid eatin' at my insides, that feeling of somethin' hot and itchy and suspicious happening right in front of my snot locker. My beloved wife and my, well, hell – I might ought to go on and admit it once and for all, my best friend. MY BEST FRIEND AND BUSINESS PARTNER... AND MY SARAH!

It still burns at me. It singes me at my core. That blackness that steals the colors from my sight and makes all music seem like white static noise. It makes my tears sting as they run from my eyes and burn down my cheeks. It creeps into me and brings its asshole best buddies, Loneliness and Paranoia, with it. Nothing tastes good or smells pretty anymore. Even my favorite smoke and whisky tasted like char and sour piss, back when I still had those. This thing steals pieces of my soul and patches it up with hatred and despair.

For, you see – I come to hate Albie Donavan. I hated that sorry son-of-a-bitch plum to death!

The holidays had ended and we was just puttin' up the decorations and the tree. Sarah made Albie a scarf and wool hat set. He gave her a large cross-stitchin' kit with hundreds of different colored threads all skeined-up, and various sized needles and cloth patches to practice on from up the handicrafts store in Portsmouth. He gave me a jug of real smooth, real 'spensive corn. I gave him extra wages as a bonus. We had a big ham supper together and he helped to polish off all that was left over as the days raced from the Lord's Birthday to the New Year's starting point. I watched the two of them together, gigglin' and singin' carols and fetching each other some of this and that. It really fanned the embers in me. I started to smolder and catch flame.

Then he told us come the week or so after New Year's he'd be leavin' to go up North to some family he had in Drake's Branch and wanted to thank me and Sarah for all our kindness and generosity. Sarah looked about ready to cry and throw her arms around his scrawny neck and beg the son-of-a-bitch to stay and the only thing holdin' her in her chair was the bona fide ass whoopin' I'd have dealt her (and him, come to think it) if she moved from her spot at the table. She didn't move a cricket flinch. That's about the only thing that saved her (and him, come to sayin' it, by God!) from meeting an untimely end right then and there.

So that night, Albie tells me he's headed into town to try and find some female companionship for the night and give me and Sarah some time to ourselves. I reckon I figured this to be the ideal opportunity to get some payback on Ol' Albie Donavan for eyeballin' my missus and needing some Sarah replacement therapy for the night.

While he was off fornicatin' and frolickin' in town, I set out on the front porch for a piece, smoldering slowly in the cold January evening, fueled by good Christmas whisky and quiet rage (way too cold for my Sarah to set out in), formulating a diabolical plan. It was a delightfully evil plan so perfectly revengeful that even I shuddered from it. Maybe it was the cold winter breeze taking hold of my bones and rattling them like a wind chime. Maybe a shot glass full of both. I know I was grinning like an old Halloween jack-o-lantern into the evening wind on that porch and probably glowed nearly the same color orange from the embers of hatred fanned damn near to flames in me. I rocked on knowing just how easily Ol' Albie was gonna pay for his piss-poor pathetic attempt at cuckoldin' me with my sweet Sarah.

First, a bottle of my finest hooch and two glasses, I figured. Then, a little music on the front porch radio just a tad louder than normal. My Hyster 2060 keys and my work gloves, I reckoned ought to do it. Keep it simple, Son-of-a-Bitch. Slow and steady wins the race. Patience is a virtue. Love is a many splendored thang. Revenge is a dish best served colder than penguin shit.

It WAS cold that night, setting on that porch in my rocking chair, waitin' for that sorry-assed Son-of-a-Bitch Albie to come stumbling back from town half shit-faced and bouncin' off everything, all played out and laid out, tore out the frame from playing too much of the game and fucked up in the head and ready for bed. It was biting cold. The Hawk was out, as we used to say. I had hatred to keep me warm, though—hatred and whisky. I rocked away the evening, whisperin' to myself, 'patience, John Jack, just have patience,' to the cold, indifferent Hawk wind with every sweet stinging sip of my corn. It whispered back after a piece. Whispered raspy little evil barbs of meanness and hatred for Albie, whispered goads and go-aheads to go find him and kill the Son-of-a-Bitch once and for all. I listened to its evil prodding and poking carried to me on the breezes. Listened intent and forthright, by Golly. It brought a shit-eatin' grin to my jaw as I listened to it egging me on. Each time I heard it in my head, I'd damn near squeeze my whisky glass to shards. My rocking pace picked up and my feet tapped the porch boards unbeknownst to me. That's what they call adrenaline, I reckon, pure adrenaline coursing through my veins like lit fuses cracklin' and spittin' fire as it consumes.

I got up from the chair around two in the morning and went for a stroll around the property. It was quiet 'ceptin' for a coon party tearing through the trash dumpsters over at Forney's Firewood. Gusts of January's icy wind whipped up long enough to smack my coat flap into my cheek then settled back down as I checked that my gloves were next to the seat of my Hyster. I climbed into my seat and started her up on the first turn of the key. She moved ahead slowly and I picked up the first YANG MING forty-footer that I came across off the top of a four-stack and set her down near the entrance of the yard, forks still under her, door side facing away from my slumbering, beloved angel, Sarah. I clipped the aluminum seal and opened the container door with the handle but left its twin brother locked down. I went and got the fresh whisky fifth and two glasses, a flashlight and a fresh pack of coffin nails all from behind the seat of my truck. I could hear the porch radio blaring country classics from the truck so I knew my Sarah wouldn't hear me out by the YANG MING container. As I slammed my truck door shut, I could hear Ol' Albie singin' something all slurry and mumbly and knew my plan was about to go into motion.

I hurried to intercept his stumble-bumblin' behind by the container. After scaring the tea-totallin' shit out him, coming up on him while he was pissin' on the side of one of the containers at the entrance to the yard, he screamed like a mouse-frightened housefrau, fell down, partially in his own puddle o' piss, pulled up his trousers and asked what the hell I was doin' up so late.

I laughed and said I reckon I just couldn't sleep and before I knew it, I was drunk as a mule and fixin' to break into a bottle of my best, most expensive corn and did he want to join me in a glass? I was gonna go sit in the container and get shitty-pop drunk on the finest hooch money could buy. Ol' Albie's eyes lit up and a sly smile crept over him. I had practically sobered his ass up just scarin' the bejesus through the pores of his skin so he was tempted to join me. For the slightest of moments, he hesitated and looked at me through his rheumy reddish-pink eyes (that couldn't seem to focus on me or anything else in particular), then he looked over at the YANG MING with the door open and I quickly said it needed some work on a door hinge and I'd deal with the welding of it tomorrow.

Albie shrugged and followed me into the container. We opened that fifth and poured it by the glassful down our throats. In reality, I let Albie out-pour and out-drink me two-to-one on that fifth and before long, he was rip-roarin', soarin' and finally snorin' drunk. I quietly left him sleeping it off and gently, ever so softly, sealed up that container with a new aluminum tie. Then all quiet-like and smoothly so as not to wake the Son-of-a-Bitch, my Hyster cradled him in its loving arms and gently placed the container at the bottom of a four stack at the back of the property between several other four stacks. It was some of my finest and quietest work, and in no time that YANG MING container was obscured on all sides, never to be seen again, as far as I was concerned.

I'd tell my beloved if she asked, and in time I'm sure she would, that Ol' Albie just figured on making a clean break, I reckon. He probably wasn't real big on 'Good-byes' and figured he'd be better off leaving this way. In the course of a couple of days, Sarah asked, as I reckoned she would, and I told her what I figured and it was a done deal, explained away good.

Then, that very same freakin' evening, after supper was finished and I was just sitting down to my first shot of cool burnin' corn on the porch, with Sarah sitting next to me practicing her cross stitchin', that damn noise started up...

TOOONG! TOOONG! TOOONG! TOOOONG!

...from the back of the yard.

TOOONG! TOOONG!

That sorry-assed, low down dirty...

TOOONG! TOOONG!

Son-of-a-Bitchin'...

TOOONG! TOOONG! TOOONG!

Wall pounding asshole had finally sobered up and obviously woke up enough to realize his premeditated, permanent, perfectly performed predicament. Fuckin' Albie Donavan; I plum forgot he wasn't dead yet—just dead drunk.

I had some quick thinkin' to do, 'cause Sarah was standing with her hand up to her forehead, shielding her eyes and wondering what the commotion was all about. I quiet-like and smoothly told her that Forney 'cross the way was probably stackin' a freshly split load of fire wood fagots against the side of a container on his side, and that seemed to nip her curiosity in the pantaloons just peachy-fine.

Next morning though, by golly, I knew I'd have to silence that confounded noise, that TOOONG! TOOONG! TOOONG! shit once and for all. Who'd a thunk I'd be tortured with that devil's poundin' for the rest of my miserable life.

6

Next morning, during breakfast, that 'Albie-goin'-ape-shit crazy' poundin' resumed. Again, I had to come up with something smooth and nonchalant to tell my beloved to keep her from wondering what the hell. I said that Forney's boy must be tryin' to make him some overtime this week, startin' that fag stackin' so early.

Sarah threw her hand up and said she reckoned as much, from over at the sink. I told her I'd have a talk about the noise and she told me not to worry about it; that they have to make their money too. I gave her some money and told her to go shop and get her hair done if'n she wanted and of course she said she did. She kissed me on the cheek and snatched up the two twenty dollar bills I held out for her. She took off to the bedroom to get gussied up to go out. I had my work cut out for me today and I needed a couple of hours alone to get it done.

Sarah left about a half-hour after breakfast. I went to the shed and got a heavy duty drill and a large steel cutting bit, an extension cord and a half bucket of water. After starting up the Hyster and taking down the four-stack with Ol' Albie on the bottom, I set up the cord and the tool and climbed to the top of the container and drilled a huge hole in the steel, cooling the bit in the water bucket every few minutes. Albie started screamin' to let him out, let him out. I just ignored him for a time, until finally, when I'd broke through the top, I softly told Albie Donavan to shut the fuck up. Then I took a well-deserved piss, aiming it into the freshly-drilled hole. Albie screamed and begged some more, frantic for me to let him loose. I told him I didn't appreciate him trying to steal my beloved Sarah away from me and fuck him. He pleaded with me to let him out, offering me money and promises of never seeing his sorry ass ever again. He screamed more obscenities and blubberin' that I couldn't make out and then he just started crying. I don't mean little boo-hoo whimperin' and snifflin', I mean bawlin' out-fuckin'-loud, hysterical crying, like his Mama had just whooped his backsides with a willow switch. It was those screaming cries that started to wear on me. I felt myself softening and getting a bit misty-eyed my damned ol' self. To say it was plum pitiful was as understated as saying Ol' Moby Dick smelled a tad bit fishy or that our Lord and Savior Jesus Christ was good with his hands and made great kitchen furniture. I'm telling you, Ol' Albie Donavan was pathetic. I had to jump down and leave him to his sissy fit baby cryin'.

I headed over to my truck for a roll of duct tape and our garden hose. I ran the hose up my exhaust pipe, taped her off, started the truck up, revvin' the engine a few times for effect, then did the same with the other end of the hose, securing it to the top. I rearranged everything with my Hyster, hiding the container and the truck from general viewing.

Ol' Albie's bitch-screamin' and sissy bawlin' had ceased. Everything got real quiet for a time. I sat on the Hyster and smoked about six coffin nails, then got thirsty and went into the house for a glass of cool-burnin' maize mash. I had a bottle hid in the back bedroom for emergencies like this one. Soon as I tipped the bottle to pour me a shot, that damn death cadence started up again...

TOOONG! TOOONG! TOOOONG! TOOOONG!

...over and over for a good solid hour, he banged on that container and for a good solid hour, I thought I'd go stark raving bat-shit. I couldn't drink it away. I couldn't smoke it away or find a pill (or twelve) that would ease that pounding pain in my soul.

TOOONG! TOOONG! TOOONG!

It just kept poundin' into my head and throbbing into my bloodstream and coursing constantly through my veins and arteries, beating loudly into my wayward soul...

And then mercifully, it stopped.

For a time, everything was still and silent.

I poured another drink and downed it.

Then another.

I lit another smoke and walked outside, mindful not to smoke in the house.

I shut off the truck and disconnected everything from both ends. I fired up the Hyster and stacked every container up the way I had it. I rolled up the extension cord and re-coiled the garden hose to hang on the wall beside the spigot. I tossed the water out of the bucket and put it back.

And that's when I saw my beloved Sarah watching me from the corner of the driveway, pretty much hid by the weeds and the tires and the junk stacked up right at the entrance to our yard. She had never left, apparently. She had forgotten something and had decided just to shut off her car and walk back to the house to get it, to save on gas, I reckon. That's when she saw me and what I was up to. She saw the whole thing.

She never mentioned it; acted as if she hadn't seen me or that I hadn't seen her crouched down behind all that scrap iron and junk. She turned and ran back to her car. I heard it start back up and drive away. I was petrified for a time, wondering what she would do. I had a feeling she was coming back a cold one with a law dog chaser. Then she returned from her outing and went about her business, putting up groceries, tying on her apron and saying nothing as if nothing had transpired, so I left it be. I let sleeping (actually, dead) dogs lie. The name Albie

Donavan was never spoke of in our house ever again, not even as she lay dying on <u>her</u> deathbed.

***

John Jack dropped the pen. He winced and gurgled something inaudible in his throat. His eyes shut tight and his neck extended. It was coming for him one last time.

My Beloved Sarah…

TOOONG! TOOONG!

Pounding on the side of that container…

TOOONG! TOOOONG! TOOOONG!

Close to her boyfriend's container…

TOOONG! TOOONG! TOOOONG!

And begging me to let her out…

TOOOONG!

"Please let me out of here!"

TOOOONG!

"John Jack, *please*! Let me out!"

TOOONG! TOOONG! TOOOONG!
TOOONG! TOOONG! TOOOONG!

Tooong! Tooong!

Tooong……………

The Undiscovered

Jeffrey B. Burton

"**I** killed all of those prostitutes, sir. Officer Schussler, too."

"Goddammit, Billy, you sure as hell did not!" Lieutenant Ross slapped the top of the table with an open palm.

"Please, Lieutenant," I said, "let me ask Officer Monroe some questions."

But where to begin? It was three o'clock in the A.M. For the past hour or so, I'd been drinking stale coffee in the 76th Precinct off Union in Brooklyn South, and bringing myself up-to-date on a grim series of waterfront killings as well as trying to unravel tonight's most disturbing sequence of events. I consult with One Police Plaza as a forensic psychiatrist and spend no small amount of time evaluating suspects' competency to stand trial. Most often, I'm utilized by the district attorney in criminal proceedings as an expert witness for opinions on mental state—you know, whether a defendant knew right from wrong and was able to understand the nature of what he or she was doing at the time of the crime.

So imagine my surprise when my deep slumber was shattered by a phone call at 1:00 A.M., followed by a loud banging on my front door, followed by a fifteen-minute, siren-blaring, roller coaster of a ride to Union Street, only to find out that the defendant in question happens to be one of New York's Finest. Imagine my further surprise when Lieutenant Ross and Captain Dietrick—both having been around the block enough to see what's coming—pushed strong for me to consider NGRI. Not guilty by reason of insanity.

"Officer Monroe, I notice they call you Billy. May I call you Billy?"

"Yes, sir."

"No need to call me sir. My name is Gerald Keiffer, but please call me Jerry. Now, what I'm here for is—"

"You're that shrink."

"Yup," I said and smiled. "I'm that shrink."

I'd followed pretty closely with the muzzled news reports—prostitutes being murdered, cut up, near the waterfront—but, of course, the murder file that Captain Dietrick let me thumb through contained stunning police photos that evaporated any thoughts of my returning home to peacefully complete my night's sleep. Although the police had held their cards close to the vest on this one, some scribe at the New York Post had referenced Jack the Ripper . . . if they only knew the half of it.

Over the course of the last several weeks, five ladies of the evening had been found dead near the waterfront. Two in alleyways hidden behind dumpsters, two in rooms that rent by the hour, and one poor soul laid out on a doorstep. But the manner of death—and I'd just paged through the equally stunning autopsy findings—absolutely boggled the mind and curdled the stomach. Their heads were split apart, each one perfectly halved, like a walnut shell. The medical examiners were at a loss as to what could have made such a cut so cleanly, so evenly, slicing *dead center* through the hairline, down the forehead, between the eyes, dividing the nose, and through the upper jaw, mirroring the same in the back of the skull as well as splitting the victims' brains perfectly into left and right hemispheres. No surgical instruments, such as the Gigli saw, used to remove the top of skulls in autopsies—or any type of bone cutter, sternum saw, or laser scalpel in their arsenal—could have accomplished this feat. Much less, the perp having done so while harried and stooped over a doorstep or in a dark alleyway.

Substantial traces of *water* were noted at all victim sites, puddled with the blood about the split skulls, dampening the victim's hair, and slopped onto exposed brain matter, indiscriminately, like a baby splashing. This led one detective to theorize that the killer was utilizing some type of wet saw, I guess something like a portable tile saw—a wet saw with an out-of-this-world kryptonite blade. Tests indicated a salinity of 3.5 percent or 35 parts per thousand.

In other words, *seawater*.

It was a mystery all right, but like any great mystery, it contained a double twist. The photos I'd rushed through were disturbing, difficult to look at, and the only thing missing from each victim was not money or purses or any of their rhinestone garters or cheap jewelry, but something strictly held back from the press. Each victim was missing their hippocampi—or, to be more descriptive, one hippocampus was missing from each side of the victim's brain.

"Billy," I continued, "your friends, here, are very concerned about you. But what you are telling them gave them pause to...," I paged through the sheets in front of me, "administer a breathalyzer, which indicates you've not been drinking alcohol. And to also take a blood sample for a toxicology report in case there's been some drug use."

"They're wasting their time."

"I suspect you're right. Regardless, what you went through tonight was traumatic. *Exceedingly* traumatic. Billy, please trust me when I tell you how well-versed I am in how the mind attempts to cope with such painful events. I could wax on, as I'm prone to do, about all sorts of psychoanalytic theories about our various defense mechanisms; how the mind unconsciously works to protect one's personality from terrible unpleasantness. You've probably heard of such concepts as displacement, regression, or repression."

"I ain't crazy, Doctor. I murdered all of those women, sure as I'm sitting here in front of you. In cold blood. I can still . . . smell their blood on my hands. I can't say why I did it, perhaps that's where some of your mumble-jumble comes in, but I killed them. And I also killed Officer Karen Schussler."

I watched as a single tear swam its way down the side of Billy Monroe's nose and came to rest on the corner of his lip.

"Well, Billy, they let me look through your file, and I must say, I'm very impressed. You appear to be on the fast-track for Detective. Several commendations, already." I scratched my cheek. "If any good is to come from this, perhaps you could let the doctors know what type of tool you used on the six victims, because, quite frankly, Billy, they're stumped. A tool like that might someday be used to save lives."

"I—um. Let me think." Billy stretched out both of his hands and fingers as though he were holding a bowling ball in front of him, digging his nails in, and began to twist.

"Jesus Christ, Doc," Lieutenant Ross said. "Billy's telling us he popped their heads using his fingertips. We've got to be able to Durham rule this."

A Durham rule excuses a defendant whose conduct is the product of a mental disease or defect.

"Is the Lieutenant correct, Billy. Are you telling us that you were able to perfectly halve their craniums with your fingers and nails? As though these women's heads were Russian nesting dolls?"

Officer Monroe shook his head and shrugged. "There are gaps. I must have gotten rid of some evidence."

"Must have gotten rid of evidence? Billy, you called in from the undercover site and have spent all night confessing to the waterfront murders, but now you say you decided to dump some of the evidence prior to your confession?"

Officer Monroe shrugged again.

"Tell me what you know about the hippocampus, Billy?"

"It's part of the brain. Humans have two. That's about it."

"Billy, you're confessing to having killed six women, split open their heads by means unknown, and stolen a hippocampus from each side of their brain. And that's all you have to say on the matter?"

Billy waved his hand. "Stuff from the briefings. They're kind of curved. Shaped like a small banana or something."

"Well," I said, beginning a lecture as though I were on the witness stand, "the hippocampus is one part of the forebrain. It's located in the medial temporal lobe, to be exact, and actually belongs to the limbic system. It's a very old part of the cortex. But you're right about the shape, Billy. The name derives from the Greek word for seahorse—*hippos* equals horse and the word *kampos* equals sea monster."

"What are you getting at, Doc?" asked the Lieutenant.

"I just find it rather ironic as this case deals for the most part in *memories*. Billy Monroe's memories of the waterfront slayings and his subsequent confession, Officer Schussler's newfound love, Officer Jensen's multiple repressions—all of which burst through to the light of day at a most absurd time."

"That nonsense Jense was sputtering about before he died . . . it was just more fucked up shit in a night of fucked up shit. What's this got to do with anything, anyway?"

"There are three main schools of thought regarding hippocampal functions that dominate the medical literature. The first being the behavioral inhibition theory, how some animals with hippocampal damage tend toward hyperactivity and have difficulty learning to inhibit responses previously taught. A second line of thought relates to spatial functions, the hippocampus as a cognitive map, if you will, with spatial coding playing an important role."

"Doc, we already know that whoever *really* cut up the brains of those dead hookers is one sick fucker," said Lieutenant Ross.

"Just hear me out. The third school of thought is what I'm getting at; the third school of thought is how the hippocampus relates to memory. Human memory is an endlessly complicated phenomenon and involves other regions of the brain. However, information is transferred from short-term memory to long-term memory through the hippocampus."

"Christ wept." Lieutenant Ross dropped his head into his hands. "So, you're saying that Billy really did eat Officer Schussler's hippocampus and that's why Billy's memories are all fucked up?"

"No, Lieutenant." I shook my head. "Just pointing out how the hippocampus is the catalyst for long-term memory, in a case where the memories of our three officers have been *interesting,* to say the very least. And in a case where the two hippocampi in each of the six victims are . . . missing."

"Craig Jensen had a meltdown right in front of our eyes." Staring straight ahead, Billy suddenly blurted to no one and everyone in particular. "Went from being my best friend and ex-jock superhero to some kind of collapsing nova in about ten seconds flat. Screaming a lot of psycho-babble about his past and his wife leaving him and even *crazier* shit, before putting the gun in his mouth."

"You're right, Billy. I've listened to the tape." Officer Karen Schussler had been wearing a wire while walking the streets and the motel room had been wired for sound as well. "It's as though a thousand years of repressed memories smacked your friend, Officer Jensen, full in the face. I think we should listen to the tape together. Billy?"

"Nothing on that tape changes anything, Doctor Keiffer. I wish to God it would."

"Let's give it a listen, Billy. Let's see if we can both give it a fair assessment."

Officer Schussler worked vice. Ambitious girl. So it was fitting that she be pulled to walk the waterfront. Only after the recent murders of the five prostitutes, she was in search of something a little more serious than your basic, love-starved johns. Billy Monroe, costumed up as a low-rent drug dealer, was Schussler's tag. On the street, she was never out of Billy's sight, and they were wired in together, as was Officer Jensen, sitting in the rent-by-the-hour motel room where Officer Schussler would bring any men who solicited her for certain services. She'd already brought two gentlemen back, who'd received the surprise of their lives, once money had changed hands. They were arrested and hustled out the motel's back exit to a waiting squad car, while Officers Schussler and Monroe returned to the streets. It was the third visitor to that flea-bitten motel room that captured my interest.

I pressed the play button on the device in front of me, so we could all listen to the recording that had originated from Officer Schussler's wire.

***

Officer Karen Schussler: You look a little lonely, sweetie.
Inaudible background noise.
Officer Karen Schussler: Sweetie, wanna little company?
Inaudible background noise.
Officer Karen Schussler: Yes, sweetie, you pay, we play. Sugar's got us a room.
Inaudible background noise.

***

I pressed stop.

"Billy, why can't we hear this john's responses—his offer of cash?"

Billy Monroe just shook his head.

"I've played it several times now, and all I get is that indecipherable susurrus."

"What's that mean?" asked Lieutenant Ross.

"Whispering noises, edge of consciousness. What is that sound, Billy?"

"Feedback, maybe. There can sometimes be distortion or some interference."

"So, Officer Schussler was getting picked up, right? A verbal transaction had taken place."

"Yes. There was *someone else* there with her . . . at first, anyway."

"At first? So, you're saying he left?"

"Yes."

"But why would this *someone else* leave, Billy? Why would you *let* him leave?"

Billy scratched at his ear. "He just left. Cold feet, I guess. Whatever. He hadn't paid her yet, and we didn't want to blow our street cover chasing him down, so we decided to head back to the room and have a sandwich break."

"Let's think hard, Billy. What did this *someone else* look like?"

"Obviously male. Caucasian. Pretty nondescript. I only saw him from across the street. He probably thought about the wife and kids and lost his nerve, I guess. Why does it matter? It was after he left that I decided to murder Karen . . . just like I'd done with all the others."

The three of us sat in silence for a minute. I could feel Captain Dietrick's eyes watching us from behind the two-way mirror. I couldn't imagine him liking the ebb and flow of the conversation thus far.

"So, a sexual transaction begins, but is immediately broken off. Then you and Officer Schussler decide to head back and have dinner with Officer Jensen?"

"Yes."

"The recording from Officer Schussler's wire of your walk back has more of that indistinguishable murmuring, but we're able to pick up the rest from Officer Jensen's mic at the motel room. Now, this next part isn't pretty, Billy, but I think we'd best listen closely."

I set the tape and pressed play again.

**

Officer Craig Jensen: Hands in the air, motherfucker!

Pause

Officer Craig Jensen: (Inaudible) . . . dripping Nosferatu motherfucker! Back away from him, Karen!

Inaudible background noise.

Officer Craig Jensen: Get away from him, Karen! Goddammit, I've got no angle!

Officer Karen Schussler: I love him, Craig. I always have. We're going to be married, Craig. You know that. I won't let you hurt him.

Officer Craig Jensen: Fuck are you saying? Back away, Karen!

Officer Karen Schussler: We're to be married, Craig. I won't let you shoot my fiancé. We're to be married.

Officer Craig Jensen: Goddammit, Karen! Move your ass!

Inaudible background noise.

Officer Craig Jensen: Oh God! Oh . . . My . . . God!

Inaudible background noise.

Officer Craig Jensen: I can't . . . I fucking can't.

Inaudible background noise.

Officer Craig Jensen: Marie's leaving. Packed and gone, she fucking knows. (Sobbing) Oh God help me, please God help me—she fucking knows.

Officer Karen Schussler: What are you saying, Craig? Put your gun down and we'll talk.

Officer Craig Jensen: (Sobbing) That bastard had at me since age six. Whenever mom was away—had me on their own goddamned bed! Good God! (Sobbing)

Officer Karen Schussler: We can get you help, Craig. Just put down the gun.

Officer Craig Jensen: You know it's a fucking circle, Schussler, you know that. (Sobbing uncontrollably) I've done things . . . and Marie knows.

Inaudible background noise.

Crashing sound.

Officer Billy Monroe: Craig!

Officer Craig Jensen: Fuckin' ends with me.

Officer Billy Monroe: Craig! Noooo!!!

Gun discharges.

Inaudible background noise.

***

I hit stop.

"Sounds to me, Billy, that *someone else* was in that room, that you followed Karen back to the motel per protocol. You heard the commotion from the hallway and burst into the room right when Officer Jensen was placing his service revolver into his mouth and pulling the trigger."

"That's not what happened, Doctor. After Craig killed himself, I murdered Karen, just like I did all the others." Billy's blue eyes drilled into me at maximum force. "You like listening to tapes, Doctor, turn it back on so you can hear me butchering her. Karen's . . . shrieks . . . will be with me to my dying day. That's all I'm able to think about. I was covered in her blood when the squads arrived, for Christ's sake."

"Look, Billy," the Lieutenant began.

"No, sir! You do your job and lock me up. Either arrest me, or I'll get a lawyer and we'll hold a press conference on the front steps, and force you to do your job."

"Okay, Billy, you want to dive headfirst off that cliff? Fine! Fuck it!" Lieutenant Ross stood up. "But you're not taking the department down onto the rocks with you. That's for sure. I'll get that dipshit, Baldwin, to Mirandize you."

The Lieutenant left the interrogation room.

"So you and Officer Schussler were going to be married?" I asked.

"No."

"Of course you weren't. It's my understanding the two of you only met last week as the taskforce ramped up. So why would Officer Schussler say such things?"

"She was trying to save me. And look where it got her."

I cleared my throat. "I'm only seeing small pieces of the puzzle, Billy, little glimpses, but let's assume that you did all of these killings. Funny thing, though—you don't look like a 'dripping Nosferatu motherfucker.'"

Officer Monroe stared back across the table at me, but said nothing.

***

I stood behind the two-way mirror with Captain Dietrick and Lieutenant Ross. We watched as Billy sat motionless at the table and listened to Officer Baldwin read him his Miranda rights.

"What do you say, Doc?" Captain Dietrick asked.

"I believe him."

"Bullshit," Lieutenant Ross piped in his two cents.

"I should say; I believe in the sense that Billy believes himself. And his non-verbals and head turns all appear to be that of a man telling the truth. In fact, Lieutenant, I believe Officer Monroe would pass any polygraph test."

"So we push hard for a Durham?"

"A mental disease or defect, combined with the grotesque nature of these killings, would probably help Billy before a jury. But it won't catch your killer, Captain. At least we can all agree that it was anyone but Billy who murdered Officer Karen Schussler and those five other women."

"Agreed."

"ViCAP or the other databases hit on any similar M.O.s?"

"Only hit was from the turn of last century. This area, believe it or not. Killer was never caught, but at the time, the perp was considered to be some kind of an expert with a broad axe."

"How many were there?"

"Six," Captain Dietrick answered. "All female."

"Six of them. Hmm. Anything regarding missing hippocampi?"

"That case was a hundred years ago, Doc," said Lieutenant Ross. "It's colder than a witch's tit."

"Humor me."

"Nothing on any missing hippocampi, but the waterfront had an epic rat infestation back then. Sadly, none of those victims had been found any time soon. The reports indicate that the rats had a bit of a field day on the remains. Sketchy autopsies, but," the captain stared at me and continued, "the skull fractures, or the splittings, were similar in all cases."

"Yes, very unfortunate that Teddy Roosevelt went off his meds back then," Lieutenant Ross added, "but if we could bring the focus back to the 21st Century."

"Rats, huh?" Something glimmered in the back of my mind. "Either of you ever watch those nature shows on The Discovery Channel or PBS? I eat that stuff up and have always marveled at what nature has thought up, for different animals to be able to defend themselves. You know, how skunks' secretion—their spray—deters predators; how a porcupine's coat of quills deters predators—and a porcupine is just a rodent."

"What are you driving at, Doc?"

"Not much, really. Recently, I heard that we haven't even begun to come close to discovering all the species of animals in the oceans. In fact, there's this new species of box jellyfish they named Malo Kingi after some poor bastard tourist who died after being stung by one. Remember that TV Crocodile Hunter who died after a stingray barb went straight into his heart? Mother Nature provides her children with all sorts of defense mechanisms. And also a million ways that creatures can camouflage themselves so as not to be seen by their natural predators. Even those seahorses we talked about earlier change color to hide from predator fish. Just as there are endless manners of killing and subduing prey, there are endless manners to elude predators."

"You're getting a little random here, Doc," the captain replied. "Is there a point?"

"Just how memories are incredibly powerful things, gentlemen. It was Faulkner who said, 'The past is not dead. In fact, it's not even past.' Now, just imagine the ability to insert *fictitious* memories into others as though you were a blackjack dealer slinging cards. Imagine what would occur, Lieutenant, if, say, suddenly you had an overpowering and very distinct recollection of Captain Dietrick having slugged your mother in the nose. It'd probably take three of us to pull you off him. Now, consider the impact that *fraudulent* memories of true love or pedophilia, or even *murder* would have, if suddenly introduced to your average Joe."

"But, you heard the tape, there wasn't any time for mass hypnosis or anything to indicate something like that," the captain said.

"The defense mechanisms of the creatures I've rattled off are relatively mundane and ho-hum. We've known about skunks, porcupines and jellyfish our entire lives and never give them a second thought. But, just for another example, consider the sheer complexities involved when an Octopus releases melanin—it's called inking—which, when you really think about it, is pure subterfuge; provides a smoke screen, while the Octopus jets away." I finished my coffee in one long sip. "I go back to the seawater found at the scene of all these murders, mixed in with the blood and brain tissue . . . and I just can't help but realize that beyond the waterfront, it's a deep and relatively unfamiliar ocean out there."

The three of us stared at each other for several seconds, before Lieutenant Ross burst out laughing. "Jesus, Doc, you had me fuckin' going there for a second."

"We called you in to help Officer Monroe sort through last night's insanity, Doctor—or lay the groundwork for M'Naghten, Durham, or the ALI test—not to hear a Grimm Brothers' fairy tale."

"Just mumbling aloud, Captain. Just mumbling aloud."

***

I stepped out into the pre-dawn morning and waited, alone, for the squad car to appear that would take me home. And, after that last exchange, it was quite unlikely that I'd be called back to the 76th Precinct any time soon. I could smell the water and turned to face the harbor. The burgeoning sun busily chased away shadows and other such cobwebs. There was a tickle in the back of my mind, an inkling about the case.

But then it was gone.

Pan-Dimensional Monsters Hate Anger Management

Michael Shimek

He stood at a podium in front of a group of twenty people seated in metal folding chairs. Most eyes stared at the tall and rail-thin man, a flannel shirt and jeans hanging off him like clothes on a hanger, but others darted around or glared with furrowed eyebrows at the ground. The overcrowded room stank of coffee and stale donuts, stationed on a rickety table in the back. Motivational posters were pinned to the walls, and two ceiling fans wobbled with rusty squeals of white noise. The standing man took a breath and then began his introduction.

"Hello. Some of you may know me, and some of you may not. My name is Keith Richards—yes, unfortunately, my mother was a huge Rolling Stones fan when she had me—and I am here because of some anger management issues I've had trouble dealing with since being diagnosed with cancer."

As the Emotions Anonymous group greeted Keith to their monthly meeting with nods and hellos, a more familiar voice drowned them out.

You are a liar. Tell them the truth.

Shut up, he mentally sent Pan, the name he had given the pan-dimensional monster living in his stomach. *Go away. You're not wanted here.*

Am I wanted anywhere?

Keith tried his best to ignore the voice and the gnawing at his insides. He pushed the monster away and continued with his introduction.

"Ever since I was a little kid, I have had a slight temper problem. I don't remember much, but my folks told me I used to hit other children if I didn't get my way; sometimes, I guess, even just for fun. It was never a huge problem, but it was something I had to keep an eye on.

"Then, about three years ago, I began developing some stomach problems. For the first year-and-a-half, there wasn't a single doctor who could find what was causing the problems. It was horrible. These terrible pains would wrench my stomach with cramps. When I wasn't vomiting acidic bile, bowel movements tore through me like razor blades. I had all kinds of tests done: x-rays, ultrasounds, endoscopies, colonoscopies, CT scans... everything. They eventually found something.

"It's funny how such a tiny tumor can cause so much grief."

I am not a tumor. If you don't stop lying, I'm going to burst from your stomach right now so they will know the truth.

I told you to shut up. Just let me be.

I could, you know. I'm stronger now. Your insides have given me healthy nourishment. Scratch, scratch, tear. Mmmm... delicious.

A searing pain stabbed at Keith's internal organs. He almost buckled over from the torture, but he gritted his teeth and powered through it, knuckles white from clutching the podium. A few people jumped from their seats to offer support, but he waved them off. Keith took a few deep breaths before continuing on.

"I've come to terms with my diagnosis, and the doctors are hopeful that the chemo will take care of it, which makes me hopeful, too. Staying positive helps.

"I guess that's really all I have to say today. And thank you, everyone, for your support."

Keith ended his time with a nod before stepping away from the podium. A few claps followed. He passed the several open chairs, instead preferring to stand to avoid any further pain in his abdomen. He took a position against the wall in the back, next to the table of snacks. Stacey Thistle, group leader for the night, bolted from her front row seat and hustled to the spot Keith had just occupied.

"Thank you, Keith," she said through a bright smile and fast-moving lips. "We appreciate you sharing with us tonight, and we are all here to offer you our support." Some of the people nodded, while others kept to themselves, waiting for their turn to speak. "Okay, then. Why don't we move on to the next..."

I want coffee. The beverages in this dimension are very tasty.

I'm not thirsty.

Keith's insides twisted, as if barbed wire had squeezed around his intestines. The weekly meetings helped soothe his anger and stress, but it sure didn't help with the root of the problem. He ignored the ongoing meeting and reached for an empty cup and the pot of coffee. He fumbled with both, spilling the warm and dark liquid all over his hand. After dropping the pot back down and wiping his hand off on his jeans, he choked down the beverage without any cream or sweetener. He hated black coffee, or any heated drink for that matter, but it soothed the creature dwelling inside his body. He'd rather eat something, if he could, but liquid had a better chance of staying down.

There. Are you happy?

Yes... for now.

Keith could only shake his head in disgust. Three years, now. Three years of daily pain from an invisible monster that had randomly showed up one day and only gave knowledge of itself to Keith. No doctors could find anything wrong. No machine could locate the source of his pain. No priest, shaman, or sorceress could cast the demon from his body. The pain was real, though, and so were the problems it caused. He had to lie to his friends. He had to lie to his family. He couldn't keep a steady job, or even a steady boyfriend; they all soon questioned his illness when the doctor and hospital visits had ended. His life had spiraled downward, and if it weren't for the support of the Emotions Anonymous group, suicide probably would have won. Instead, he gave up to the fact that a monster from another dimension inhabited his gut—he was not insane.

"At least the coffee is decent, right?" The deep voice startled Keith, and he jerked around in surprise. The man, big and burly with a belly, hefted up his sagging pants and turned red behind his thick and brown beard. "Sorry, there. Didn't mean to startle you. The name is Alan."

Keith took Alan's outstretched, beefy hand and pumped it up and down. "Nice to meet you. I'm Keith." He turned a little red as well, especially since he found the man quite attractive; bigger, bearish men always caught his eye.

Alan spoke through a grin. "Yeah, I remember from when you spoke."

Duh, smarty-pants.

Shut up.

Keith felt his skin warm even more, but he tried to force the embarrassment away. "Right." He returned the smile. "I haven't seen you around here before. Is this your first night?"

"Yep," Alan said, picking up a donut. He took a large bite and wiped away the crumbs from his beard while he chewed. He continued on after washing it down with some coffee. "My therapist thinks these meetings will do me some good."

"Well, they've definitely helped me out." Keith poured another cup of coffee, hoping it would keep Pan preoccupied, at least while he talked to Alan. "So, Alan, tell me about yourself. You already know a bit about me."

The man frowned. "Oh, yeah. Sorry about the whole tumor thing."

"Nothing to be sorry about. Shit happens. I try not to let it ruin my life."

"Positive thinking is good for the mentality," Alan said in agreement.

Even though it won't work.

Keith took a large sip from his cup, ignoring the voice from his stomach. "Yeah. I try to stay positive, though it can be tough."

"I hear that, which is why I guess most of us are here, huh? Anyway, I try to stay positive, too. I'm a high school teacher and, man, let me tell you; sometimes those kids just make me want to erupt. Don't get me wrong, I love working as a teacher. But life can be a little too much every once in a while, you know?"

"I do, I do," Keith said, while nodding. "Kids can be fun, but they can also be a handful."

"Which is why I became a teacher. I like kids, but I never want any of my own. This way I can just give them back to their parents at the end of the day."

Keith felt the same way about children. He also felt his attraction growing the more he conversed with Alan.

He let the large man finish his donut and drink while giving some attention back to the group. A woman named Trinity something-or-other stood behind the podium, talking about her troubles with relationships or some topic about guys that stressed her out. Keith didn't care, focusing mainly on the man giving him notice.

Keith's luck with men usually ran dry. Problems always arose, and they were always because of the pan-dimensional parasite. Pan would never let him get close enough to form a lasting relationship, to love another human being. Small flings were all he could handle with his affliction. He wanted more, but he wasn't sure more was a possibility. Even so, he still liked the company of others.

The creature took a wrench to his stomach and twisted. Keith closed his eyes for a moment and cupped his stomach with his free hand.

I don't want to be here. I don't like your anger management get-togethers. Take me home.

I will in a while.

He tried to calm Pan with the rest of his coffee, but the pain only subsided to a dull throb. He did want to leave, though, and decided to take the monster up on its demand.

Keith turned to Alan and said, "Hey, you wouldn't want to leave and get a bite or a drink somewhere, would you?"

A chubby and bearded smile filled Keith with a happiness of jittery butterflies. "I would like that," Alan said.

Keith responded with a step closer and said, "There's a bar down the street that we could—"

The stabbing returned. An intense pain tore at his insides. The room spun, and he grabbed the snack table to stop from tumbling over.

I told you, I want to go home. I don't want to go to a bar.

Why won't you leave me be? I want my life back. Give me back my life.

Your life became mine once I chose you as the host to bring me into this new dimension. Your fate was unfortunate, but a necessity for my rebirth: a life for a life. And now I'm ready to be born...

A large and gentle arm steadied Keith's failing body. He looked up and saw Alan with a concerned face. "Are you okay? Do you need help?"

Keith felt his stomach churn with vomit. "I'll be fine. I just need to use the restroom."

He hurried out of the room, leaving the Emotions Anonymous group and attractive man behind. His shoes echoed against the empty hallway's linoleum floor with loud squeaks. He located the men's restroom a few doors down and burst through the door. Thankfully, the place was empty, and he stumbled into the farthest stall in just the nick of time.

Black coffee sprayed from his mouth and nose. The undigested liquid splashed into the porcelain bowl, followed by another burning heave from his stomach; the second helping was even darker, mixed with a maroon tinge. He tried to breathe, but the powerful expelling had numbed his esophagus into a thin tube.

What are you doing to me?

I told you. I'm ready to come out.

No. Please. Not now.

It's too late. This place bores me. This way, I'll be able to roam free to my liking.

Keith's stomach exploded with pain. He vomited one last time, all red with chunks. His head swirled and a burning fire ravaged his throat, but nothing compared to the razor blades slicing at the organs in his gut. Death whispered in his ear. The monster in his stomach was finally making true to its word.

Although he would never feel the warm and caring touch of another person, the kindhearted affection from someone—one last time—gave him a little happiness.

The pan-dimensional creature roared.

Keith lifted up his shirt and watched something bulge from inside him. His skin stretched taught, sending a disturbing pain throughout his body and soul. He tried to scream, but only gurgled chokes came out. A bloody, needle-like talon poked out just below his sternum. Pain raged as it traveled down towards his belly button, a line of gushing red trailing behind.

Darkness shrouded over him, and at last, the pain vanished. Everything disappeared, and Keith was at peace.

***

Alan stood outside the restroom, his sausage fingers nervously tapping at his wide love handles. He had followed Keith, the cute man who had spoken to the group, worried the sick man might need help. After some disturbing grunts and soft screams from the closed bathroom door, a worrying silence nagged at the large man.

He decided to act, opening the door and cautiously walking inside. "Hello? Keith? Are you okay? Do you need some help or anything?"

A steady drip and wet rustling sounded from the far stall, its door hanging wide open.

"Keith?"

Only when he approached did he notice the pool of crimson and syrupy liquid, spreading along the dirty-white tile. Panic washed over him, and he rushed into the stall to help his new acquaintance.

Alan found the skinny man from Emotions Anonymous as a motionless, bloody heap slumped against the toilet bowl; his skin was as white as the porcelain. His stomach had been ripped open, entrails strewn about as if a horrific piñata had burst open.

Alan reared back and gasped. He wanted to run, but his legs felt as solid as rock.

The body jerked. A shadow moved from behind the corpse and toilet.

A raspy and slithery voice spoke. "Finally, freedom."

Ebony claws stretched into view, talons glistening, as long and ferocious needles. Alan closed his eyes and felt a warm liquid trickle down his legs. He sensed movement in front of him. The voice spoke again, this time closer, reeking of death, decay, and viciousness.

"It's unfortunate I filled up on Keith, you look quite tasty. Maybe we'll meet again."

Like metal scraping across tile, the thing scattered from the stall and echoed out of the bathroom.

Alan never opened his eyes, not until an hour later, when an EMT slapped him awake. He instead opted to faint again, in case whatever monster had mutilated Keith decided to return. After re-awakening, it took another EMT to help sedate the heavy man.

Cookies

Matthew Weber

Emmy Beemer tiptoed with her footstool through the deep shadows of the dark house. She quietly placed it on the floor in front of the kitchen cabinet, climbed the two steps and stretched to open the cabinet door. The hinge squeaked, and she froze, praying the noise had not stirred her sleeping stepfather from his bedroom down the hallway. After a moment's hesitation, she slid a paper plate from the shelf and placed it on the countertop. She leaned over the counter and carefully lifted the lid from the cookie jar, which sealed around the rim with a rubber ring. The steel lid gave an airy ping as it pulled free, and she winced. She pulled out three chocolate chip cookies, added them to the platter, then grabbed a banana from the nearby fruit bowl.

Emmy liked bananas, so maybe the thing in the trees would, too. It definitely liked cookies. But a diet that consisted only of cookies was not a healthy one; she had learned that at school when her teacher taught about nutrition and the basic food groups.

She stepped off the stool and crept out of the kitchen with the plate held flat in front of her. She passed through the living room and neared the front door of the house. Slowly and steadily, she pinched the deadbolt latch between her fingers. This was always the worst part. With teeth clenched tight, she gave a twist. The deadbolt slid back with a *thunk!* that echoed throughout the house.

Emmy held her breath and listened. The black of night hid everything beyond the reach of the pale windows. Her heart thumped in her ears. The old refrigerator hummed from the kitchen. But that was all she heard—not the heavy footsteps of a grown man disturbed from his sleep.

She pulled on the thick front door, which popped and creaked as it opened. She drew it halfway back, just enough room to slip past and push open the screen door.

A cool breeze rushed into the house and ruffled her curly brown hair. Emmy placed the plate on the deck just outside, then looked up to an overcast sky. Few stars shone above, and the moon looked fuzzy. She found it difficult to make out the inky branches of the skeletal trees that loomed above her back yard. That's where the thing lived, somewhere up there, crawling around, leaping from limb to limb, and watching. She wouldn't see it. Not tonight. The light had to be just right, and she had a hunch that when the thing did not want to be seen, no one would see it.

She had gotten her first glimpse of it two weeks ago from the deck of her house. It had made a noise that caught her attention. She'd sat alone on the steps that clear autumn night, blowing bubbles through a small plastic ring, when a low, chattering sound, almost a buzz, came from the trees. At the time, a few dead leaves still clung to the tree branches, and Emmy peered up to see an odd shape perched among them on a thick limb far overhead. It moved with quick, jerky motions and had long, slender limbs—more than four—like some strange, gangly insect that might hide in your slipper and crunch beneath your bare foot. But this thing was much bigger than any bug she'd ever seen.

Its head, if that's what it was, shook from side-to-side and gave a string of soft chirps, which sounded in no way dangerous to Emmy. In fact, it sounded cute and put her at ease. She took the noise as a greeting.

"Hello," Emmy answered the thing in the trees.

A twinkle in its eyes told her she'd made a new friend. Then the shadow's head wiggled and chirped again, and the creature leapt up to the higher branches, climbing the tree with cat-like speed and grace. It disappeared as it shot over to a neighboring tall pine.

Since then, she had been leaving it snacks. And it had been eating what she fed it—at least some of the food. Always the cookies. And she caught glimpses of the creature only once in a while. On the lucky nights.

Emmy closed the doors. She twisted the deadbolt, which clicked with a smaller noise than when unlocking it, and tiptoed back to her room.

***

Cold air swept over Emmy. She opened her eyes to the raging voice of her stepfather as he ripped away the bedsheets that covered her.

"What have I told you!" he shouted. "Time and time again, I told you! No sweets in the middle of the night. NO SWEETS!"

He hit the light switch, and Emmy squinted from the painful glare.

"But whad'ya know! The first thing I find when I wake up is the damn cookie jar left open in the kitchen," he said. "Now all the cookies have gone soft and shitty. That's why you're supposed to seal 'em up and not leave 'em open!"

Emmy stuttered and grunted.

"What's the problem, Dale?" asked her mom in a groggy voice from somewhere down the hallway.

"Nothing I can't handle!" Dale shouted to her over his shoulder. He turned back to Emmy and frowned through the grainy beard that circled his mouth, staring down at her with cold gray eyes. "If I'd wanted the cookies to be all soft and shitty, then I'd have bought the soft and shitty kind at the grocery store. As far as I'm concerned, these are now ruined. You ruined 'em 'cause you disobeyed. I guess I just wasted money on this brand-new pack of cookies I bought yesterday. Which is just par for the course around here, since I'm the only one who BRINGS IN any money! No wonder I'm the only one with any goddamn appreciation for it!"

"I told you," called her mother from the other end of the house. "I'm looking for a job."

He turned toward the hallway and roared, "SHUT UP, MAUREEN!"

Emmy rubbed her eyes and realized Dale was holding the open cookie jar. He raised it in front of him with both hands and flipped it upside down. All the remaining cookies tumbled out and spilled all over her bedroom floor in a crumbly mess.

"Clean those up," he said. "And get ready for school."

***

As Emmy walked up to her porch from the bus stop after school, Dale's raised voice boomed out of the walls. The thump of stomping feet rumbled from one end of the house to the other. He shouted and cursed about his job, calling his boss a son-of-a-this and a mother-that. Emmy decided not to open the door. She turned around and sat down on the front stoop.

Beneath her, on the cracked concrete walkway, a single black ant carried a quarter-sized piece of potato chip that dwarfed the little critter. Emmy bent closer to the ant and studied its fierce determination.

"I wish I was as strong as you," she whispered to it.

The ant ignored her.

Big things almost always took advantage of little things, except the ant was different. Not like her. She had to put up with Dale because he was stronger. She was just like her friends who rode the school bus. Red-headed Phillip had a mean mother who would sometimes lock him in the closet. Her friend Bethany, whose Mom would give her the most beautiful braids, also had a father who would rub her in uncomfortable ways and make her sit on his lap funny. Emmy, Red-headed Phillip and Bethany had to put up with such things because they were weaker than the people who did it to them, and they were afraid to do anything about it.

From somewhere inside the house came another voice—her mother's. Emmy had hoped that Dale was yelling into his phone. Her mother was not always home when she arrived from school, but it appeared she was today, which put her right in Dale's warpath.

She left the ant and went into the house. She'd learned that Dale was less likely to strike her mother when she was around to witness the abuse.

Dale continued his tirade in the master bedroom, so she shouted, "I'm home, Mom!" then headed into the kitchen. Two grocery bags sat on the counter, still full. Dale must have ambushed her mother with news of his bad day before she could stock the shelves. Emmy lifted her step stool from its place in the corner and carried it to the counter. She placed it on the floor and climbed up to unload the bags and sort things out.

Among the items from the store, she found a new package of cookies, the shortbread kind with fudge stripes. For the first time that day, she smiled.

***

Dale eventually hollered his throat hoarse and left to get beer with a slam of the front door. Emmy walked to the other end of the house to check on her mother. Sobbing came from the bathroom. She approached the fist-sized hole that Dale had punched through the door a couple of months ago. Instead of fixing the damage, he had only thumbtacked a hand towel over the hole to give the bathroom back its privacy.

The jagged edges of the wood formed the open jaws of a hungry mouth. She leaned into the hole. "Mom, are you okay?"

A hiccup and a sniff were her only answers.

"Mom, are you hurt?"

"I'm okay, hon. Don't worry about me. I'll be fine."

Her mother's soft cries passed right through the thin linen, and Emmy took in every hushed sound.

"I'll be right back," she said.

Standing atop her step stool, she pulled a tray of ice cubes from the freezer. She walked it to the sink, held it over the basin, and twisted the plastic tray. With a sharp crackle, the ice broke loose of the little square cups. She dropped three cubes into a plastic Ziploc baggie and sealed it up tight.

She moved the step stool further down the counter to reach the paper towels. She unspooled two and wrapped them around the plastic-covered ice. After folding over the paper several times to pad the compress, she returned to the bathroom.

"Here you go," Emmy said to her mom through the door. Ice in hand, she pushed past the towel curtain and reached through the hole into the bathroom. After a sniffle, her mom came over and took the cool bundle. She then returned to her spot on the toilet lid, where she always cried alone.

"Thanks, hon."

"You're welcome."

Mom often needed ice after Dale had been yelling.

***

The front door parted with a pop and a creak. Emmy pushed open the screen door, and the familiar gust of chilly air blew through the cotton fabric of her t-shirt. Twinkling stars and a full moon lit the midnight sky with a purple glow that outlined the scraggly trees overhead. She stepped onto the deck with a plate of cookies in hand, and eased the door closed behind her.

Almost barren of leaves, the wide web of overlapping branches bent and split and crisscrossed to form a busy patchwork, like the sky had shattered and the broken shards had yet to fall to earth.

High above her, and perched near the trunk of a tall oak, she made out a shape. When it moved its spindly limbs, all jerky and weird, she knew she'd found the creature.

"Hi," she greeted through a cupped whisper, hoping with her biggest wish that it would greet her back, that it would somehow acknowledge her presence. "I brought you more cookies. And an apple, tonight."

The shadow in the tree tilted its head and wiggled its body.

"Apples are good," she said. The thing didn't eat the banana, but she hadn't thought to peel it. She'd found last night's plate with only crumbs of the cookies but the full banana, with small gnaw marks on the tough stem of its peel. The creature hadn't made it to the sweetness of the soft fruit inside. The thin peel of an apple would be easier to get past.

With the squeal of a hinge, the front door flew open. A loud bang, and the storm door swung outward. Bright yellow light poured onto the deck behind the dark shape of big Dale Roberts, who rubbed his eyes while muttering words that Emmy was not allowed to say.

"You woke me up, ya little dumbass," Dale said. "Goddammit. And looky here. Caught red-handed. Disobeyin' me, just like we talked about."

Dale seemed to grow in size while Emmy shrank. She stared at the plate of cookies, having known the sight of it would light Dale's fuse. Now, there he stood, looking at it, right above her and ready to blow his stack.

He batted the plate out of her hand. The apple bounced across the deck and rolled right off the edge to the ground below. The cookies lay scattered everywhere. She dropped to her knees and snatched them up, collecting three in the hem of her t-shirt. Dale lifted his knee and stomped the other cookies into powder with snarling curses.

"I told you NO SWEETS!" he shouted. "NO FRIGGIN' SWEETS!"

The wood shook beneath her. She backed away and clutched her shirt together.

"What is it about the word 'NO' you don't understand!"

Her eyes clouded and hot tears rolled down her face. Part of her so badly wanted Mom, but another part didn't, because then Mom would get hit again.

"I'm sorry," Emmy said. "Please don't be mad! I'm so sorry!"

"You're always sorry! You and your mom both, the sorriest people I ever met!"

Maybe Mom would hear and come, anyway. Or, maybe Mom had taken a pill and wouldn't wake up.

"I've had it with you two," Dale said. "I really have." His nostrils flared, and his whole body heaved with his bull-like breaths.

"Don't hurt me," she said. "Please, Dale."

"Why not?" he said. "'Cause it don't seem to me that anything else is gettin' through to you. I've told you time and time again. But you keep right on disobeyin' me."

He leaned closer, just inches from Emmy's face. His body heat clouded around her.

"Maybe," he continued with his breath stinking of beer and tuna, "maybe I oughtta blister your little bottom."

Emmy backed into the corner where the deck railing met the house wall—trapped with nowhere to run. The tears were beyond her control. She could barely breathe.

"Maybe," Dale said, "I oughtta bend you over and jerk down those panties. Take off my belt and show you how my daddy used to punish me."

He lifted his hands, working his fingers eagerly. He was coming for her, plain as day, and he was so *huge*. She clutched her ears and sank down into a ball.

He grabbed her by the shoulders.

But a heavy thump on the deck made him freeze. He turned his head slightly and squinted, listening to a reedy, chirping noise behind him. He released Emmy and spun around.

"What the hell?!" Dale lurched back, nearly falling onto her.

The thing from the trees stood upright on the deck atop four hind legs. Maybe five feet tall, it had a segmented body with a shiny underside. Shell-like armor covered its skinny legs and torso, and its upper limbs floated in front of it like angry, jointed snakes. Two long, thin antennae extended above two huge eyes that looked like black tomatoes, their surface shimmering with countless gleaming lenses. And two pincer-like jaws twitched at its mouth as it made the chirping noise.

"He's my friend," Emmy said.

The thing took a lurch forward, stretched its head at Dale and gave a furious hiss.

"Like hell!" Dale snatched a nearby broom from where it leaned against the house. He swung it in a wide home run arc that clobbered Emmy's friend. With a crunch, the creature slammed into the house siding from the blunt force of the thick wooden handle.

"LEAVE HIM ALONE!" Emmy screamed.

Dale drew back and flipped the broom. He struck again with the handle end, thwacking it into the thing's limbs, crashing it back into the wall.

Emmy leapt onto Dale's back and clawed at him. He shook her off, lifted a foot and kicked her square in the chest with his slipper. The blow shot her backward like she'd been jerked with a rope. Her bottom pounded onto the deck, sending a sharp jolt through her.

Back on the creature, Dale beat it mercilessly where it had fallen. Its limbs thrashed and squirmed. Dale cursed and spat as he caned the thing. The creature's angry hiss became a frightened moan. Then Dale lifted the broom handle, brought it down like a spear and skewered the creature.

"NOOO!" Emmy wailed, and the creature's moan deflated to a weak, voiceless rattle.

"This ain't no sort of friend," Dale muttered, catching his breath. "Some freak of nature! Mutant grasshopper or some shit."

She threw her hands to her mouth as the creature went silent and still. The twinkle in its eyes went dim like a cooling ember.

Something fragile inside her cracked apart and collapsed to pieces.

"You ruin *everything*!"

Dale gave a raspy laugh. "Whatever it was, now it's DEAD." And with that, he gave a final stomp to the creature's mid-section—and he howled as soon as he did.

Dale jumped up and down on one foot.

"OW! SHIT! WHAT THE HELL!" He bounced over the thing's body while groping his other leg. The tail of the creature clung to his calf as if somehow attached. "Goddamn thing stung me!"

With the husk of the creature tangled beneath, Dale shook his leg and kicked outward, but it was still stuck against him. Finally, he stamped his foot down on its midsection, gripped the tail like a beer can, then twisted and pulled. The tail tore away from a long, spiny thorn that remained snared in his flesh. Where the hard shell snapped off, an oozing slime leaked from the squirming organ that wiggled on the end of the stinger. Dale grunted and fell on his rump. His eyelids peeled back from the whites.

"What the hell is stuck on me?!"

Emmy wondered the exact same thing, as the wriggling tail shortened. The head of the stinger burrowed into Dale's calf as he whimpered and clutched his leg. It swelled his flesh as it dug beneath the skin, raising a quivering lump beneath the fabric of his ratty sweatpants. He swatted at it in a panic. The lump traveled up the knee, and Dale screamed. It appeared further up his thigh, and he rose to his feet and chased it with clutching, frantic hands.

"STOP IT! STOP IT! STOP IT!" he cried in a high, shaky pitch.

Emmy followed Dale's frenetic slapping, toward the crotch of his pants, and that's when the *real* cursing and bellowing began. She'd never heard such a racket from a grown man. He socked himself in the crotch as though he hated himself. He drove a fist into his gut. As the lump climbed higher, pulsing and growing, Dale used his powerful, muscular arms to slug himself in the ribs and beat himself about the chest. The blows were brutal, and his faced twisted with each wallop to his body.

The swelling reached his neck, and Dale stopped breathing. He clutched at his collar. He dropped to his knees as snot ran from his nose and sweat rolled down his cheeks. His throat expanded like a balloon, stretching to twice its size. Dale looked up, and his once-white eyes went cherry-red and rolled backward. His whole head shook and his mouth stretched open. A quivering black mound surged outward with a glut of thick mucus, ripping Dale's lower jaw from its hinge. His cheeks split open as a fat, veiny blob slithered out of his throat, bringing with it a short tail that wagged behind. It plopped down onto the deck.

Emmy had never seen such a monstrous tadpole.

Dale lay next to it and did not move at all. Blood spilled from his face. His eyes went glassy.

The tadpole-thing stopped shuddering. Emmy watched and waited. She knelt closer, inching toward it without a breath. The dark skin suddenly rippled and then peeled from around the top like a budding flower. Inside, six gnarled clumps rolled out onto the deck and began to uncurl. Slowly, each revealed several slender, insectoid appendages.

A gasp escaped her. The six little creatures took form and looked around, scuttling in circles. They explored one another, trading close looks and curious sniffs. One gave a prod to Dale's body, then immediately lost interest and returned to its brethren. The little pack huddled together and appeared to devise a plan. Then they all scurried together, over to one of the discarded cookies lying on the deck. The shortbread kind with fudge stripes. They devoured it enthusiastically, and Emmy clasped her hands with joy.

They moved a few feet over and shared another cookie.

Quickly, Emmy shot into the house, ran to a hall closet and returned with a shoebox. She collected the creatures into it—along with another cookie—and took them inside. She hid them under her bed before waking her mother to tell her that something terrible had happened to Dale.

**

Emmy stayed home from school the following week, having been excused to mourn a parent. *Step*-parent, she would always add.

She didn't do much mourning, though. Neither did Mom, although her mother made sure to fluster and pout when certain adults were present. The week they spent together was magical; they picnicked, and flew kites in the park, and danced in the sunshine. They stayed up late, painted each other's nails, ate ice cream and shared secrets.

But Emmy didn't tell *all* her secrets. She returned to school the following Monday and carried two gifts in her backpack for her friends on the bus ride home. She'd been feeding the babies, and they'd grown to the size of grapefruits.

After school, she took the bus seat ahead of Red-headed Phillip and Bethany with the braids. She pulled out two folded paper lunch sacks, leaned over the backrest and handed one to each of them.

"Here, I brought you presents."

They both smiled and took the sacks, unfurling the tops. They peered inside, and Phillip's face brightened. Bethany looked confused.

"Thanks," Phillip said. "But what are they?"

Emmy smiled. "They're pets."

"Oh, wow," Bethany said. "Neat pets!"

"Be nice and feed them, and they'll grow a lot bigger," Emmy said. "And maybe one day, they'll protect you when you need it."

Phillip and Bethany looked at each other, and then back to Emmy.

She winked. "They prefer cookies."

Axe Murders on the Harpeth Turnpike

B. C. Nance

John knew the rule, unwritten though it was. His mother had always told him not to stop for strangers. *You never know which one of them might be a pervert or an axe murderer, Johnny.* John had been driving for twenty years now, and his mother had been dead for twelve, but as he pulled to the side of the road, he still remembered that argument.

"Who the hell murders with an axe anymore, mom?"

Don't be insolent with me, Johnny.

But how could he refuse to help his fellow man – or, in this case, a beautiful damsel in distress? She was tall with long, shapely legs and flame-red hair. John pulled in behind her car, stranded on the Harpeth Turnpike by a flat tire. Not a good place to be stranded because his mother had been right. There *was* an axe murderer on the loose. Of all things, an honest to goodness, genuine, bloodthirsty axe murderer.

"Looks like you could use a hand," John said. He approached slowly, with his hands in plain sight. She had, no doubt, heard that an axe murderer was in the area, and John didn't want to frighten her.

"Actually," she said, bending down to pat the flat tire that leaned against the car's rear bumper, "I was just finishing up, but I'll still give you credit for the chivalry, Mr. White Knight."

"At least let me help you put that tire in the trunk," John said. "I'd hate to see you get your nice clothes dirty." She wore a black skirt that might be a tad too short for some offices, and a sleeveless black blouse. A scarlet jacket lay on the top of the car beside a grimy cloth.

"Don't bother," she said, reaching for the cloth. "I like to finish what I start."

"I insist," John said. "I like to be helpful." The key was still in the trunk lock, and, deciding that he would not take "no" for an answer, he gave the woman a quick smile and turned the lock.

"Please, don't," she said, but it was too late.

The sight of the bound and gagged woman in the trunk and the click of the revolver as it was cocked beside his ear must have registered in John's mind at the same time, but it took a few seconds for him to sort them out.

"Chivalry is dead for a reason, Mr. White Knight," the woman said.

"My name is John Goodwin." He thought his voice sounded calm, but he smiled at how out-of-place his words seemed.

"My name is Trouble," was her response.

"It's not safe out here, you know," said John. "There's an axe murderer on the loose."

"What makes you think that *I'm* not the axe murderer?" the tall woman said.

"You're carrying a gun."

She gave a slight laugh. "It's easier to hide than an axe."

The captive in the trunk had looked relieved when she saw John, perhaps expecting a rescue; now, tears began to roll down her face. John looked at her and she at him.

I told you so, Johnny. Mommy knows these things.

The captive's eyes grew large, and John felt a thud at the base of his neck accompanied by a flash of light that seemed to come from behind his eyes. For an instant, he recalled a recent headline, "AXE MURDERER STRIKES AGAIN!"

***

John's boots clunked on wooden steps as his would-be killer dragged him down into a basement. "Damn," she said, "You're heavier than you look. Why don't you wake up and walk?"

John tried not to smile at the trouble he was causing. He had regained consciousness shortly after they had started down the road and found himself bound but not gagged like his trunk mate. She was Fiona Allendale, reporter for The City Chronicle. John had learned this after removing her gag with his teeth. Even under these circumstances, he took a secret delight in performing this task. "Don't tell her I'm conscious," John told Fiona, when their mobile prison cell came to a stop.

When his captor had finally lifted him into a chair and tied his hands and feet, John moaned, pretending to awaken.

"Well, welcome back the world of the living," the woman said. "Or, in your case, the world of the short-lived."

Fiona sat in a chair next to John, her gag removed and her hands and feet bound like his. John looked around the basement. The floor was concrete, and the walls were cinder block. Black paint covered the basement's few narrow windows, and a fluorescent light fixture hummed softly above them. A small workbench was strewn with mundane tools, and a large metal cabinet stood next to the bench. John saw a crude shower and large drain in one corner of the basement, but no curtains, doors, or screens to hide it.

The tall redhead placed her revolver on the workbench, then opened the metal cabinet and turned to look at him and Fiona. Fiona's eyes grew wide. The cabinet held several knives and saws and a large, shiny axe. John scanned several newspaper clippings hanging on the cabinet doors as his captor strode toward him. She stroked him under his chin and said, "I need a shower before I start work. I like to be clean when I kill."

She walked to the shower and began undressing, occasionally glancing back at her captives. She was breathtaking, and John stared with no pretense of looking away. Fiona looked at John contemptuously. He strained at the ropes holding his left hand, and Fiona saw that his bindings were loose.

The red-haired beauty finished her shower and pulled on a large t-shirt that clung to her wet body. "Much better," she said.

John's hand was almost free as the woman went to the cabinet. "The city councilman beheading was a real work of art," John said, looking at the newspaper clippings. "But I think my favorite was the dismemberment of the two lawyers." His hand slipped from the ropes. "But," he spoke softly, "Those weren't yours, now were they, Liz? Or should I call you *Annie*?"

He smiled. She didn't.

"Now, don't look so surprised," John said. The redhead fumbled with her collection of cutting tools. John's left hand was free now, and Fiona watched as he strained to reach his ankle, where a small knife was sheathed in his boot. "I've been stalking you for some time, Liz," he continued. "But you're more resourceful and much more beautiful than I had imagined." He pulled a thin-bladed knife from his boot, then tucked his hand back into the ropes, concealing the weapon.

Liz stood with her head down, still facing the cabinet. She turned toward John with a butcher's blade in her hand. "*You*," she said. "*You're* the other one."

"No, Liz," John said. "*You* are the other one. I am the original axe murderer." He turned his head and smiled at Fiona, then looked back at Liz. "I must admit, Liz, that having you for competition has brought out the best in my own artistry, and I think the police are only just beginning to suspect that there are two of us."

"You bastard," said Liz. "You deceitful, bastard." Liz walked toward John like a lioness stalking her prey. She clutched the stainless steel fang. He gripped his own knife, still concealed under his bindings. Liz leaned forward and held John's head firmly, the cold blade pressed against his ear. She looked intently into his eyes, her face inches from his own.

"The banker," she said. "In his own home with all of his family there, and no one heard a sound as he was dismembered. How?" John just smiled, and she kissed him. Fiona whimpered and pulled at her ropes.

Liz pushed away, nearly knocking John backwards. "So, what now, John Goodwin?" she waved the long knife in the air. "Do I kill you as planned and become the only show in town?" She stepped back toward him and placed the point of the knife under his chin. "Or do I show you some professional courtesy and let you go? Maybe," she said, turning to Fiona, "we could carve up Miss Allendale together. She was stalking me, too. Did you know that, John?"

"Yes," he answered. "She told me in the trunk, a nice place for an intimate conversation. In fact, Fiona seems to know more about your early life than I do."

"Oh, is that so?" Liz walked to Fiona and stroked her chin with the tip of the knife. "Why don't you regale me with this tale of *my* life."

Fiona was dry-mouthed, and her words creaked from her throat. "I know that you are Annie Booth from Des Moines, Iowa. You were in and out of foster homes until you were sixteen. That's when you killed most of your foster family. And you've been on the run ever since."

"Leaving a trail of corpses," Liz added. "But, honey, I killed *all* of my foster family, not most. Every. Last. Wretched. One of them. I cut their miserable throats while they slept, then burned that damned house to the ground."

"No," said Fiona. "*Not* all of them."

Liz regarded the younger woman. She looked deep into Fiona's eyes, and John smiled at the little melodrama. Liz reached toward Fiona and pulled at her high collar. There, on Fiona's neck, was a long scar.

Fiona returned Liz's burning gaze and said, "I've never forgotten you, *sister*."

"Well, isn't this quite the cozy reunion," John said as he stood. While Liz had been occupied with Fiona, he had cut his bindings. "Two competing axe murderers and the stepsister bent on revenge." Liz stepped back and held out the knife. John raised his own small blade. All three of them looked at Liz's revolver lying on the workbench. "We're quite the trio," John continued. "Or quartet if we count Liz and Annie."

"Let's make a deal, Mr. White Knight," Liz said. "I'll carve the girl, you walk away, and we forget that we ever met."

"Oh, no," John said. "Now that I've found you, I could never walk away."

Liz lunged forward and grabbed the gun, and John grabbed her by the wrist. Together, they held the weapon above their heads. John leaned forward, bending his face toward hers until she plunged the knife into his ribs. He pulled her closer and slid his own thin blade into her back.

John stumbled backwards and ran into the cabinet of weaponry. He grabbed the axe and smiled at Liz. She had sunk to her knees, but she managed a smile for John. He started forward with the axe, but Liz raised the revolver and fired. John stumbled as the bullet hit him in the stomach, but he lurched forward, toward Liz. She tried to pull the trigger again, but her strength was failing. John brought the axe crashing down on Liz's left shoulder, cutting deeply into her flesh.

"You don't keep this thing sharp enough," John wheezed to Liz as he collapsed on top of her. They lay motionless for a moment, then Liz raised the gun again, aimed it at Fiona, and squeezed the trigger.

***

A rusty truck rumbled to the side of the road, stopping behind a stranded car. The pot-bellied driver stepped out and adjusted his pants, then sidled toward the other vehicle. Fiona self-consciously pulled her hair to the left side of her head to hide the scar made when a bullet had blown off a portion of her ear.

"Looks like you could use a hand, little lady," the man said to her.

"I sure could, Mr. White Knight," she said. "Could you get the spare tire out of the trunk for me?"

"My pleasure, darling," he said with a smile. He took the key that Fiona offered and unlocked the trunk. "I haven't seen you around before, are you new in town?"

"That's right," Fiona answered. "I came to take over my sister's business."

The man opened the trunk and saw only a large, shiny axe. There was a dull thud at the base of his neck, then all went black.

Romero & Juliet

Liam Hogan

Don't get me wrong, I knew the risks. We all did.

Sure, like everyone else, I never thought it would be me – right up until the moment it was. And certainly not in such a goddamn, dumb-ass, *Comedy of Terrors* way.

If this is to be warts and all, I should admit that I wasn't originally a fan of the genre. It's hardly something that befits someone with a degree in English Literature, even if it is only from community college. Financially, I could see the merits, but before me, it was just a few poorly-lit, shakily-held, brutish and downright nasty YouTube clips. Not that mine aren't brutish and nasty when the story calls for it, which is often, but I'd be very disappointed if you thought they were poorly lit.

I might have to brain you with one of my two ZAFAs.

Joking.

I do wonder who exactly I'm talking to here. I mean, I'm not talking to *those* two, not the 'actress' whose brains are decorating the far wall, nor her crippled 'girlfriend' propped up at the exit. If things had worked out differently, I'd be talking to my Assistant AD, Claudia, who'd be winking back at me from behind the camera, but as it is, she's... indisposed. I guess I'm talking to whoever stumbles across this footage. I'm hoping that you'll have the wits to piece it all together, maybe put it out as a making-of documentary, or director's comments, or something. In which case, I'm also talking to a much wider audience, assuming they ever get past the main feature; my first and only starring role. Maybe I'd better backtrack; some of you might not even know what a ZAFA is.

Ever seen two zombies having sex?

You have to make sure they're both well fed, which is... ethically *dubious* at best, and it helps if you dose their meal with Viagra, but once you do, it's pure paywall gold!

George A. Romero zombies don't fuck. The question is: why not? Sex is a primitive, base urge; you don't need to be able to hold a conversation or know how to handle a knife and fork. All you need is a guy zombie and girl zombie, with their rotting brains not entirely focused on food.

I guess that's why Romero's zombies don't fuck – they're *always* hungry. That and they're fictional, of course. On film, they're too busy chasing the few remaining bits of live flesh. No chance to sit, to scratch at their wounds and turn brain-mush to more romantic thoughts.

I wasn't the first to make zombie porn, and despite this cautionary tale, I won't be the last. But I reckon I was and still am the best, and those two Adult Film Awards (Zombie category) – or ZAFAs – back me up. I had high hopes of a third, but things have gone a little off-book. So this; this is my improvised and final gift to you, my sick and perverted audience, but it'll have to be someone else who does any post-production editing.

My first ZAFA was for *Romero & Juliet*. I guess that thing about Romero zombies not fucking had been on my mind a while. Sometimes I wish I'd been a little less clever-clever with the name though. What's in a name? you may well ask. But it's not *Schindler's Fist*, is it? Or *Pokeahotass*. Or even *Clitty Clitty Bang Bang*. And it's definitely not *Shaving Ryan's Privates*. *Romero & Juliet* is just a tad *too* subtle. The sort of thing you might pick up and not even notice the changed spelling. The sort of thing my grandma might pick up, when she saw my director's credit on the cover. She has not spoken to me since. But then, a stroke will do that to you.

So, anyway. *Romero & Juliet*. It was an uncomplicated thing, a mere thirty-seven minutes long. Three cameras, two zombies, one blood-smeared balcony scene. But it set a new standard, without which there probably wouldn't even *be* a Zombie Adult Film Award.

It's all about quality. Proper sets. Proper lighting. Candles, a four-poster, silk sheets. Not actual silk – anything that looks like silk will do, but remember you're gonna want to burn them; you're gonna want to burn the whole damned set. Now picture a zombie chick in a nightgown, lounging on that four-poster. It's best to find a girl-z already in her nightgown, because trying to dress a zombie... well that's a whole different genre of snuff flick, and one with an even shorter life expectancy for the director.

It also helps if the girl is quite obviously a girl. Sometimes, depending on the state of decomposition, it can be kind of hard to tell. So, for the more mainstream of audiences – if there *is* such a thing with zombie porn – choose one with long hair and big tits, and your casting work is done.

You might think I'm relaying this kinda calmly, under the circumstances, given the *outrageous fortune* that has led me here. My calm is of the bottled, pharmaceutical variety, and I'd not be able to record these last *mortal thoughts* without its assistance. I did, I admit, initially panic when the supposedly bullet-proof glass shattered, but it didn't take long to realise how this would all turn out. There were never more than a couple of outcomes, really, and in both of them, I don't live long enough for the drugs to wear off.

My second ZAFA was for *MacDeath.* And for anyone who's just starting off in the industry – the plural of ZAFA is, "Fuck, yes. I have *two* awards!" As I'm the only one who does, it's my name that gets projects greenlit, which brings me neatly back to my comatose assistant, Claudia.

She worked with me at the tail end of the budget production of "*Tits and Groan-icus*". My usual AD had to be replaced halfway through the shoot – torn limb-from-limb during the zombie orgy scene while trying to right a toppled camera. His own dumb fault – well-fed, my ass. At least I gave him an acting credit. Not that he was acting.

When Claudia said she had an idea for my next film, I was happy to listen. Said she'd already done the ground work – scoped out a location, sourced props, even knew where she could get hold of the two zombie actors required. The two *girl* zombie actors required.

That made me pause. I mean, for starters, where was she going to get lesbian zombies from? How was she even going to know they were lesbians?

But I didn't kick up too much of a fuss. If it tanked, I'd just pull my name from the project, which, depending on how the filming went, was either going to be called *The Taming of the Screw*, or *A Midsummer Night's Scream.*

The set up looked okay, cameras already in place, a big, panoramic window for us to film through. At first, it was *Much Ado about Nothing.* The two girl-z's just lurched around the room, ignoring the couch, the bed, the various medieval-looking dildos. I shot Claudia a "What did I tell you?" look, but she just shrugged. "Give it time," she said.

And then, one of them fell onto the bed, tits up, and lay there flapping her limbs in the air like a beetle on its back.

This is the thing about the zombie apocalypse, another difference between reality and Romero: zombies are brain-dead. Like, *totally fucking* brain-dead. They starve away to nothingness unless food happens to wander within a couple of uncoordinated steps of them. This is why most of the outbreaks were so easily controlled, why the lights are still burning, factories still running, internet still up, porn industry still filming. Hardly the sort of apocalypse that has us re-inventing slings and arrows. More people died in the stampedes than actually got bit by zombies. There are still flare-ups, of course, but generally speaking – good hygiene, interval training and a decent handgun should see you safely through.

Unless, of course, you go looking for them. Unless, of course, you decide to *film them having sex.*

Anyway. Back on set, the ineffectually struggling girl-z had attracted the attention of the other one, who'd stopped banging her head against the wall long enough to swivel it in the direction of the bed. Clambering onto it, she nosed her way towards the prone figure until they were in a 69 position, and then they went to work.

Colour me surprised. Colour me fucking *amazed.*

Until I realised that if I were to tell you they were "eating each other out", this wouldn't be a euphemism. My heart sank.

Then, I felt a hot breath against my neck, and a gentle, soft pressure against my back. It was Claudia, her pupils wide and her cheeks a-flush.

So what if the zombies were munching rather than licking? It all came down to what they *looked* like they were doing, and it was obviously working its icky magic on my bisexual AD. I tweaked the remotes to make sure the close-ups didn't give the game away, and turned to give Claudia my full attention.

So I couldn't really tell you when the zombies gave up doing what they were doing and decided to go looking for fresh meat, instead. Maybe I give them too much credit – they might have simply got bored and gone back to banging their heads against the wall.

Against the supposedly bullet-proof glass.

Three times is all they knocked, I know that, from the coitus-interrupting noise. And then it splintered, and then it *shattered* – showering us with shards.

We might have survived if I hadn't had my pants around my ankles at the time, and along with them, my 9mm semi auto.

I still got to it before they got to us, but only just. Blew one of them away as the other seized hold of my arm. Didn't have enough in the clip to do more than cripple her, but by then, it was too late.

Ragged teeth marks oozing blood on my wrist. A pale echo of Claudia's torn-out throat. I didn't even see that happen, didn't see the fatal blow. I placed the reloaded gun into the gaping wound, angling it up towards her brain, but I couldn't... just couldn't pull the trigger.

What right do I have to decide whether being dead is better than being just undead? *Zombie or not zombie*? That is the question.

Instead, I got busy. Laid Claudia's twitching body on the bed. Propped the still-struggling girl-z up against the door – to stop any unwanted interruptions.

I can feel the poison burning up my arm. Up to my shoulder now – it hasn't got much further to go. Blissfully, the rest of me is going numb, except down below, where it appears the handful of little blue pills has started to kick in. Time to wrap up, time to stumble over and join Claudia, where the lights still blaze and cameras still point, ready to capture whatever happens next.

Like I said – there were only ever two outcomes. Will Claudia revive hungry, or horny? If she's peckish, then that'll be the end of me, the freshest meat in the room, and this will be a short. If she's patient, and waits for me to revive, then perhaps we'll still get to finish what we started earlier, and you're in for a rare televisual treat – the perfect zombie screen couple. Silver linings, right? And – as far as it can possibly go on a fucked-up day like today – '*All's well that ends well.*'

Fading fast, now. The things I do for you guys. Still, it's better than shooting myself in the head, I guess...

Lights! Camera! And... *urghhh... Action!*

PERIODS

Florence Ann Marlowe

"It's going on three weeks, now."

"Mm-hmm. And there's no chance of you being pregnant?"

"Oh, no!" Nancy shook her head. "I haven't even been with a guy in a long time."

"Good." Doctor Mason stood up, his eyes still glued to Nancy's chart. He flashed her a quick smile. "One less thing to worry about."

Nancy nodded. "So, what could it be?"

The doctor seemed lost in thought. He pressed the butt-end of his pen to his teeth. He then quickly shifted his seat, uncrossing and re-crossing his legs. Nancy suppressed an impatient sigh.

"I know exactly what it is," he finally said.

Nancy was surprised. "Oh."

"Endometriosis." He waited to let the big technical-sounding word sink in. "It's nothing serious. You have a problem with your ovaries, really. Nothing serious."

Nancy sat up quickly. "You're not going to take them out, are you?" She could see a whole life go by without children, maybe without a husband. She was already thirty-six, but she had never ruled out the possibility of a family. "Is it – like menopause?"

Dr. Mason tapped at his incisors with his pen. "Oh, no – not at all. It's very different."

Staring at his long, pale face and long, delicate nose, Nancy realized suddenly that she didn't really like this man very much. She should have gone to the GYN her sister had recommended. Watching his smug face, the tight smile was pissing her off more and more, and she wanted to get out of there, go home and take a shower.

"You see, when a woman has problems with ovulation, usually caused by stress or hormone problems, she'll develop endometrial tissue on her ovaries which will cause her to menstruate constantly." Nancy's face betrayed her confusion and the doctor continued, "Your body thinks it's time to menstruate all the time. So – you do!" He spread his long hands wide and shrugged.

I hate this man, Nancy thought.

"So, what happens now?"

"Well, we can give you hormone pills that will counter-balance the hormones that are causing you to ovulate." He pulled a small pad out of his desk drawer and took some time choosing a pen from the bouquet of writing instruments jammed into a mug.

"How long before I stop bleeding?" She picked up her bag thinking how expensive hormone pills sounded.

The doctor sighed, "Oh, about ten days."

"*Ten days*?!" Nancy cried. Dr. Mason looked up, his eyebrows arched. "I can't take this for another ten days!"

He stopped writing and folded his hands in front of him. Nancy felt a surge of anger. *If I hear one patronizing word of comfort from those slimy lips...*

"What can't you take?" he asked.

"Ten more days of bleeding! Shit! *One* more day of bleeding! I've been bleeding for *nineteen days*, dammit!"

"The pills will control that," he began calmly.

"I've gone through twelve boxes of super absorbent tampons! That's two hundred and forty tampons in less than three weeks! I'm ready to shove a friggin' rag up there!"

The doctor was staring at her, his face frozen. Nancy felt her throat tighten. So, she was a little edgy; she hadn't meant to offend him, but this was becoming pathetic. Couldn't he see she was suffering?

"Do you fill each one to capacity?"

The question threw her off. "What? Oh, yeah! Definitely! More than capacity. I'd get the super plus, but they don't always carry them." He was regarding her oddly. Nancy could feel a seed of worry working its way into her brain.

"Are you serious about that or is that just a number you made up?" He took a spiral notebook out of his desk and turned the pages, searching for something.

"No, that's for real. I buy four boxes every time I go to the drug store."

He found the page he wanted, ran his finger under some important line and then slammed the book shut. "Really?" He seemed genuinely interested. "That's quite a bit of blood loss."

Nancy's eyes widened. "I'll say it is! That's four hundred and eighty grams worth!"

"Excuse me?" The doctor eyed her curiously.

Nancy laughed. "That's what the box says. Each tampon holds twelve grams of blood. How much is that in ounces?" she kidded.

"Actually that's almost four liters," he replied. She stared back at him and he said, "It's a lot."

"I thought it was."

The doctor had gotten up and was slowly walking towards her, prescription pad in hand, his dark eyes never leaving her face. Nancy thought he had a rather predatory stroll. He stopped and perched on the edge of the desk right in front of her. He smiled, a slippery thing that slid the flesh around on his thin face.

"Do you usually have heavy periods?"

"Yeah. All the time."

Dr. Mason crumpled up the prescription he had been writing and lightly tossed it into the wastebasket. "Well, we'll have to take care of this right away." He began a new script. "This should do it. I'd like to see you back here again in three days."

"Three days?" Nancy could hardly believe what she was hearing. What happened to two weeks, call me if you have any questions? She took the prescription from him and glanced briefly at the ink scratches he had made.

He was still smiling. He looked like a sharp-beaked bird, hovering over her. His nostrils flared and quivered and Nancy thought he was sucking some dark aroma deep into his lungs.

She shrunk back from him. "I smell, don't I?"

Mason blinked. His visage softened and he shook his head. "No, no. Well – all women are fragrant during their time of the month."

Nancy sighed and sat back in her chair. "I feel like it's all over me. In my skin, my cuticles, even my hair."

Mason stretched out a long, lean hand as if to stroke Nancy's hair. She ducked her head out of the way. She wanted sympathy, but she didn't want him touching her. She felt dirty. Not Courtney Love dirty, but rolling in a loaded dumpster in the middle of August dirty.

"It's the concentration of iron and protein in the blood," Mason said as he sat back on his perch. "It can be very aromatic at times. Which reminds me," he began to scribble on his pad again.

"I'm also giving you a prescription for high potency iron tablets, you'll need to take them three times a day."

Great, Nancy thought as she plucked the new prescription from his pale hands, *another forty bucks.*

"And I'd stock up on those super plus tampons," he said. "You'll start to bleed more at first."

Nancy moaned and dropped her arms at her sides in defeat.

"Only at first, only at first," he soothed.

Nancy trudged unhappily to the door. His chipper voice called her back.

"One other thing. Before you start taking those, I'd like you to run over to the clinic for an HIV test."

Nancy spun around. "What for?"

"It's all right, it's nothing. Just a precaution, that's all. Just to be safe." His smile was absolutely fulsome. Nancy wanted to take her bag and bash his long, white teeth in.

"I want you to take this to a Dr. Roman Haledon at the clinic. He's a friend and he'll get me the results right away. They're very discreet there. After you've had the test you can start those pills. Every six hours."

Nancy whacked the door with her fist on her way out. She trod down the corridor, prescriptions crumpled in her fist. *Male doctors,* she thought. *They think it's all a joke.* She stepped out into the waiting room. Karen, the receptionist, had her ear pressed to the phone. She motioned to Nancy with one finger. "She's right here. I'll find out." Hanging up, she opened a file on her desk.

"Nancy? Are you married?"

"No."

"Living with someone?"

Nancy stared at the woman behind the counter. "No. Why?"

"Just for your records. So, you live alone?"

Nancy was losing patience. "Yes, but I don't see what that has to do with my period." She glanced at the other patients in the waiting room, another woman and an elderly man who was probably waiting for his wife. Probably.

The receptionist glanced up. "It's just for your records. Now, you just moved to town a few months ago. Work related?"

Nancy could feel it was time to run to the bathroom. The changing of the guard, so to speak. "Yes. New job. Is that all?"

Karen smiled. "Yep! Today's Monday – is Friday at seven good for you?"

***

Nancy shook the stout little amber bottle of pills. The name at the bottom of the label meant nothing to her. Just a long, multisyllabic word she wouldn't even attempt to pronounce. The other bottle was full of large, deep magenta tablets. Three times a day, she was expected to swallow one of those baby torpedoes. Her throat clutched at the thought of it.

The guy at the pharmacy had given her some look. With a wad of cotton taped to her elbow and five boxes of super plus tampons under one arm, she had handed him her prescriptions. Did he have to check them out before giving them to the pharmacist waiting in the balcony above the counter? It was none of his business what her doctor was giving her. She didn't like the way he seemed to study the tampon boxes before ringing them up. He picked up each blue and white box, reading the labels, the content, instructions whatever could have caught his eye. And what was it with those blue and white boxes? Every brand name seemed to restrict their packages to blue and white and green boxes. It was as if they were purposely avoiding the color red on their packaging.

Drawing a glass of water from the faucet, Nancy tossed back one of the hormone capsules. It felt dry and papery on her tongue. She swallowed some water and then wrestled with the child proof lid on the container of iron tablets.

Ten days. Maybe less. She padded into the bedroom to change her tampon. She could feel the fullness of it in her crotch. They were giving up quicker and quicker. Every two hours or so she was changing them. At the clinic, she had to balance on the edge of the toilet, one foot in the air, her fingers stretching impossibly long to push the damn thing up there. A dog shouldn't suffer like this.

She changed her tampon four more times before going to bed. A girl in high school, Wendy, swore she could use two tampons at once on really heavy days, but Nancy thought that sounded dangerous. Could you still get Toxic shock? She unraveled the paper from the plastic container as thick as a cigar. What if two was too much and it sucked all the moisture out of her? They could get stuck up there. She pictured herself having to go to the hospital to have them surgically removed, explaining that Wendy Pooles had told her to do it.

In her sleep, Nancy drifted in a sea of scarlet. It was cloying, the metallic smell, the sticky liquid tugging at her. She twisted, only to find her face submerged in the thick, red ocean. She gasped, swallowing a mouthful of the stuff. Her body convulsed, her chest hitching. The air was gone from her lungs and in its place, hot liquid rushed in.

Gasping, Nancy bolted upright. She heard a loud squish. Between her legs there was a puddle of red. Leaping from the bed, she saw an oval of blood in the center of her mauve sheets.

"Aw, shit!" she hissed and peeled the sheets off the bed. The blood had soaked through to the mattress. Nancy tossed the bloody bedding onto the floor and sprinted to the bathroom for a cold, wet towel and some liquid cleanser.

The fibers of the mattress began to fray as she worked the cleanser in and she stopped scrubbing. The dank odor of her own blood made her eyes water. A dark trickle skidded down her leg.

"Shit!" Nancy squealed and dropped her towel. Running to the bathroom, leaving a wake of bright red, she grabbed a new box of tampons.

"Things had better improve in the next three days," she snarled as she liberated her soaked tampon. It hung by its cord like a red mouse. Nancy's mouth twitched. She dropped the offensive thing into the garbage and ripped the new box open.

***

There was no point in going to work the next morning. Nancy couldn't keep a tampon inside for more than an hour. She felt the swelling begin forty-five minutes after she'd put in a fresh one and fifteen minutes later, had to rush to the bathroom before it popped out on its own. An ever-growing pile of stained clothing made her give up on wearing underpants. She felt gruesome and unclean.

By evening, her crotch was sore from the constant pushing and pulling. She could hardly sit straight in a chair. Her back and chest had hurt for weeks, but now they felt as if they were bruised, her breasts swollen. The smell was everywhere. Every time she raised her hand to her face, she caught a whiff of metallic filth. The beds of her nails were tinted deep red and she spotted stains in the whorls of her skin. Like Lady Macbeth, she scrubbed her hands constantly.

The second day was worse. Not caring to explain her condition to her boss, Nancy told them she had chicken pox. This was going to last a while. She changed tampons nearly every half hour. They slid from her body, anxious to be free. The only comfortable position to do this was lying down. Towels covered every piece of furniture now. She slept on a bare mattress protected by the thickness of two terry cloth towels and prayed she'd awaken before her tampon filled up.

For the sixth time in four hours, Nancy was lying down, changing her tampon, when she felt something crawl out of her. It wriggled from the lips of her vulva and past her thighs, making her shriek in terror. The image of some parasitic worm burrowing in her bowels tore through her brain. Throwing herself from the bed, she collided with her dresser, a shower of bottles and nick-nacks cascading to the floor.

Afraid to turn around, Nancy peeked at the bed. A long dark object like a piece of liver lay on the towel in a pool of blood that was slowly sopping into the towels. Nancy moaned, recognizing it as a huge blood clot.

"I can't take this anymore," she whispered. Pawing through her bag, she found her address book. "I'm bleeding like a stuck pig." She dialed up Dr. Mason, but the woman who answered claimed to be the service. He wouldn't be in until tomorrow, did Nancy have a message?

"I've got a message," she growled as she slammed the receiver down. Tears burned in her eyes. *This isn't fair,* she thought. Her crotch felt hot and full, and she buried her hands in the damp, bloody hair. One more day and then she was going to give it to that doctor. He had some nerve subjecting her to this.

Again, she was floating in red. The liquid seeped into her mouth and she was suddenly heavy, bloated. Her body sank. Her nose, her eyes filled with blood. She could smell it, taste it, clawing at her throat. Her arms beat at the rich redness as she swam, frog-like through the river of gore. Nancy couldn't tell which way was up or down. She could smell the coppery odor, strong in her nostrils. Why didn't she die? she thought, as she treaded the red water. A pale figure seemed to be moving towards her. Nancy floated, expectation rising in her chest. The figure had a face, a keen oval of whiteness. It seemed to speed towards her, its body undulating rapidly like some blanched flagellum. Nancy felt an urgent need to flee, but she was dead weight, drifting. It darted towards her, the pallid face growing closer, until its eyes met her own.

She jerked from her sleep. There was a hot thickness trying to escape her crotch and she fished the swollen tampon out. A ribbon of blood sprayed the mattress. Nancy felt an animal sound gurgle up in her throat. Then the phone rang.

She flicked the tampon into a plastic bag she had left lying on the floor near the bed. It landed with a splat next to its spent brothers. Hooking the phone with two fingers, Nancy threw herself back on the soiled mattress.

"Hello."

"Good morning! Nancy? This is Karen, Dr. Mason's receptionist."

Nancy grunted in reply.

The cheerful voice on the other line continued. "I just wanted to let you know that we got the results on your HIV test and they're negative." The woman sounded as if she had just awarded Nancy a new car. "So, we'll be looking forward to seeing you tomorrow night for your appointment."

"I can't stop bleeding," Nancy said into the phone.

"The doctor said you'd be bleeding a bit more at first."

"It's not a bit more!" Nancy shouted. "It's twice as much. Ten times as much! I sit on the toilet and it just pours out!" She began to sob. "I can't stand it anymore."

"Just one more day," the receptionist chirped. "We'll see you tomorrow at seven."

The receiver went dead in her hands and Nancy felt a shriek of outrage boil up inside her. She bashed the phone down and jumped off the bed, ready to dial back the doctor's office. A rush of liquid shot out from between her legs, running down her thighs. She stared down her legs, watching droplets of blood spatter on the floor. They were everywhere. Little circles of brownish red sprinkled in the bathroom, out in the hall, on her sheets. She sat down with a wet squish. Her face puckered up and she began to cry.

***

For the first time in three days, Nancy was out. She had finally conceded to Wendy Pooles' double-tampon theory and she walked like a cowboy. Dr. Mason's office was empty. Karen wasn't even at her desk. For Nancy, sitting was a new adventure in pain. Gingerly, she eased her butt onto the vinyl cushioned chair. The familiar sting raced up her spine, into her teeth. *Please, God,* she thought, *let it be over soon.*

She was about to grab a copy of *People* magazine when the inner office door opened and Dr. Mason poked his head out. His nostrils looked huge and he took a deep breath.

"Good, you're here." He flashed her that huge smile. "We'll be ready for you in a minute." Before she could reply, he ducked back out of sight.

Nancy grabbed the magazine and started flipping through it. *Male doctors,* she thought. *Bastards have no respect for women's problems.* "Women's Troubles"; that's what her father always called it. When her mother went through menopause, her father told them she was having "Women's Troubles." How could a man understand what women suffered? Nancy knew she'd been crotchety for the last two weeks, but who wouldn't be? Anybody would feel bitchy if they had to shove cotton bullets up their crotch every two hours. She fiercely turned the pages. She should have seen a woman doctor. Even her sister's GYN was a man. If Mason didn't do something to relieve her from all this bleeding, she was out of there and into another doctor's office, pronto.

The door clicked open and Dr. Mason motioned her in. Nancy got up too quickly, forgetting her sore bottom and she cringed. The doctor smiled as she hobbled carefully into his private office.

"So, how are we feeling today?" he said as he closed the door behind him.

"I don't know about you, but I feel lousy." Nancy gently settled into a chair. "I can't even keep a tampon in me. I've got two stuck up there, now."

The doctor shocked her by laughing. Nancy saw a slight movement out of the corner of her eye and realized that Karen, the receptionist, was standing in the corner. The young woman was flicking a plastic syringe with one finger. She smiled brightly at Nancy.

"Have you been taking the iron?" Mason asked. He sat on the edge of his desk, his former roost, and shrugged out of his lab coat.

"Yeah," Nancy said. She watched Karen prepare a cotton ball with alcohol. "Am I getting a needle?"

"Yes, you are," Mason answered promptly.

Karen brought the injection over and handed it to the doctor. He studied the gauge.

"Did you call the office?"

Karen nodded, "Yes, I did."

"And?"

"No problem. She called in sick two days ago."

"I thought she would." He smiled at Nancy.

"What's that for?" Nancy unbuttoned her sleeve. Mason approached her, needle in position.

"Let's just say," the doctor smiled again. "You're going to need it."

The injection was cold and Nancy's arm immediately went numb. "Is this going to stop the bleeding?"

"Oh, no," he answered, handing the syringe back to Karen.

"What do you mean, 'oh, no'...?" Nancy's tongue felt thick. "You've got to do something. I can't keep bleeding."

Mason pulled out his notebook. He quickly jotted something down.

"Can you smell it?" It took Nancy a moment to realize he wasn't speaking to her.

Karen nodded, smiling at Nancy as her vision softened. "It's strong."

Mason was undoing his tie, "and did you set up a room for her?"

"All set." Karen flopped down in the chair behind Mason's desk.

"Did you call Roman?"

"Done."

Nancy's eyes felt heavy in her head. They felt like they might just roll out of her skull and drop to the floor. Mason looked up at her for a moment and then returned to his notebook.

"Get me some tape," was the last thing she heard before she surrendered to blackness.

***

When she first regained consciousness, Nancy thought her mouth was full of blood. She gagged, bucking wildly, only to find her arms restrained. Her eyes were misty and she struggled to see straight. Her mouth moved, but no words came. Her lips felt as if they'd been erased from her mouth.

Mason stood by a small cart. She could hear something bubbling, like coffee. There was an odor, dark and distasteful, so familiar. She attempted to move but her arms were fastened to metal poles that stuck out on either side of her. She tried to pull them free. A painful pinch of the skin cautioned her and she gave up the fight. Silver tape strapped her arms down. The same pinch tugged at the corners of her mouth. Looking cross-eyed she could see a plastic tube extending from her mouth, curling over her head. More silver tape held the tube in place. Above her, hung a bag of pulpy, brown liquid. A thick moan escaped her throat.

"Hi," Mason said casually. He smiled and walked towards her. "Just relax."

Nancy's eyes snapped open. She shifted her legs and noted that her feet were taped to the legs of the chair. But it wasn't quite a chair...

"I know this isn't pleasant, but it could be worse." His lips slid back from his teeth. He looked positively carnivorous. "Trust me. It could be much worse."

Nancy felt weak. A nylon harness dug into her flesh. Cold metal rings and chains were lying against her naked skin. The sudden realization that this was no medical facility made her feel ill. Her head dropped forward as she fought a wave of nausea. She could see her bare legs. The chair she sat on was made of wood, a hole cut out beneath her bottom. The soreness was still there, only now, it was accompanied by a burning sensation further up her crotch. Her eyes strained to see what was there. More tubes projected from below, leading away to several different machines. One tube was filled with a pale yellow liquid, the other was filled with what looked like red ink.

Mason juggled a few bottles from the cart and chose an empty one. He glanced up at her amiably.

"This won't be so bad, Nancy. I've had great success with this process before." He strode over to one of the machines Nancy was hooked up to and checked the gauges.

"It's really worked out well for us." He looked back at her. "For me, and others like myself."

Tapping a few buttons on the machine, he set the glass under a nozzle. The thing made a noise like a cappuccino maker.

The machine made a loud fizzling sound and a squirt of crimson drained into the empty glass.

"Over the years, we've found it more and more difficult to find what we need to survive. You can't count on superstitious villagers any more. The police hunt you down so efficiently nowadays."

About two inches of the red stuff filled the glass before the machine became silent. Mason picked up the container and held it to the light for scrutiny.

"And everything is so modernized these days. It's amazing what technology can teach you. Things like filtering, homogenizing and pasteurization, for instance." He jiggled the contents of the glass and smiled. "The resources you find online would amaze you."

The impossibly red fluid swirled in its receptacle and Mason shook his head. "Your blood – menstrual blood – is so rich. It's heavy with proteins and iron, stripped from the deepest, inner parts of your body. The bits needed to create life, all concentrated in a capsule of red nectar." He glanced up at her and winked. "Kind of like a shot of the best espresso."

The door opened and Karen stepped in. She barely glanced at Nancy. Turning to Mason, she said, "Who says you get the first taste?"

He grinned back at her. "I always get the first taste." With that, he brought the glass to his lips and sipped.

Karen watched with expectation. "Well?"

The doctor licked his lips and nodded. "Good. Sweet."

Nancy felt her vision slip. The croaking sound she made in her throat caused Karen to step forward and check the tubes sticking out of her mouth.

Mason continued. "As you can see, we'll feed you and look after you like a vascular cow." He gestured at the tubing. "The restraints, unfortunately, are necessary, but you'll get used to it after a while. And if you want, we could sedate you, although I'd rather not." He held up his glass. "It does involve another step in the purification process. Gets a bit expensive."

Karen was writing something on a chart. She glanced at Nancy. "What was her name, again?"

"Nancy," he answered. "I meant to put up a little sign."

Karen shrugged. "Listen, Roman and Betty are outside, and a few of the others are coming. Michael can't make it. We're going to use up what we have in the fridge."

Mason drained his glass and nodded. "That's fine. We should be getting a little better than a liter from her after today. I've upped the hormone shots."

The two busied themselves with cleaning up, checking the machinery and Nancy's tubes. She watched them, wild-eyed, her breathing quick and erratic. Mason checked her chart again and made a notation. From far off, Nancy heard a doorbell ring. Karen slipped out the door and a moment later, Mason followed, clicking off the overhead light without a backward glance.

Nancy sat in the dark. Voices tittered from outside. She could hear the common noises of an evening with friends; doors opening and shutting, laughter, the tinkle of glasses. Her face felt tight. After a while, all she could hear was the hum of machinery and the dripping from her tubes.

She hoped they would realize that she would need to be sedated before the night was through.

Cuppa Joe

Craig Faustus Buck

I wake up feeling logy. I head for the kitchen and grab the mix from the freezer, throw it in the blender and give it a whirl. Then I dump it in Mr. Coffee and turn on the drip.

The brew takes a while to cool to 98.6 degrees but the smell warms me all the while. It feels good to be alive. I swirl the rich liquid in my mug. My morning cuppa Joe. He was my brother-in-law, until I switched from cappuccino to decappuccino. But he's been missing for two weeks now. I'm running low.

***

My sister and Joe were pretty happy before he and I had our little falling out. It happened on my day off. Joe had stayed home from work, feeling fluey, so my sister asked me to look in on him. He was feeling better by the time I got there, so the two of us grabbed our fishing gear and drove out to the lake.

We were bobbing for bass, sharing a thermos of Java, and he was going on and on about how my sister blows her paycheck on hair products when he could be doubling her money in Vegas. (The only clod dumber than this bozo is my sister for hooking up with him). He was yammering on, driving me nuts, when all of a sudden we both got a strike. After a few minutes of struggle, we figured out there was no fish involved. Our hooks were entangled. Joe made some lame joke about our worms fucking and as I gave him a guffaw, just to be polite, a huge bass took the bait. I never dreamed that two men could catch the same fish at the same time, but it happened. Joe started in about how he caught it first and I told him to eat shit because he wasn't about to be eating *my* bass, and one thing led to another and I found myself garroting Joe with his own fishing line.

A dripping ring of blood bloomed around his neck when that thirty-pound-test broke his skin and I became fixated on the physics of the thing. Would the line break before Joe did? Would thirty pounds be enough tensile strength? Would he die by asphyxiation

142

before the line got deep enough to sever his carotid artery? Would his tendons be cut? My enquiring mind wanted to know.

So many questions, so little time – though in the moment, it seemed like an eternity. Thank God I wore gloves or the monofilament would have sliced my fingers off. Damn if he didn't linger a good five minutes before the light finally drained from his eyes. I thought he'd never stop breathing. Just to be safe, I didn't let up until he turned blue. I was sweating like a pig and the next day, my biceps ached like a son-of-a-bitch.

I felt lucky he'd brought the thirty-pound because I doubted my own twelve-pound would have withstood the strain. I'd choked him as hard as I could but it probably still took longer than it should have because I wasn't in the best of shape. Then and there, I resolved to go back to the gym.

I wound up releasing the bass and gutting Joe instead. It was not easy. I wanted to avoid making a mess that some hiker might find, so I drained him into my bucket. Luckily, the bass I'd set free was the only fish we'd caught that day, so the bucket was clean. That's how I wound up tasting his blood. Can you imagine sipping a cuppa Joe that smells like fish? It would have been undrinkable.

I'd never killed a person before. I'd hunted deer but it's a lot easier to drop a buck with a bullet than to strangle your brother-in-law with a garrote. It was an eye-opening experience – for me, not for Joe. Dealing with the body wasn't too bad, either. Not all that different from dressing a deer, except you don't collect a deer's blood.

Most of Joe ended up in the garage in my roadkill freezer, along with two possums and what was left of a succulent fawn. But there was something hypnotic about the blood, so I brought it inside to the kitchen. It separated pretty fast as the red stuff coagulated and the clearish serum rose like cream to the top. But when I tried putting it in the blender, damn if it didn't reconstitute like silky red gravy. So, I figured, what the hell? And took a slug.

I expected it to taste like biting the inside of my cheek, but there was something about it being Joe's blood that made it taste foreign. And I mean that in a good way, like Thai food. So I divvied it up into Tupperware and stored it in my kitchen freezer.

My first cuppa Joe was a religious experience. The angels sang in five-part harmony and my incomprehensible life finally made sense. Thanks to Joe, the purpose of my existence was revealed to me. I now knew why I was put on this Earth: to fulfill my biological imperative, which is killing for sustenance. Man has been doing it since we were

Paleolithic. Our species evolved to hunt, and among our prey were rival tribes of homo sapiens. Over the millennia, we became civilized to excess and that essential humanity was encased in a cultural shell, a screaming pearl in an impenetrable oyster. Luckily, Joe came along to shuck my oyster, release my essence, reintroduce me to the perfect local source of sustainable food.

*　*　*

But I digress. I've become addicted to my morning pick-me-up. Yet, one good exsanguination only goes so far. The average man contains about 4.7 pints of blood. After spillage and coagulation, I only got three out of Joe. And of that, only a few cups are left. I need to restock.

I've given the matter considerable thought and have come to the conclusion that a woman might be a better choice next time. Don't get me wrong. I love my morning cuppa Joe. But he's just a maintenance drug, like taking a statin. A woman! Now we're talking recreational drugs. Something with a kick, some sex appeal. Not to mention the joy of dismemberment. No offense to Joe, but his rough, hairy skin made mine crawl. Joe's flesh is to a woman's like sackcloth to silk.

A cup of feminine essence in the morning. The thought makes my breath flutter like first love. I imagine her on my kitchen table with her long blonde hair cascading over the edge like a golden waterfall, her slender body parts strategically placed to approximate what she looked like in life, freckles intact, legs long and lean, breasts frozen forever pert. I wonder if postmortem nipples react to the cold. Only time will tell.

There's definitely something arousing about the thought of drinking a woman's blood. I reach down to feel myself starting to harden beneath the heather cotton of my sweatpants. Joe may have been my first, but he was an opportunity, not a selection. A woman would be a feast of my own choosing. It feels so right. I can already taste her.

My doorbell chimes.

I wipe Joe's blood off my lips and close the kitchen door behind me to hide the blender and coffee pot. Joe must remain my little secret. I head to the door and look through the spyhole. It's a woman, standing with her back to me. Her hair is blonde and stringy like corn silk. I picture my fingers running through it to grab a firm handhold as

I let her body fall away from her severed head. The image brings a giddy smile to my lips.

"Who is it?"

She turns and tries to peer through the wrong end of the peep hole. Her eyes are red and teary. "Open the door, jerkoff."

My sister, Lurlene. I open up.

"You've been crying," I say.

"You should have been a detective," she says. She's being sarcastic, seeing as how I'm a Detective II with LAPD. She sweeps past me and throws herself on my couch. "The cops aren't doing shit. They think Joey probably ran off with some lover. Are they idiots? No woman in her right mind would want that asshole."

"Except you." I hate stating the obvious but it had to be said.

"Fuck you, Ernest."

"I thought you loved him."

"Why are you talking in past tense? Do you think he's dead? Did you hear something at the station?" There's real panic in her voice.

"I didn't hear anything. It was just a figure of speech."

"Well, for your information, I *do* love him. What do you know about love, anyway? Nothing, that's what."

We've been replaying this scene in one form or another since Joe went missing into my freezer. Lurlene claims she loves him but acts like she hates him. I can never tell. But her life has been an endless stretch of misery since he disappeared, so maybe she *did* love him. Would it be an act of kindness to kill her? To lift her out of her depression? She does, after all, satisfy the primary requirement of being a woman.

Is it incest to drink your sister's blood? Maybe roast her loin for Sunday supper? There's no sex involved. No danger of inbreeding. In a way, it would reunite her with her beloved Joe. It's got a poetic ring to it. A renewal of vows in my bowels.

My stomach rumbles. I realize I'm not feeling a hundred percent. Is that my conscience poking around? Maybe it isn't morally ideal to feed on one's sister. Still, she is a bird in the hand. And even if it is incest, isn't that a petty crime in the shadow of sororicide?

"Love is complicated," she says. "Too complicated for your sorry ass."

My eyes are drawn to her throat. Lurlene's body is trim from teaching Pilates five days a week, but she's got a triple chin. Just like our Mom. There's a crease in the fat just above her neck that might as well be one of those dotted lines that show you where to cut. I start to salivate.

A woman is softer than a man. I wonder if that makes her flesh more tender. Maybe the twelve-pound-test would be strong enough for Lurlene. Though, a good, sharp knife would take much less effort and probably be just as fun. The only downside would be that her death wouldn't last very long. There's something very satisfying about the lingering part. Maybe I should tie her down and bleed her out slowly? But even if I did it in the basement, one of the neighbors might hear her screams. I guess that's what gags are for.

Is it worse to kill your sister than to kill a stranger? I weigh the pros and cons. A stranger might have a husband or boyfriend who would miss her. My sister, thanks to me, does not. A stranger might have a happy life that would be cut short. My sister, thanks to me, is depressed and likely to become more so as the weeks without Joe turn to months and then years.

My stomach growls again. This time, I feel a little queasy. Is it my cuppa Joe? I've been drinking him for over a week now with no problems. I'll bet it's the tuna salad from yesterday.

"I need some water," I say and head into the kitchen.

As soon as I open the door, I see the bloody appliances. Shit! I grab the coffee decanter with one hand, the blender jar with the other, and jam my foot on the garbage can pedal just as I hear my sister drag herself off the couch. I lower the glassware carefully into the garbage so nothing breaks. The lid falls closed just as she walks into the room.

"He's been stealing from me for years," she says. "Did I ever tell you that? He thinks I don't know but he's been skimming our vacation savings and blowing it at the poker tables in Gardena."

"Isn't that money community property?" I move to the sink to drink sideways from the tap. When I lower my head for a sip, I get dizzy.

"Community property means it belongs to both of us," she says. "When he sneaks it out, knowing I wouldn't allow it, it becomes stolen property. It's in the law."

I stand up straight and use both hands to steady myself against the counter. One hand falls on the handle of my boning knife.

"Can you cite the statute for that?" I say. "Because we didn't learn anything about it at the Academy."

My eyes return to the line across her throat.

"Shut up, Ernie. You're not funny."

I wasn't trying to be, but I keep my mouth shut. I think I can see her pulse beating in her neck, like a little drummer urging me on. My toe starts to tap to the beat.

Then I realize she's still talking and I haven't heard. I've zoned out. Not something I usually do. Am I being sucked so far into my blood fantasy that I'm losing touch with reality? It's almost like I'm blacking out. I force myself to tune back into the conversation.

"...last week I found a motel receipt. Not only was he cheating on me but he was spending my money on her!"

"Who?"

"Are you not listening? His secretary-slash-whore!"

"Joe had a secretary?" I'm shocked he could afford one. He told me his business was in the toilet.

"Hey!" She snaps her fingers in front of my face. "Focus on the 'whore' part." Her face seems to melt and her eyes tear up, finally breaching her lower lids. She whispers, "I thought he loved me."

I feel awful for her but I can't tell if it's because I know Joe's not coming back or because Lurlene was betrayed by him. Either way, I think she's my sister and deserves better. The little drummer in her throat is throbbing, calling me to rescue her from the quicksand of her despair. My fingers snake around the knife handle like a python around a stripper.

"I thought he loved me!" she shrieks, then erupts into sobs. I'm getting a migraine from her agony. I've got to make it stop. I slide the knife off the counter and hide it behind my back.

Lurlene forces back her tears and grabs a paper towel to blow her nose.

"He's dead," she says. "I know it."

"You don't know for sure."

"Yes, I do." She starts crying again.

My hand tightens on the knife.

"I've been feeding him cyanide," she wails.

I feel a surge of reflux as my stomach acid torches my esophagus.

Lurlene steps on the pedal of the garbage can to toss her phlegmy paper towel. The lid flips open and her eyes widen at the sight of all the blood. She turns to me in shock.

"Whose blood is that?"

I have to end this before comprehension breaks her heart. I lunge toward her, knife extended. But my stomach clenches like a choke chain. I manage only one step before the pain slams me to the floor. The knife skitters away. I can't breathe.

"Ernie, what's wrong?"

A scream of agony struggles to explode from every pore in my body, but my muscles are locked tight and I can't get it out. If this is death by cyanide, it's taking for-fucking-ever. I'm dying for a cuppa Joe.

The Punchline is Cthulhu

Jamie Wahls

Della pushed the button and killed another ship full of babies. There was a collective sigh of relief in the control room and, a moment later, some uncomfortable glancing around and self-awareness.

"Well." said Juliet, with a sense of finality. "Glad that's settled. I didn't want to be changing diapers."

Relieved laughter from the staff, except for Della. Juliet clapped her on the shoulder like a drinking buddy, and they both glanced at the screen where a green blip wasn't.

Everyone got back to work, except for Della. She went on break.

***

"It's a very important job, sweetie," First Magister Clementine-Who-Was-Also-Mom said. She punched the buttons to order some soup. "I'm sure it's hard. But I'm afraid it's a necessity. You'll get over it."

Mom didn't say anything about grades. Della didn't say anything about mom's lover. They had to live in the same villa, after all.

"I'm going to the park," said Della.

And as she sat in the park underneath the stars, staring into that blackness through maybe meters of glass or maybe just seeing a projection, she wondered just *why* she had to kill so many babies.

***

She noticed a coincidental tally: the day that Mendicant politely informed her of her thirteenth birthday, and played her an odd and tinny tune, was also the same day that she shot down her fiftieth ship.

Fifty ships times fourteen babies a ship equaled seven hundred babies. The record number of people personally killed by a serial killer was, what, one hundred and fifty? So, Della had incidentally become the most killingest person, well, surely not *ever*, but definitely under the dome. Depending on if she considered babies to be people.

***

The next day, Della accidentally opened a com-channel to the ship, so for a few seconds they heard a miserable choir of screaming babies, as everyone waited for Della to push the button. She did. It stopped.

***

"It's not pleasant, but it needs to be done." Magister Clementine gestured at her with a fork as Mendicant wheeled up with another course. "The Earth is overpopulated, we aren't. Consequentially, we can live our lives at a much higher standard, but only if we can keep our numbers low. Now, Earth is jealous of us, so they sometimes send ships here to try and join us. At first, we let some people in. But that was a mistake. They kept sending more, and there's no end to the Earthbound. So, our requirements got stricter, naturally, since we only wanted the best of their best.

"But since we weren't accepting as many people as wanted to come join, they got mad. They were always a jealous bunch, and after they ruined the planet with filth and fornication, they decided they wanted the moon, too. And they use all kinds of tricks to get up here, sending ships filled with works of art, or gold, or... other means of seducing our decision-makers." She delicately dabbed at her mouth.

"We decided that we couldn't accept any more refugees, and that we had to shoot down any ships that came. We told them that, and they kept coming. They may not be as smart as us." She smiled at Della, who was expected to laugh, so she did.

"And over time, they concluded that the best way to try and wear us down—attempting to hurt our feelings, Della—was to send ships carrying babies. Well, no one *wants* to shoot at a baby, but of course, we *have* to, for the reasons I just explained. So, well, the actual work of shooting down the ship wasn't something anyone really *wanted*, but everyone has to have a job, and you know, dear, with your test scores..."

Della's face was burning. "I know."

Mom reached over and tousled her hair. "We'd like to be able to let more people live like we do. But we simply cannot afford that, and—" she had a strange expression. "The stars aren't yet right. It would be *calamitous.*"

She stood up curtly. "I have work to do, dear. You may finish dinner without me."

***

The ships full of babies came every two weeks. There were sometimes other ships carrying different things, but the baby ships came like clockwork.

***

"Mendicant, what's 'old age'?"

The shiny metal faceplate was impassive. Mendicant continued to wash dishes with its spindly metal limbs, without facing her. "Old age consists of ages nearing or surpassing the life expectancy of human beings."

Della sat down on the kitchen floor. "What's life expectancy?"

"A statistical measure of how long a human may be alive."

"Look up 'alive'." She paused. "Please."

"A characteristic differentiating physical entities having biological processes from those who do not. Contrast: Dead."

"What's 'dead'?"

"The termination of all biological functions which sustain a living organism. Common causes include old age, injury, disease, suicide, homicide—"

"People can die from old age?"

"Yes."

Della chewed her bottom lip. "That doesn't seem right."

Mendicant didn't reply, and Della held her breath, afraid that she'd tripped the operator call—

"Insufficient data," it said, which was basically a shrug. Della breathed a sigh of relief.

"Mendicant, where do new people come from?"

It had been nagging at her for a long time, but no one was willing to talk about it.

Mendicant's voice was tinny and flat. "In human reproduction, pregnancy is the development of one or more offspring—"

"How do people get pregnant?"

"Fertilization is the fusing of gametes resulting in the creation of a new embryo. As sperm and ovum—"

"Sperm?"

Mendicant paused, and even though Della knew it was a machine, she still felt like it was disappointed in how slow she was.

"The male reproductive cell."

She furrowed her brow. "Mendicant, what's 'male'?"

"A male organism is the physical sex which generates sperm. Comprising approximately fifty percent of the human population—"

"Fifty?" she asked skeptically.

"Fifty percent of the human population, a male cannot reproduce sexually without an ovum from a female."

Her expression was perturbed. "Really, fifty? Then why are there no males here?"

Mendicant paused, and the silence stretched on, far too long. She cursed herself.

"Della?" came mom's voice, metallic and strained through Mendicant's speakers, but still sharp. "What are you asking about?"

Della clenched her fists tight. *So close.* "Hi, mom."

"You asked about men, and reproduction and—" Della knew mom was looking through the records as she spoke.

A small, disappointed sigh. "And old age."

"Yes, Mom," she said, in a small voice.

"Della..." a silence. "Where did you hear about old age?"

She swallowed. "In a book. Juliet left it at the house."

"Ah." She made a *tch* noise. "I see. I'll have a talk with her." And Della winced a little in sympathy.

"Well," said Magister Clementine-Who-Was-Also-Mom. "Old age is a thing that happens on Earth. People's bodies wear out over time. It doesn't happen here, though. You don't need to worry about it."

"Their bodies wear out and they *die*?" asked Della in horrified fascination.

A slight pause. "Yes."

Della searched for words. "That's awful!"

Mom chuckled, and the speakers made it echo funny and sound mean. "You are a very sweet girl, which I suppose shouldn't surprise me. My little Lamb. Don't worry about it. It won't happen to you."

"Because of the moon?" asked Della.

"Because of the moon. We're taken care of here. Now, go study, instead of wasting time asking stupid questions."

Della flinched slightly. "Yes, Mom."

***

The ship streaked in on the screen. They had disabled most of the panel in front of her, so there was no way she could accidentally patch them into baby screams again.

Maybe I could let this one land? she thought distantly. *We could raise some kids, that'd be nice. I'm tired of being the youngest.*

As the ship grew closer and the silence in control stretched out, Juliet cleared her throat. "You see it, Della?"

She couldn't say anything.

***

"She froze!" shouted Juliet. "She almost didn't do it!"

"Della," said Mom sternly, "what happened?"

Della couldn't say anything. Her face felt stiff.

Juliet shook her head. "She's a ridiculous liability. She's the point of failure for the whole colony."

"She needs more time," said Mom firmly. "She's a good girl. She'll come around."

Juliet made an irritated face. "Fine. Let's have our partners change the delivery schedule, so we can send more volume less frequently."

They're talking around me, thought Della. *It's like a joke, and I don't get to know the punchline.*

Della swallowed. "I thought the Earth people were sending babies to hurt our feelings?"

Juliet scoffed incredulously. She looked at Mom with a touch of scorn.

"Hush, Della," said Mom. She turned to Juliet and her face was hard. "Our partners on Earth can't change the schedule. They've paid a price, like us, and they're also reaping the benefits. But we're paying down the interest, here. ANY deviation and the debt comes due."

Juliet's voice rose with anxiety. "I understand that. Which is why it's absolutely critical we find someone else to push the button!"

"We *can't*," said Magister Clementine, with a strange bitterness. "It has to be *her*, willingly. The blood of my blood. *The Lamb.* Anyone else would be *calamitous*."

Juliet's eyes widened very slightly. Her voice was barely a whisper. "Oh."

***

Two tense weeks passed. A ship was inbound. Della was sweating.

"Della, buddy."

They had changed her panel again. There was no screen, any more. She had a light, to tell her when she should push the button. She had the button. The light was on.

153

"Della, come on. You've gotta do this."

"Why does it have to be *me*?" she burst out. "This just doesn't *make sense!*"

Juliet shook her head, a little angrily. "It *has* to be you. Anyone else would be—"

"*Calamitous*. I heard. What does that even *mean*?" Della asked, scathingly. "You and Mom keep saying that, and I don't think anyone else knows what that means." She stared accusatorily around the control room, vaguely aware of people besides herself and Juliet. Other staff watched, bewildered.

Juliet, eyes clenched shut, shook her head. "A few people know," she said, the tension rising in her voice, "and we can talk about it later, but Della, buddy, it's very important that you push that button and that you do it *right now*."

Della's finger hovered near the button. And then, she simply said, "No."

Juliet gritted her teeth. "I'm sure you have good intentions but you're being a little idiot—and this will kill us all—and we can explain everything in just a minute, but Della, I absolutely *need* you to push that button right now!"

Della threw up her hands. "*Please*, just tell me what's going on? Are you really this scared of overpopulation? That's... very silly."

"*Please*." Juliet whispered, and her face was white.

Della stared at her, bewildered. "No."

Juliet glanced at her, then at the button, her fingers clenched tight into fists. She lunged for the control panel, and *just* as she did so, the ground began to shake.

"What is it? What's happening?" exclaimed Della.

"I'm sorry!" shouted Juliet. "We're *all* sorry! Mercy!"

Juliet suddenly froze, and then quickly brought her hands up before her face. Her fingers were running like melting candles, drooling down to the floor in drips of undifferentiated flesh tallow. She gazed at Della in horror as the skin on her face began to bubble and pop, oozing a thick, pale yellow slime. Her mouth was open— maybe she was trying to scream—but all Della could hear was a high, tight, gasping noise, repeated endlessly as Juliet slowly sunk into the expanding pool of her own melting body.

Della stared, mouth agape. The ground quaked more violently, now.

"No," Juliet hissed, with the last of her voice. Her head was almost on the floor now, the rest of her body subsumed into the mass. In barely a whisper that Della was only just able to make out, Juliet's head spoke directly to her.

"The pact is broken. He wakes… ia, ia! You will *envy me*—"

Xmas

Calvin Demmer

Damian Pennington heard a commotion downstairs. He rolled out of bed, straightened his superhero pajamas, and traversed the dark passageway to the top of the staircase. He was filled with a mixture of both joy and disappointment when he recognized the booming laugh. It wasn't Santa, but it was his grandfather.

He began his descent, only to stop a few steps down. His mother had told him to go to bed so that Santa would have time to bring his presents. Inhaling deeply, he summoned the courage to go on. There was a slight wheeze when he breathed. He felt his pants' pockets, but they were empty. He had forgotten his inhaler in his bedroom—another complication he didn't need. His grandfather's laugh bounced all along the walls up to him, and he wondered what he was missing out on. Forgetting about his mother's warning and his heavy chest, he continued on down.

He turned into the living room and couldn't resist smiling. It was Christmas Eve, and the tree lights illuminated the world around him—no darkness. To his surprise, there were already presents all around the bottom of the tree. Damian figured Santa must have visited already. He looked on the table alongside the single chair near the tree. The cookies and milk he had placed out earlier were gone, confirming his conclusion. He looked back at the presents, wanting to do some scouting so that he would know exactly where his were when he woke up. Taking a step forward, his eyes sought the biggest of the lot.

A hand gripped his shoulder.

Damian turned around. His mother was standing behind him. Her pretend angry face was dialed into her visage, not her serious one, where her cheeks would flare red.

"What are you doing out of bed?" she said.

"The presents are here, was Santa here?"

"Yes, but it's not too late for him to fetch them if you misbehave. Now tell me, what are you doing out of bed?"

"I want to see Grandpapa."

His mother frowned. "Very well, but Damian, listen. There is an animal in the kitchen, and I do not want you touching it or getting too close under any circumstances. Do you understand?"

Damian nodded, and then stopped. "But, why?"

"Your asthma for one, but also because the animal is very ill."

"What animal is it?"

"Go look," his mother said, shooing him along. "Remember, no touching. And then I want you straight off to bed. You hear me?"

"Yes."

***

A potent medicinal smell singed the interior of Damian's nostrils as he entered the kitchen. His grandfather and father were seated at the far side of the kitchen table, near the back door. They were looking down at something, oblivious to his appearance. He strained his neck as he tried to peer over the table to see what they were looking at, but it was no use. Another idea came to his mind. Damian snuck around the table, keeping low, while hoping to get a better view before his father noticed his presence.

"Do you think he'll make it?" his father said.

"Not sure," his grandfather said, scrunching his shoulders. "I would have taken him to the veterinarian, but the storm has already hit town, don't want to get stuck."

"Yeah."

"If he makes it through the night, I'll take him first thing, hopefully everything will have cleared up by then."

Damian paused behind his father. He looked towards the kitchen window. It was raining outside, and he could hear the howl of the wind picking up. He knew one more step and he would have a clear view of the animal. His mind raced with the possibilities of what it could be. He took the step, only to feel a hand come down on his shoulder, harder than the grip of his mother.

"Whoa, easy there, fella," his father said. "Where do you think you're going?"

"I want to see the animal." Damian didn't turn to look back at his father. His focus was on the animal, which lay on its side on a pale yellow blanket a few feet from him. He could see its chest move up and down, but its breathing seemed to take great effort, which reminded Damian of the worse times with his asthma. He knew this to be a bad sign. His father had not released his shoulder, which forced Damian to whip his head from side-to-side as he tried to get a better view of the animal's face.

"What is it?" Damian said.

His grandfather chuckled. "It's a caribou, well, a reindeer. You'll know what that is. And it's a little boy calf. Found it in my backyard this afternoon, thought it was a good sign, it being Christmas and all, until I realized how sick he was. I always get animals wandering in from the woods, never a sick one though."

"What's wrong with him? Asthma like me?"

"No, Damian. I think his sickness is worse. Your father helped me bandage a spot on his leg, where it looks like he was cut by something. The wound looks a little infected."

"What's his name?"

"Ah, he doesn't have one, but we can call him X. You see that patch of missing hair there on his thigh. It kinda looks like an X."

"What about Xmas?" Damian said. He looked up at his grandfather, who was nodding, and then gave Damian the thumbs up.

"That's a great name, Damian. Xmas it is."

"I hope Xmas gets well," Damian said.

Before his father or grandfather could agree with him, a pair of footsteps could be heard approaching.

***

Damian's mother entered the kitchen, her face crinkled when she saw him, and he knew she was getting closer to the real angry.

"Damian, did I not tell you just to look and then be off to bed?"

"But, Mom…"

His mother shook her head and made her way towards Xmas. Damian shrugged and his father released his grip on his shoulder. He took a few steps back, hoping that peering from behind his father's body would shield him from his mother's thoughts. His mother knelt down next to Xmas, touching the animal's side.

"His hair feels so dry, and it keeps coming out," his mother said. She lifted a bunch of Xmas's hair to prove her point.

His father nodded. "We've done what we can, dear."

Damian took a step out from behind his father. Everyone had been allowed to touch Xmas but him. He could not accept this and decided to rectify the situation. He figured if he could just get down and start patting Xmas, his mother would give up and let him be. He readied himself, imagining his legs to be like springs; ready to propel him forward. His mother stood up and turned to face his grandfather.

This was his opportunity.

He launched himself forward and was about to slide onto his knees, in the hope of ending up next to Xmas, when his mother turned back on him with ninja-like reflexes. His mission was too late to abort. His mother had gotten between him and Xmas. Instead of sliding next to the animal, Damian found himself crashing into her legs.

He felt her grip the back of his pajama top. "Stand up, Damian. You're a bad boy, what did I tell you? Stand up, now."

Damian stood, glancing at his mother. It was as he feared. The real angry mask had taken over her face. He looked down, pouted his lips, trying to act innocent.

"Oh no, mister. You're not getting away with this. I want you to head straight up to your room. I'm going to check up on you in a few minutes, and you'd better be in bed. You better listen. You wouldn't want Santa to come back for all your presents."

Damian could feel the tears building. Not only had he been scolded in front of both his father and his grandfather, but the threat of losing his presents was just too much. He spun around, breaking free from his mother's grip. He bolted out of the kitchen and made his way to the sanctuary of his room.

***

The torture was unbearable. Damian could hear his mother, father, and grandfather downstairs laughing and talking. Yet, he had to suffer alone. He turned from side-to-side. There was no way he could go to sleep. Not only was he too excited for his presents he would be opening in the morning, but he still could not get over the fact that he hadn't been allowed to touch Xmas.

Later, he heard the creaking of the stairs. Someone was coming up. He wondered who it was, hoping it was his grandfather coming to say goodnight. He heard a cough and frowned. It was his mother. She coughed again, this time a deep, raspy hack.

His bedroom door, which stood ajar, opened further. He looked up and saw his mother standing in the doorway.

"You should be asleep, Damian. You wouldn't want Santa to think you're a bad boy on Christmas Eve."

"Why couldn't I touch Xmas?"

"He's sick, and I've told you with your asthma, animals are a no-go. It's just something you need to accept."

Damian shook his head.

"I can't tuck you in tonight. I think I'm coming down with a cold. So I want you to close your eyes and go to sleep. Tomorrow, when you wake up, you can open all your presents and we're going to have a nice lunch in the afternoon."

Damian didn't reply.

"Damian, did you hear me?"

"Yes."

"Now, sleep."

Damian waited for his mother to leave. Once he heard her descending the stairs, he shook his head and kicked his legs against the bed. Reluctantly, he turned on his side and closed his eyes. He wondered if all his family had gotten the cold, as he could hear his father and grandfather coughing every now and again while he counted sheep.

But all thoughts soon faded.

Damian fell asleep.

***

When Damian awoke, there was a potent energy circulating all through his body. All he could think about was his presents. He sat up in bed, his chest heavy, his breathing labored. He reached for his inhaler and took two hits. He sat, feeling calm, and controlled his breathing as his father had taught him to do. Once he felt better, he shot straight out of bed and flew down the stairs.

The living room was empty. The Christmas tree lights were still on, but shone dimly as the early morning light found gaps through the curtains. Damian called out to his parents but got no reply. He wondered if they were still in bed.

If so, he realized, he may have an opportunity to pat Xmas, if his grandfather hadn't taken him to the veterinarian yet. The thought of patting Xmas and then coming back and opening his presents was too exciting to contain, and he grinned from ear-to-ear.

He snuck into the kitchen.

The putrid smell that greeted him was like a whack to the face from a tree branch. He pushed through, only to be greeted by an even worse surprise. The pallid, gaunt bodies of his family were lying in an ocean of blood, which had pooled all over the kitchen floor. Damian looked down at his slippers, now bloodied. He held his breath and walked towards Xmas. The animal's pelage was almost gone, though some gray tufts remained, while spots of some green fungus seemed to grow in sensitive areas.

Damian knew this was bad. He looked at his parents, and then his grandfather.

They were dead.

Damian felt a pain explode in his chest. He wanted to run and hold them, but he knew something wasn't right. He figured a disease or something must have been transmitted from Xmas when they had all touched him. The teachers had often spoken about such things at school. Clenching his hands into tight-balled fists, he fought back the tears.

Unable to bear the scene any longer, he ran out of the kitchen.

Once he entered the living room, he took off the bloodied slippers, throwing them behind him. He looked towards the coffee table and saw his mother's cellphone. He knew he needed to dial 9-1-1. This was an emergency. He picked up the cellphone and pressed the 9, then the 1, but he paused. He felt calmer in the living room and told himself he would phone, but there was something else that required his immediate attention. Placing the phone down on the table, he looked towards the Christmas tree.

Damian decided he would open his presents first.

Sinker

Robert Hart

It was cool and misty, but it was still early. It was the earliest Billy had been up all summer, unless he counted the nights he'd spent at Mike's house, or Troy's, but he didn't. It didn't count if he stayed up all night; that was cheating. The challenge was to go to sleep, not too early because that was cheating, too, and get up when the alarm buzzed and not hit the snooze bar. It was even better if he could get up before the alarm, or not use one at all, but he wasn't that good yet.

The sun would burn off the mist before another hour was through. The grass was slick and wet and it soon darkened Billy's sneakers with damp. The sun would burn that off, too.

His parents were still asleep; wouldn't be up for a good couple of hours. He had noticed a few times lately that they'd still been up when he turned his TV off, after some late-night Creature-Feature or other, arguing in the hissed tones of angry parents in the middle of the night. Everybody argued, Billy knew, but at least his parents didn't hit each other or throw things. He didn't think he could get used to that. He thought of the bruise high up on his dad's cheek and the surprised look in his mother's eyes that told Billy she knew as much about it as he did. It was going all yellow, now. He must have got it at work the other night when he'd stayed late. Construction sites are dangerous places, floodlights or no.

This morning, the object was to get down to the lake and have a day's worth of mischief before everyone else had the same idea. School was back in tomorrow, and Billy knew this was his last, best chance to have the run of the place in the warm sun. He'd packed his Wrist-Rocket, a big bag of Doritos and a canteen filled with orange juice, and left the house before anyone would have thought possible. Now, he rounded the gray condominium block at the end of the road and headed for the train tracks.

The neighborhood Billy lived in consisted mainly of one wide street with a greenbelt running down one side and a dozen or so smaller streets branching off the other. The neighborhood was all

162

townhouses, great for trick-or-treating, the creepy gray condo block, not so much. The lake was through the woods that ran along the greenbelt side.

The train tracks ran through the woods parallel to the greenbelt, and the woods were about two hundred feet deep. Tall oaks and maples crowded with dozens of other types of trees that Billy didn't know the names of. The undergrowth was thick in places, but there were loads of paths. In a couple of hours, the place would be overrun with kids. Right now, Billy was alone.

He stepped from the woods onto chunky chippings and looked both ways down the tracks and listened. He knew he'd hear any train a good mile off because they had to sound their horns at certain places along the line – the nearest, well within earshot. Parents always bitched about how kids got killed by trains because they weren't paying attention, but no one Billy knew had ever heard of any kids around here getting hit. He'd have to be deaf not to hear the things coming and they were all slow.

There was a guy who got caught on the bridge down by the dam and got knocked off and squashed. That was true, Billy knew, because his friend Mike's older brothers knew the guy. Mike said the guy committed suicide, but Billy didn't believe that. It sounded like a stupid way to kill yourself.

Sometimes, Billy and his friends put pennies on the tracks. When a train came by it would smoosh the pennies flat and Abe Lincoln would look like the Elephant Man. Once, his friend Jeff had made a sandwich with two pennies and a nickel in the middle, but that was a bigger investment than anyone else wanted to make.

Smooshing pennies was how Billy found out about iron ore pellets. Freight trains went by with big dumper cars full of iron ore and some of the pellets always bumped out. Some were bigger than others but they all looked like little rocky marbles. They were heavy; dense was the word his friend Troy used. They were great for Billy's Wrist-Rocket, like they were made for it. They fit into the little leather sling like a burger in a bun and when he let fly, they zinged and hit hard.

Once, when they'd snuck out at night, he and Troy had hidden in the bushes and taken a shot at a late-bus. The noise was fantastic and it sent them running, scared shitless but trying to keep quiet and not wake anyone. The next day, they'd gone into the woods with a stolen real estate sign, a metal one. The pellets clanged and punched straight through, like bullets. After that, Billy had practiced for accuracy and taken care to look after the slingshot properly. He'd saved his allowance to buy replacement slings and extra surgical tubing. He was fascinated that a slingshot could be so powerful and that he, a boy of eleven, could walk into K-Mart and buy one unaccompanied and unsupervised. He was careful to restrict his targets to inanimate objects like cans and bottles, enlisting a friend to throw one high if he wanted a moving target.

He crossed the tracks on an angle, taking his time. He collected a few dozen pellets for his stash, but he hadn't come out to practice today. He wanted to play some 'Clinkers and Sinkers' and the games were too short and predictable if he used his Wrist-Rocket. He'd use stones and his hands, to begin with, at least. If his aim was off, he might relent, but only if the place was getting busy.

He hitched his pack further up his shoulder and went down the other side of the railway embankment to a narrow path into the woods. The foliage swallowed him like a vast, verdant fog.

The path to the lake was well worn, but this time of year it was thickly overhung. Billy was always mindful of the possibility of snakes and spider webs. He lived in fear of the brown recluse and the black widow. Panic ensued whenever he brushed a gossamer strand. Snakes, he liked. He and his friends often beat the undergrowth with sticks in the hope of flushing one and the exalted cry of 'Snake!' was responded to with military precision and cultish zeal.

The neighborhood record was held by Lex, a kid from the Catholic school who'd bagged a six-foot long black rat snake in a patch of ivy further down the tracks. It was docile and unconcerned, and Lex took it home, but his father killed it and put it in the garbage can at the curb. By majority consent, Lex was never allowed to take a snake home again, even if he'd been the one to capture it.

The neighborhood record for a lucky escape was held by Jeff, who had tried an Indian snake charming trick he'd seen on TV and wound up holding a copperhead by the business end. At the time, nobody knew what he'd got hold of, so they had trudged, en masse, from the beaver pond where he'd caught it; through the woods, over the tracks, across and up the street, and into Jeff's basement, where they'd consulted a wildlife encyclopedia. On realizing that he held writhing death in his hand, Jeff quickly became terrified of letting the thing go. In the end, it got dropped into a pillowcase, which was then dumped into an empty hamster cage with a brick on the lid. The next day, they took turns carrying the cage with the brick on it back down to the beaver pond. Very long sticks were procured and escape routes planned, but when Jeff got the big gloves on and removed the pillowcase, the snake was gone. In the world of pre-teen boys, this constituted divine intervention. Those present decided among themselves that, henceforward, no snake would be removed from its place of capture.

Billy wasn't after snakes today, however. He took a plastic grocery bag from his pocket and walked along with it, ready to carry any whole bottles he might find. He turned off the path at a point that only someone who spent the better part of every warm day and every other cold one in these woods would recognize as another path. The new trail was narrower, but soon after it left the main path, the undergrowth thinned a bit and the going got easier. It emptied into a small, circular clearing with an improvised fire pit at its center. On the far side of the fire pit laid a mattress, which fostered a lively patchwork of slime – part moss, part algae – over a sodden surface the mottled pink-gray of dead bodies left outside. Billy thought that if he were a girl, he wouldn't lie back on that abomination for anyone, and wondered if anyone actually had. After all, someone had gone to the trouble of hefting the thing all the way out to the clearing.

He came there most times he and his friends played 'Clinkers and Sinkers'. The teenagers who came after dark had a penchant for forties. Some purists thought it was cheating to play with such big bottles, but most forties were screw-tops and the clearing was littered with caps. Billy took the purely practical view that if the bottle had a cap on it, it could not sink of its own accord; an occurrence which in regulation play would earn a foul. Three fouls and a player was out. He collected a half-dozen, empty forty-ounce bottles (carefully avoiding those that had been refilled with liquids other than malt liquor) and another half-dozen caps, and made his way back to the main path.

Moving gently downhill, he came to a fence, which was more hole than chain link. Why anyone would have the idea to put a fence around a lake was beyond him; it wasn't like it was something anyone could steal. Even if it was, no one would want to, the shape it was in. The water looked like chocolate milk with bits in it. There were fish in it, but nothing edible, just carp and bullheads and a few eels; bottom feeders. Besides, if anyone actually fished in it, they were far more likely to hook an ancient spare tire or an old shopping cart. Billy knew this from experience.

It was called Lake Tincotac, which someone once told him meant 'Great Toilet' in Choctaw or Chickasaw or something. He didn't want to believe such an obvious load of crap, but the water and what it contained made it seem like a reasonable translation. About half of the lake was made up of a lazy network of swollen streams, which had been backed up by the dam to make the rest of the lake bigger.

The depth used to vary a bit due to the silt brought in by the streams, but last summer the county had dredged the whole thing. Billy and his friends had watched a lot of the dredging, fascinated as young boys always are by loud workmen and even louder machinery. They had asked a foreman what was going on and he'd told them a bunch of boring nonsense about tonnage and man-hours and other things they had no interest in. Troy asked if they hauled up any dead bodies because he'd stayed up late and been scared stiff by that part at the end of the first 'Friday the 13th' movie. The foreman said between the fish and the microbes in the silt, all they'd find if there were a dead body in there would be the fillings from its teeth or the rings from its fingers. They did find a whole '42 Dodge Super-8 and all the rubber had been eaten off its wheels.

Now, the depth in the middle of the lake was about a hundred and fifty feet and about ten or fifteen, twenty in a couple of spots, back in the streams. The deepest spot in the streams was where they usually played 'Clinkers and Sinkers'. It was called the swimming hole, but no one knew why. Everyone knew they'd need a tetanus jab and a psychiatric evaluation if they actually wanted to swim there.

Billy walked through what was meant to be the fence, crossed the cinder path, which circled the lake. He pushed through a narrow gap in the foliage on the other side. This way led to the wide streams with currents so slight that flotsam took whole minutes to pass a bystander.

He reached the edge of a gravelly ledge about ten feet high. Below was a crescent of shore five or six feet wide, which disappeared into thick brush at one end and bent around a big dead elm at the other. The elm was tattooed to a fair height with the drunken or belligerent or horny musings of several generations of local teenagers. He hugged the tree and used its exposed root system to ease his way down to the tiny dirt beach.

Billy brought his dad down here for the first time about two weeks ago and had been genuinely proud at his father's fascination with the place. He had been tearing around the woods and the lake as long as he could remember. All of his rambling dinnertime anecdotes seemed to contain some reference to woods or brown water, especially in the summer. But his dad had only occasionally ever seemed politely interested until the other week. When they had gone through the fence and crossed the path and Billy showed him the narrow, single-file walk through bushes and low-hanging trees, the questions had started in earnest.

"Do a lot of kids know about this spot?"

"You guys come down here much?"

"Good fishing?"

"Ever get any hassle from rangers or park police or game wardens?"

Billy was excited by his father's interest. It ended up being a great day and they hadn't seen a single snake or frog, or baited a hook or thrown a rock. They had just talked – about all kinds of things – school and work. His dad said they might need to move before Christmas because he wanted to expand his business and there were already too many houses in Springfield. Billy said he didn't like the idea of moving, but if it was important, he'd manage it somehow. His dad said he knew he could count on 'Big Bill' and asked a few more questions about the lake. In the end, they'd gone home sweat-filthy and mosquito-bitten, with ravenous appetites. Billy's mom had called for pizza.

He shook off his backpack and laid out some smaller bottles. He went on a quick scrounge and came back with two double-handfuls of pebbles.

The sun was rising quickly, and Billy knew that before long, only his proximity to the water would keep the worst of the heat away. Soon after that, nothing would.

He tossed the first bottle in. With a half-dozen stones, it was a Sinker. One point. In regulation play, each Sinker scored an extra point if it was sunk with the first rock to hit it. A Clinker was a bottle hit, possibly more than once, but either didn't break or for some reason broke, but failed to sink. If a bottle was clinked several times by the same player and then sunk, that player was awarded one point. In a game with more than one player, where each player was limited to a certain number of throws, a player who sunk a bottle which his opponent had already clinked was awarded points for his opponents' clinks as well as his own. A bottle that was clinked repeatedly and refused to sink earned no one any points as a Clinker was worth nothing unless it became a Sinker. Occasionally, simply to clear the field for a new bottle, a persistent Clinker could be sunk by slingshot or the largest rock available. Multiple bottles confused scoring, except in the case of a Lightning Round, which wasn't scored anyway, but merely served as a means of clearing away multiple bottles. Cheating was not an issue. No one Billy knew or had heard of was a good enough shot to cheat effectively.

Within fifteen minutes, he had earned twenty points between nine Sinkers, twelve Clinkers and a foul from an old rectangular bottle with 'Hoyt's' moulded into one side, which had gone straight to the bottom when Billy had chucked it in. He threw in his last forty and it bobbed invitingly. His first two stones missed, but his third cracked the bottle in two with a muffled crunch. The two halves subsided like a torpedoed boat.

It was still relatively cool and completely deserted, so Billy decided to head over to the swimming hole. Teenagers sometimes drank there which meant possibly finding more bottles. He shouldered his pack and kicked his way through the brush with a contented sigh. Clearly, most of the other neighborhood kids had taken the opposite view to his, and were taking advantage of the last day of summer to stay in bed most of the morning.

He crossed the tiny creek and emerged from the bushes onto a flat ribbon of grass beside one of the fat streams, which flooded every spring. He'd once come down after the flood had ebbed and saw a big carp mating-ball. About thirty or forty fish writhed around at the surface of the water, releasing eggs and sperm in a scaly-slimed orgy. They were all different sizes and colors, probably descended from pet goldfish or Koi, let loose in the lake to breed with wild carp. The spectacle made Billy feel decidedly strange. He had found it both sweet and vile and couldn't reconcile the disparity in emotions. When he set off walking again, he'd nearly trodden on a thick, dark snake, which had stretched itself across his path in the grass. He recognized it as a cottonmouth from its delta-shaped head and since he'd nearly stood on it and it hadn't killed him, he assumed it was dead. He flung it in the water with a big stick and it had swum lazily away. It hadn't been quite as close a brush with death as Jeff walking home with a copperhead wrapped around his arm, so he hadn't told anyone about it.

There were no snakes today and Billy reached the swimming hole without encounter. It was really no more than a slightly wider spot in one of the already-wide streams, a bulbous little bay in the brown, nearly stagnant flow. It was known as the swimming hole because it was deeper than the water around it and because it gave a hole-like impression. There was a tall oak at one point, on its own among the reeds and elephant grass, with a rope swing attached by an ambitious cluster of knots to its lowest bough, about twenty feet up. As far as

Billy knew, the object of the rope swing was to run with it in one hand, leap out over the water, swing in a wide arc and touch down on the grass on the other side of the tree, as dry as when you took off. The fact that the rope swing had always been there lent credence to the place's name. It had always been assumed that people had once swung out, but not swung back. Although, this option was now seen as a form of punishment.

Billy started looking for more bottles. He found a long, thin, very straight birch branch and used it as a staff, imagining himself as a Magic-User from Dungeons & Dragons. As he found bottles, he threw them in and sunk them with his slingshot, no longer bothering to keep score.

As he bent to fish a wine bottle out of the shallows, he found – with a strange, creeping realization – that he was looking into a face. Not *his* face in reflection, but someone *else's* face, *under* the water. It was inverted so that the forehead was nearest to him and the mouth was at the top.

His breathing became rapid and he could hear his heartbeat, like the angry footsteps of a giant coming to crush a trespasser. His vision grew blurry and he slowly came to the knowledge that he was crying.

When his brain had sorted all this input, it began telling him that, even upside-down, this was a face he *knew*. This was *Uncle Ed*. Uncle Ed who wasn't really his uncle, but who he just called Uncle because he was always around and it was easier to call him that, instead of Mr. O'Brien. Besides, Uncle Ed was his dad's partner, and also his best friend. But now, he was underwater and he didn't look good. In fact, he looked like hammered shit, as his friend Mike would say. Uncle Ed had little minnows and bluegills swarming around a nasty gash in the side of his head, the fish nibbling off bits of loose, flapping flesh.

It was the fish that did it. Billy moved quickly to the side and threw up in the shallows. He vomited three times, then dry-heaved for what felt like ten years. When he managed to get control of his breathing again, he noticed a fresh and growing school of minnows, called to the chuck wagon of his vomit. Thinking this almost had him laughing – almost.

He stood and made himself look. Uncle Ed was a big guy, to Billy anyway, but never what he would call fat. Now, however, Uncle Ed looked like something out of the 'Guinness Book of World Records', or maybe a circus sideshow. His belly was bloated and round and strained the buttons of his flannel work shirt, which looked about four sizes too small. The skin peeking from the gaps in his clothes was the same color as the mattress in the woods. There were coils of rope around the top of his chest, pushed up by the bloating. The frayed ends suggested heavy things in the depths. His legs dangled down at an angle and there was another frayed rope around one ankle. Billy could just make out that he was only wearing one boot. He started to wonder where the other boot was and then his mind switched to wondering how Uncle Ed had found his way into the swimming hole and when was the last time he saw him?

Then it broke over him all at once.

It felt like the time they went to the beach last year and he had been caught under a series of breakers – one after another – pressing him down, holding him under, using his breath and rubbing him into the sand like a bully. The tide of remembered clues assaulted him; hissing arguments late at night, dark circles under eyes, a bruise high on one cheek.

Curiosity about Billy's haunt.

And inquisitions – leading inquiries – questions a person wouldn't dare ask anyone but a trusting eleven-year-old.

"Does this place get busy?"

"How deep did the guy say it was?"

"What's down there? Any big fish?"

"What did he say about the silt?"

"Microbes, huh?"

"Nothing left but fillings?"

Billy couldn't process it all and staggered backwards under the repeated blows. His Magic-User's staff fell to the grass with a soft thump; he'd forgotten he was holding it. He put his hands up to his head to keep it from spinning off like a helicopter. He squeezed his eyes shut, but he saw things in the dark behind his lids that he didn't want to, so he opened them again and looked up at the sky. Just like Uncle Ed, except now Ed's eyes were waxy and opaque and saw nothing.

This thought made Billy cry all over again. He looked down again at Uncle Ed. A minnow hovered in the cave of his open mouth. He looked like he was about to let rip with one of his big belches. This made Billy cry harder. He liked Uncle Ed – he told good jokes.

"What's green and red and goes a hundred miles an hour?"

"I dunno."

"A frog in a blender."

"What goes black-and-white, black-and-white, black-and-white?"

"What?"

"A nun rolling down a hill. What's black and white, and laughs like a hyena?"

"I dunno."

"The priest who pushed her."

Last year for Christmas, Uncle Ed had given Billy an official Army surplus canteen – the one that was now in his backpack and filled with orange juice.

He took it out and drained it in a single quaff. Then, on impulse, he threw it out into the middle of the swimming hole. It bobbed at the center of its own bulls-eye. Billy loaded his Wrist-Rocket and sunk it with two wet clanks.

He stood, arms drooped, head hung low, tears washing clean stripes in his sweat-grimed face, and thought. He thought of Uncle Ed and how much he had liked him. He thought of his dad and why he would have done such a thing, for there was no doubt in his mind as to who had given Ed that head-wound and tried to sink him in slime.

Billy's father had always been a good dad. Not the 'let's play catch while your mother bakes some cookies' type, but he had consistently listened, always had time. He'd given Billy advice and Billy had often, not always, heeded it. He had always trusted his dad. But what would happen now? Whatever occurred, Billy knew that most of it hung on what *he* did next.

If he did what every teacher and other part-time authority figure had always told kids to do, and found a policeman, his dad would go to jail. No shit, Sherlock, hurtin' for certain, do not pass go, do not collect $200, go directly to jail. Grownups were forever yapping on about running to the cops. It was their only contingency plan in situations like this. *Were* there situations like this? The more he thought about it, the less sure he was. Whenever they showed a safety film at school, or Mr. Happy did a public service message on TV, it always had to do with fireworks or downed power lines or ditches or something equally fascinating to a kid. This was a no-foolin' USDA approved Murder Scene he was standing in the middle of, however, and no public service message, not even one with Mr. Happy, had ever given instructions to sort out a snag like this. To Billy's frantic mind, this was a unique circumstance and, although murder was a particular forte among law enforcement officials, he would not be running to them. He kept seeing his dad in an orange jumpsuit, holding a plastic board with a long string of numbers on it, and the ensuing mugshot plastered all over the front pages of the local newspaper, proclaiming to the neighborhood, his friends and their parents, his teachers at school, that Billy's father was a *murderer*. And he saw the empty, lonely house, devoid of his dad; he and his mother – just the two of them – sitting down to the dinner table on quiet nights, ostracized and shunned by the world. Abandoned. He'd already lost Uncle Ed, but going to the police would cost Billy his father as well.

There had to be an explanation. Maybe it had been an accident and his dad had panicked. Maybe Uncle Ed had tried to kiss his mom and his dad had got angry. Those sorts of things seemed to happen constantly on TV. Maybe it was self-defense.

Billy's hypothesizing was broken by the sound of distant laughter. Anger flashed across his mind; jealousy at the loud expression of joy when he was sad and lonely and confused. Then, just like a cartoon lightbulb, the truth of the situation clicked on in his head. Someone was coming, kids probably, friends possibly, and if he didn't want a jailbird dad, good reason or no, Uncle Ed could not be seen.

He looked around quickly and seized his Magic-User's staff. Saying a quick and quiet apology, Billy poked Uncle Ed gently in the shoulder, trying to submerge him completely, but only succeeding in pushing him out to bob on the surface about four feet from shore. The surprised, belching look on Ed's face nearly made Billy laugh again, in spite of himself.

He heard the kids again, closer now, laughing loudly in the woods. He guessed they were through the fence already and across the main path.

In desperation, he leaned out and gave Ed another shove, sending him cruising into the center of the swimming hole, swiftly enough to leave a small wake. Now Ed was too far out for Billy to have any hope of getting him back.

There was only one thing left for it. He picked up his Wrist-Rocket, loaded an iron ore pellet.

He held the slingshot at arms-length and pulled the surgical tubing taut against his cheek. Mercifully, Uncle Ed had spun a few degrees on his travels, so Billy couldn't see his face; he might not manage if he could. From this angle, his target looked like a badly used bathrobe, and that's how he thought of it.

His first shot went in high up on the flannel mound. The noise it made on impact – something like hitting a thick steak with the claw end of a hammer – was one Billy instantly wanted to forget, but knew he'd take to his grave. The entry wound exhaled a thin stream of greenish gas, like a rotten teapot, and a proud, vaporous hiss. The farting sound made him want to laugh for a third time, but he heard the kids, closer still, near the graffiti tree now, from the sound of it, and he was sure he recognized individual voices. Mike was telling dirty jokes.

He took aim again and again, keeping his shots near the waterline. Five quick pellets and Uncle Ed was sinking to the bottom of the swimming hole in a roil of bubbles, like he had got into a hot tub fully dressed. The startled, belching face rotated back around and seemed to stare at Billy as it faded into the brown murk. He didn't know whether to interpret it as a look of gratitude or accusation.

He could see Mike, Troy, Lex and Jeff tramping along the way he had come and, as a precaution, he quickly found the biggest couple of rocks he could lay hands on and threw them as far into the middle of the swimming hole as he could. Then, he busied himself collecting bottles. He was going to challenge his friends to a grand tournament of 'Clinkers and Sinkers'.

It was the last day of summer. School was back in tomorrow. The real world was coming and it couldn't be stopped. In another hour or two, Uncle Ed would be buried under a blanket of stones and broken glass. Maybe then he would stay sunk.

About the Authors

Ken Goldman is a former Philadelphia high school teacher of English and Film Studies, and he has taught courses on Horror and Science Fiction in Film & Literature. An affiliate member of the Horror Writers Association, Ken has homes on the Main Line in Pennsylvania and at the Jersey shore depending upon the track of the sun and his need for a tan. His stories appear in over 825 independent press publications in the U.S., Canada, the UK, and Australia, and over thirty of Ken's tales are due for publication in 2016-2017. Since 1993 his stories have received seven honorable mentions in The Year's Best Fantasy & Horror. He has written five books: his books of short stories, *You Had Me at Arrgh!!* (Sam's Dot Publishers), *Donny Doesn't Live Here Anymore* (A/A Publishers), plus an e-book, *Star Crossed* (Vampires 2 Publications); and a novella, *Desiree*, (Damnation Books). His novel, *Of a Feather*, was published by Horrific Tales Publications (UK) in January 2014. Currently, he is scouting a publisher for his new novel, *Sinkhole*. (You hear that, Bantam and Doubleday?) Ken's stories haven't made him famous yet. He expects that to happen posthumously, probably ten minutes after he is in the ground, after which, universities worldwide will make GOLDMAN 101 a mandatory course for future writers. For now, you may find many of Ken's stories online and at Amazon. Stop by and scream hello.

Jenean McBrearty is a graduate of San Diego State University, who taught Political Science and Sociology. Her fiction, poetry, and photographs have been published in over a hundred and sixty print and on-line journals. She won the Eastern Kentucky English Department Award for graduate Non-fiction in 2011, and she won a Silver Pen Award in 2015 for her noir short story "Red's Not Your Color". Her serials Raphael Redcloak: Guardian of the Arts and Retrolands can be found on Jukepop.com.

Larry Lefkowitz's stories, poetry and humor have been widely published. Lefkowitz's humorous literary novel, "The Novel, Kunzman, the Novel!" is available as an e-book and in print from Lulu.com and other distributors. Writers and readers with a deep interest in literature will especially enjoy the novel. Lefkowitz's humorous fantasy and science fiction collection, "Laughing into the Fourth Dimension" is available from Amazon Books.

Ellen Denton is a freelance writer living in the Rocky
Mountains with her husband and two demonic cats that wreak havoc and hell (the cats, not the husband). Her short stories have been published in over one hundred magazines and anthologies. She's had an exciting life working as a circus acrobat, a CIA spy, a service provider in a Red Light District, a navy seal, a ballerina on the starship Enterprise, and was the first person to climb Mount Everest. (Editorial note: The publication credits are true, but some of the other stuff may be fictional.)

Luke Walker was born in Cambridgeshire, England in
1977. He grew up reading his brother's collection of James Herbert paperbacks, his dad's Stephen King collection and various editions of the Pan Book of Horror which some might say shaped him into the man he is today. Now 38, he has been writing horror novels and short stories for as long as he can remember. After leaving school with a tiny handful of qualifications and a deep love of books, Luke works full time in a library. He has also had a job as a hospital orderly and can say with some confidence that a severed leg in a bio-waste bag is surprisingly heavy. Luke lives with his wife, two cats and more horror films than he knows what to do with.

Richard W. Black is a freelance writer born and raised
in Indiana. He optioned a feature film script through InkTip and has written polished first draft screenplays for production companies from Luxembourg to Singapore to Australia. He wrote the TV show "Bible" and 6 episodes of "S.L.I.P." for RADAR in Luxembourg now in preproduction by the RTL TV network of Luxembourg. RADAR also commissioned him to write the first drafts of the feature film scripts "Sub" and "Seeds" that are currently in preproduction by English production companies. His first novel *A Cross in Time* was released by ASJ Publishing. *The Hive* is his second book, currently in the editing stages for publication. His political futuristic novel *Heresy's Child* won an honorable mention in the Deep River Book Publisher's Contest and he crafted the story as a screenplay. He wrote

the feature length screenplay "Darkness of Night" for an Indian production company that filmed in Dubai and is in post-production. He worked on "Zero Hero", a children's animated cartoon series by CreatvToon Studios and Tapir Reka Productions in Malaysia with 20 credited episodes. The short story "Mrs. Whitfield Lives Forever" was published by the *First Line* as part of their December, 2015 issue, "Perfect Beauty" was released by Silver Pen in their Fall 2015 *Silver Blade Magazine* and "Space Partners" is part of an anthology collection called *Night Lights* published by Geminid Press in 2016. Richard is a member of the Tennessee Screenwriting Association and currently resides with his wife of 39 years in the greater Nashville, Tennessee area.

Randy D. Rubin lives in quiet lunacy in a very old haunted house in Virginia. He is a very proud member of The Horror Writers of America and HWA-VA. He matriculated from Old Dominion University studying Creative Writing/English. He has two novellas published by Secret Cravings Press, *The Legend of my Nana, Miss Viola* and *The Witch of Dreadmere Forest*. His short story, "Tommy Kitty Cellar Son" is part of the anthology, *Suffer the Little Children*, published at Cruentis Libri Press and "This is a Troll Free Call" is in *Ugly Babies Vol. 1.* by JWK Publishing. His story, "The Water Got Mad" is part of Perpetual Motion Machine Publishing's *One Night Stand* series. He is the featured poet showcased in *The Horror Zine*'s September 2014 issue. He recently won the NECON E-Book Flash Fiction Contest last year and received an honorable mention for his haiku poetry this year. His flash fiction took second place in the January Short Fiction Contest at The Cult of Me.Blogspot.com this year. His dark passions and prose have been turned into podcasts at *The Wicked Library*, Episodes 417 in 2014; 516 last season; and 613 this year. His drabbles have appeared at *Hellnotes'* "Horror in a Hundred". And he's just getting started… His first dark poetry collection, "The Demon in My Head Doth Speak" was just released through *Eldritch Press* in February. His short story, "T-BONE" has just been published in the *Happy Little Horrors Anthology Vol 2 – ALIENATED* at Amazon as of Halloween 2015.

EMP Publishing will have his first collection of short stories, tentatively titled, *Warmest Regards from Austria* on the shelves in September of 2017. His second poetry collection, "The Joint" will be incorporated into EMP Publishing's *The Prison Compendium*, a tome of dark speculative and literary prison stories and poems breaking out in December, 2016.

Jeffrey B. Burton was born in Long Beach, California, grew up in St. Paul, Minnesota, and received his BA in Journalism at the University of Minnesota. Novels in Burton's *Agent Drew Cady* mystery series include *The Chessman*, *The Lynchpin*, and, coming in 2017, *The Eulogist*. Jeff's short stories have appeared in dozens of genre magazines (mystery, horror, fantasy). Jeff is a member of Mystery Writers of America (MWA), International Thriller Writers (ITW), and the Horror Writers Association (HWA). Jeff lives in St. Paul with his wife, daughter, and an irate Pomeranian named Lucy.

Michael Shimek currently lives in Colorado where he writes and has adventures in the mountains. He has stories that appear in *Sanitarium Magazine* Issue #32, *Fossil Lake: An Anthology of the Aberrant; Fossil Lake III: Unicornado!; We Walk Invisible; In Shambles: A Scarlet Nightmare Vol. II; Slaughter House: The Serial Killer Edition – Vol I; A Chimerical World: Tales of the Unseelie Court,* and more. Many of his stories can be found for free on his website: michaelshimek.blogspot.com. He also tweets @michaelshimek.

Matthew Weber is author of *Seven Feet Under*, *A Dark & Winding Road*, *The Bull*, and is editor of the *Double-Barrel Horror* anthology. He is owner of Pint Bottle Press, editor-in-chief of *Extreme How-To* magazine, and author of the non-fiction book *The Quick & Easy Home DIY Manual*. His short stories have appeared in multiple magazines and anthologies, and he lives in Birmingham, Alabama, with his wife and two sons. Visit **www.pintbottlepress.com**.

B. C. Nance is a native of Nashville, Tennessee where he works as an archaeologist specializing in historic sites. He has written several archaeological reports and articles, and in his spare time, he writes fiction and poetry. His stories and poetry have been published in: *The Writer's Post Journal*; *Inwood Indiana*; *Swords and Sorcery Magazine*; *Theme of Absence*; *The Literary Hatchet*; and the poetry collection *Filtered Through Time*.

Liam Hogan is a London based writer and host of the award winning monthly literary event, Liars' League. Winner of Quantum Shorts 2015 and Sci-Fest LA's Roswell Award 2016, he's been published at DailyScienceFiction, NoSleep Podcast, and in over a dozen anthologies.

Find out more at http://happyendingnotguaranteed.blogspot.co.uk.

Florence Ann Marlowe started out as a journalist, writing for local newspapers and radio stations. Since 2008, she has been a published fiction writer for E-magazines and hard copy publications such as *Macabre Cadaver, Demon Minds, Pseudopod, 69 Flavors of Paranoia, Dedman's Tome, Death Head Grin, Fantastic Horror* and *Wiley Writers*. Her stories have also appeared in the anthologies *Reflux, Peep Show Volume 2, The Pulpateers, Fantastic Horror's Temptations and Other Sins, Fear's Accomplice* and *Fear's Accomplice: Halloween* and in the next issue of *Black Candies* and the upcoming installment of *Ladies and Gentleman of Horror*. She has just finished her first novel titled *The Bitter Dead* and is currently looking for a publisher. Originally from Hoboken, Florence has lived from one end of New Jersey to the other and currently lives on a small farm in southern New Jersey. Her closest neighbor happens to be the Jersey Devil.

Author/screenwriter **Craig Faustus Buck**'s debut noir novel, GO DOWN HARD (Brash Books) was First Runner Up for the Claymore Award and a Silver Falchion Award Finalist. His short stories have won a Macavity Award and been nominated for two Anthonys and a Derringer. His screen writing includes an Oscar nominated short film and *V: The Final Battle*. You can find out more, and read more of his short stories for free, at CraigFaustusBuck.com.

Jamie Wahls is a writer, programmer, pianist, suicide counselor, massage therapist, mime, model, ex-millionaire, Krav Magi, scuba diver, neuroscience enthusiast, dance instructor, vegetarian, and very cautious driver.

Published stories include *Maestro*, "For The Children" in *Mothership Zeta*, and "The Button" in *Sci Phi Journal*. You can read more, but not much more, about Jamie at jamiewahls.com.

Calvin Demmer is a crime, mystery, and speculative
fiction author. When not writing, he is intrigued by that which goes bump in the night and the sciences of our universe. His work has appeared in a variety of publications including *Sanitarium Magazine*, *Morpheus Tales*, and *Devolution Z*. Find out more at www.calvindemmer.com or follow him on twitter @CalvinDemmer.

Robert Hart has worked a series of crappy jobs, both in the
US and the UK. He has written several novels and mostly-written several more. Some of his short fiction can be found in Thuglit, '*The Good Fight: A Super-Hero Monster Hunter Anthology*' from Emby Press, '*People Eating People: A Cannibal Anthology*' edited by Dusty Wallace, '*Creature Stew*' from Papa Bear Press, on outofthegutteronline.com and as part of Digital Fiction Publishing's new Sci-Fi, Horror and Microfiction imprints. He lives in England with his wife and daughter.

Acknowledgments

EMP Publishing and Creepy Campfire Quarterly would like to thank the following in no particular order. Each and every one of you has supported the CCQ and you are all responsible for helping every issue come into being.

THANK YOU.

Søren Skøtt, Marlena Frank, Jenny Koenig, Bruce Galbraith, Jessica Hogue, Lewis Crown, Damian Stout, Jeremy Thompson, Ashley Spychalla, Jaime Metoyer, Ashwini Reddy, Rachel Blackburn, Michael LaPointe, Kristin Giglio-Baldi, Dale W. Glaser, Theresa Huffman, Kimberly King, Craig Steven Herndon, Jr., Jonathan Hixson, David Hoenig, Michael Picco.

On a final note, EMP Publishing and the CCQ would like to give special acknowledgment of the hard work and efforts of our specific staff for this issue:

Jonathan Hixson: Associate Editor/Acquisitions

Craig Steven Herndon, Jr.: Associate Editor/Acquisitions

Dale W. Glaser: Copy Editor

www.ingramcontent.com/pod-product-compliance
Lightning Source LLC
Chambersburg PA
CBHW030253130626
46549CB00002B/517